The Killer in Me

THE KILLER IN ME

A BENOIT AND DAYNE MYSTERY

WINTER AUSTIN

TULE
PUBLISHING

DEDICATION

This dedication belongs to a fighter
combating a brain tumor,
who loves all things Scooby Doo
and Darth Vader, where the Force is ever with
Gabrielle "Gabby" Ford.
Every day is a day to get a Gabby hug.

PROLOGUE

E LIZABETH BENOIT SETTLED in a chair across from the two men. A carafe was placed in the center of the table and white ceramic mugs and dessert plates were set in front of each person. The *pièce de résistance* left for the trio was a square glass dish brimming with Neva McKinnley's famous pecan sticky rolls. The retired teacher took a chair next to her son.

"Well, I feel like I'm getting the royal treatment." Elizabeth poured a generous cup and served herself a fat, square roll. "To what do I owe this grand pleasure?"

Jason McKinnley, the youngest man to serve as mayor for Three Points, folded his hands and leaned toward her. "As you know, it's an election year." He inclined his head to the second man in an Eckardt County deputy's uniform. "Rafe and I have been talking."

Her antenna rose. "Have you now?"

"It's nothing bad, I assure you. We have . . . lots of concerns, and we . . . feel like you're the best person to address them."

Now this was proving interesting. "And what concerns would those be?"

"The direction this county has been going for the last three decades." Rafe Fontaine's deep rumbling timbre caught the attention of Elizabeth's canine companion, who abandoned her owner for one of her other favorite people.

Stifling the comment that popped on her tongue, Elizabeth shoved a corner of the caramelly goodness into her pie hole. Rafe's left eyebrow peaked.

"Ellie, the folks of Eckardt County are tired of the downward spiral this county has gone into." Jason pried his hands apart and laid them flat on his mother's brilliant blue tablecloth. "I became mayor of Three Points to help quell the problems, but I'm getting nowhere as long as certain people are still in control of portions of our government."

Elizabeth took a sip of coffee to ease the lump of dough down her throat and placed her mug on the table. "County council and other mayoral positions are not up for election this year."

Rafe and Jason glanced at each other. A tic in Rafe's jawline set the antenna to waving.

"Correct, those are not." Jason blinked. "But the sheriff's seat is."

Neither man flinched as Elizabeth crossed her arms and leaned forward. "Mrs. McKinnley, this wouldn't happen to be your idea, now would it?"

The retired teacher continued to sip her coffee and stay out of the conversation.

"Gentlemen, what in the world gives you the idea that I'm even one-third qualified to be sheriff?"

"Joel told me about all the online classes in criminology and law."

Elizabeth's eyelid twitched. "Is that a fact? And what else did my usually tight-lipped, no safe-cracker in the world could ever break, ex-husband tell you?"

"Elizabeth, we all remember what happened to Brendette. We were all here when it happened." Neva McKinnley reached out and grasped her hand. "Who better to find out what really transpired than her number one champion? As sheriff, you have every right to reinvestigate her death."

"And we get rid of one of the worst sheriffs in Eckardt County history," Jason said.

"You want me to run against Kelley Sheehan for sheriff? He has decades of experience over me, and let's not forget his weird voodoo magic hold on people. I'd never win."

"Don't sell yourself short." Neva squeezed her hand. "You have the very things people are thirsting for: honor, integrity, smarts, and family."

"And you look better than him," Rafe added.

"Thank you for that fine assessment, Raphael Fontaine."

Elizabeth bit down on her cheeks to quell the smile.

"Mom's right, you can win this. And once you've taken office, we can begin the process of weeding out the criminals and corruption that's been plaguing our communities for so long, starting with the drug problem."

"Jason, you act as if I already have won the election. I haven't even given my consent to do this. I need time to think about it."

"There's not much time. In order to get a good campaign going and make sure people go to the booth voting for you, we need an answer by tonight."

"Not leaving a whole lot of wiggle room there for a second option, Mayor."

"The only option is another four years of Sheehan's corrupt and perverted version of law and order." Jason pushed out of his seat and tilted forward. "What's your final answer, Elizabeth?"

CHAPTER ONE

Day 1: Wednesday

A s a child, the adults surrounding Elizabeth Benoit called her listless, a daydreamer. Names meant to cut her to the quick, but she'd owned them, let them define who she truly was as a person. Forty-five years later, she'd become a better woman than those folks from her childhood had expected.

Pressed against the edge of the counter jutting out into the center of her kitchen, she stared at the black liquid, her lifeblood, dripping from the reservoir. It would take more than a pot of coffee to sort out this new mess her intelligence had uncovered. Reaching into the cabinet above the coffee-maker, she pulled out a brown Yeti mug and a green thermos.

The black gold burbled out of the tank. Removing the glass pot, she poured the contents into her mug and then the thermos.

Last night she'd decided to wrap up a particularly turbulent Tuesday at Marnie's bar. Since winning the election and taking over as sheriff last month, Elizabeth hadn't seen much of her sister and needed a hit of whatever mojo Marnie exuded in copious amounts. Five drinks and a tottering walk home later—thank God she lived only a block away—

Elizabeth was greeted by a surprise. An unwelcome one.

The cadence of an easy swagger punctuated by the metal on metal rip of a zipper preceded the appearance of that unwelcomed surprise. Elizabeth turned as he exited the hallway.

A half-cocked grin, bare chest, and half done up jeans met her. Yep, she'd let his whiskey-honeyed voice and moves seduce her once again. Damn him.

"Morning."

Sighing, Elizabeth braced her body against the counter. "Joel."

The finely honed Delta Force operative strode past her to take a glass out of the cabinet above the sink and grabbed the half-gallon milk jug out of the fridge. After pouring himself a generous amount, Joel Fontaine, *ex*-husband, leaned against the sink and downed the entire contents of the glass. Finished, he set the glass in the sink.

"Why are you here?" she asked.

"Wasn't it obvious last night?"

Rolling her neck, she crossed her arms and dropped her gaze to the squared toes of her boots. "You can't come back from a long mission and expect a booty call every time you visit Iowa." Her gaze darted back to him. "We're divorced. Remember?"

Joel pushed off the sink's edge and inched closer to her, dipping his broad, muscled shoulders so he could meet her gaze dead on. "I didn't hear one protest out of you before or after."

Anger snapped through her. "Because I was drunk, you ass." She pushed him away. "This"—she jabbed a finger between them—"is why we divorced in the first place. Except for the sex, we're not good together, and even the sex had problems."

Joel held up his hands in surrender. "Ellie . . ."

She slashed the air. Whatever sweetness he thought to spew to soften her up ended here. They weren't teenagers deep in the throes of hormonal lust. Damn it, they were both grown-ass adults and he still thought he could smooth everything over with a few platitudes, a few kisses, and she'd just cave. That special maneuver had stopped working on her a long time ago. "Don't *Ellie* me. This can't happen. Anymore."

A huff ending with a very dog-like yawn put a pause to their standoff. Bentley, Elizabeth's red border collie and constant companion, popped up from her second dog bed by the sliding glass door and jogged over to the water bowl. She couldn't have made her point clearer: "We're done here. We've got work to do."

Elizabeth gathered up her mug and thermos. "I'm going to the department. I'm putting in a full day of work. When I get home, I expect you gone." She squared off with Joel, the heat of his body reminding her how good the sex was between them. It was always at its peak right after he got back from a deployment or after a particularly long mission.

Fire and kerosene.

"It's not that easy, Ellie."

"My house, my rules. Crash somewhere else." About-facing, she snapped her fingers to call Bentley and marched out of the house, letting the doors slam, punctuating the finality to this conversation.

Miracle of miracles, Marnie had dropped off Elizabeth's vehicle, keys still in the ignition. Letting Bentley hop into the passenger seat, Elizabeth climbed in, got settled, and started the engine. She made the mistake of looking at the porch, finding Joel propped in the doorway, staring at her.

Backing out of the drive, she pointed the truck in the direction of the courthouse and resisted the urge to look back. A part of her, the deeply ingrained part that was well aware of that man's penchant for disobeying orders he deemed worthless, knew he would not listen to her. Joel would still be there by evening.

Elizabeth didn't have time for his games. Crashing on her sister's couch might be the better option.

BENTLEY LED THE way up the courthouse steps, waited patiently for Elizabeth to open the glass door, and then trotted along the polished tile, the click of her nails echoing in the high-ceilinged hallway on their way to Elizabeth's office. Following her faithful friend, Elizabeth fiddled with her keys, fingering each one until the rough etching of a star pressed into her fingertip.

After she'd won the election and cleared out Sheehan's mess, Elizabeth had all the locks changed and a select set of keys made that only she and the dispatcher had access to. The state-of-the-art security system she'd managed to wiggle out of the county budget had been installed last week. Each deputy was given a special coded card that allowed only them entry to the main office and holding cells, tracking their comings and goings. Until Elizabeth deemed such time as she saw fit to trust the deputies, they would not be given any undue entry to certain offices and rooms in the department's portion of the courthouse.

Hot, fresh coffee hailed her as she unlocked the half-beveled glass door. Bentley slinked past Elizabeth's legs, around the corner, and darted through a second doorway into the main hall, where she was welcomed with a: "Bentley-boo!"

Bentley's short list of people she didn't like did not include Dispatcher Georgia Schmidt. Georgia had been Eckardt County's dispatcher for twenty-three years through two sheriff administrations. She edged out Elizabeth in age by a few years, but no one could tell.

Georgia had a distinct dislike for the former sheriff but never voiced her reasons.

Dropping her load on the organized clutter on her desk, Elizabeth joined her canine companion in the main hall. "Good morning, Georgia."

The curly blonde ruffled Bentley's silky red ears as the dog licked her arms. "Mornin', Sheriff."

A short stack of pink slips sat in the tray marked Sheriff Benoit. Gathering the thin sheets, Elizabeth wandered to one of the desks set up in the office's corners. "How did Lundquist and Meyer fare last night?" She rotated a file folder ninety degrees to read the typed heading: Eckardt County Sheriff's Department Budget.

Thank you, Rafe.

"By all appearances, they did fine." Georgia rolled her office chair across the floor and joined Elizabeth next to the deputy's desk. "I still can't fathom those two boys being old enough to be deputies." She tapped the folder. "He worked late on that."

Elizabeth smiled. "We all grow up." She picked up the folder. "Anything of interest I need to be aware of today?"

"Mrs. McKinnley called right as I got in to lodge a complaint that someone has been breaking into that old house out on her road. She swears up and down she hears people having a party or an orgy in there."

"I'll check it out."

"Sheriff, that's not your job."

Elizabeth gave Georgia an indulgent smile. "I know, but I won't win the next election by ignoring my voters."

Shaking her head, Georgia rolled back to her desk. "You've got four years to worry about that. Let's focus on the here and now. How many deputies do you plan to bring on to replace all the ones who left?"

"As many as I can find room in the budget for." Elizabeth waved the budget folder as she headed back to her office. "Speaking of which, I'm expecting a visitor sometime today. Let me know when they get here."

Saluting, Georgia grabbed up the phone as it rang. "Good morning, Eckardt Sheriff's Department, how may I help you?"

With Bentley at her side, Elizabeth entered her office and closed the adjoining door. The McKinnley complaint was on top of the stack. Easing into the brown leather and brass-studded chair leftover from a long-ago sheriff, Elizabeth read through Georgia's scrolled notes on the call. Mrs. Neva McKinnley, a stable member of the Eckardt community, was not a woman you disregarded, nor was she one to lodge complaints on a continual basis, according to Georgia. Yes, this situation required the sheriff's touch.

As Elizabeth shuffled through the messages that had come in overnight, Bentley hopped onto the raggedy armchair Elizabeth had shoved into a corner of the office until she found the time to dispose of it. Hind end tucked into the juncture of the chair back and armrest, Bentley cocked her head, watching. Smiling at her dog, Elizabeth traded the pink slips for the budget folder. She and the county council had an upcoming meeting about her proposed changes.

Georgia's knock stopped her from opening the file. The door creaked open. "Sheriff?"

"Yes?"

Georgia poked her head inside. "You're going to have to put your morning routine on hold. Deputy Fontaine has called in a 10-107."

For a month, Elizabeth had been trying to get a handle on these particular codes her ex-brother-in-law, Georgia, and a few of the others used. Having had no prior experience working in law enforcement, Elizabeth found her vocabulary was better suited for military than a law enforcement officer. She was frustrated, to say the least, that she hadn't had the time to study up on it.

Georgia winced and stepped inside the door. "Sorry, that's the code for a dead body."

"Where?"

"Out on the old quarry road, heading toward Three Points."

Elizabeth stood. "Car accident?"

"No. Deputy Fontaine is calling this a homicide."

She froze. A homicide. An unexplained death in a county that hadn't seen one since Brendette Lundquist's life was cut short.

"He's sure?"

Georgia turned away. "Sheriff, the final call is yours on whether it's a homicide or not. But if Rafe says it is, I'd believe it." She closed the door.

Here it was—the reason the voters of Eckardt County had chosen Elizabeth over Kelley Sheehan. Her first test.

She would not fail them.

CHAPTER TWO

H ER BODY LAY broken and twisted, curled about a stout juniper tree. Dirt and dried leaves tangled in blond hair, blood and mud caked once-youthful, unfamiliar features. The red and black flannel button-up and faded jeans were tattered and ripped, whether by design or from the trip down the steep, rocky embankment. Appearances being what they were, it looked as if she had been flung from the road at the top of the ravine. It was uncertain if she'd been alive or conscious at the moment she was tossed over like a bag of trash. One thing was clear to all who had come to this gully: she was not meant to be found.

Elizabeth rose from her crouched position, jingling the carabiners on her rappelling harness. She peered up the ravine wall, her keen eye assessing the forty-foot drop. Scrub brush, thorny vines, and saplings grew among the outcroppings of rock and slate. She could visualize the young woman's body tumbling, bouncing, and slamming into the obstructions as she made the horrific descent until crashing into the juniper's trunk, coming to rest under the needle and berry laden limbs.

God have mercy on this poor girl's soul if she was alive when she went over.

Putting her back to the ugly scene, she faced the deputy

who had rappelled down with her. "Fitzgerald, have them send down the equipment. We've got a big scene to process."

Wary lines deepened the wrinkles etching Deputy Ben Fitzgerald's bronzed face. He gave a slow nod and gripped his handheld radio, rotating to peer up the steep incline as he spoke into the bulky device.

The lone holdout left in the wake of Sheehan's ousting, Fitzgerald still didn't believe she should be in the sheriff's position. He was a fine deputy and a dedicated officer of the law, so his loyalty to the crooked bastard cut deep. She would win him over, or he'd eventually do as the other loyal Sheehan followers had done and quit. If she were honest with herself, Elizabeth wasn't sure about Fitzgerald.

She rotated on the balls of her feet, squatting as she moved, and studied the area around the body. She mentally imprinted the whole scene, absorbing the fresh, brisk scent of the fir trees, the sharp bite of dust rising into the frigid December air. The cloying odor of decay suffocated human nostrils but was attractive to vermin. She tilted her head, squinting at the sky. Beacons of death, four vultures lazily circled above, waiting for the humans to clear out and let them feast. A murder of crows perched on nearby trees squawked their displeasure at being kept at bay.

Not today, birds.

This young woman belonged to Elizabeth now. The large birds had done their duty, alerting their two-legged counterparts of the grisly scene far below them. Once the medical examiner and the team had what they needed, they would tuck her away and send her to the hospital where Dr. Olivia Remington-Thorpe would take the victim under her care. The vultures would have to find a moldering meal elsewhere.

"Sheriff." Fitzgerald practically choked on the title.

Rising to her full height—how she loved that she inched over the man who found any chance to slight her by word of mouth or facial expression—she took the offered radio and engaged the talk button. "This is the sheriff."

"Ellie." Her ex-brother-in-law's gravelly tone was the complete opposite of his brother's. "Georgia called. Your expected visitor has arrived."

Rafe was her voice of sanity. Had been right before, during, and after the divorce. Rafe's cajoling was what had brought Elizabeth back to Juniper, and into the election for sheriff.

He never treated her as a new strain of black plague.

She clicked the mic. "Prepare for me to come up. What's the ETA on Dr. Remington-Thorpe?"

"Ten minutes. I don't know that she's going to like having to rappel down there."

"I hope you told her to wear clothes she didn't care about."

"I mentioned it."

"Coming up."

"Roger."

She handed the radio back to Fitzgerald. He eyed her, most likely trying to figure out who her visitor was. Her change in the wind she'd kept hidden under her hat, that's who. No one in the department had an inkling. She dared not say a word to her dear sister for fear that someone would rip the strings from her hands.

Elizabeth Benoit was about to tip the scales in her favor with a jack of spades.

LILA DAYNE STOOD at parade rest, the deep-seated training instinctual, while the woman who held her future in her hands perused the dossier at her leisure. Off in the corner on a chair better suited for the dump, a red and white border collie watched her. Trying to ignore those brown orbs boring holes into her soul, Lila stared at the bare wood paneling above the sheriff's head.

Knock, knock, the seventies were calling.

Sheriff Elizabeth Benoit was not what Lila expected. To have a woman sheriff was rare in this country, rarer still in a rural community like Juniper, Iowa. It mattered little to Lila. She needed this job. This deputy position with the Eckardt County department was about as perfect as she could get.

"You have an impressive résumé, Ms. Dayne." The older woman's gaze lifted to meet Lila's. "It would seem taking this deputy position would be a step down from what you were doing in Chicago."

"Ma'am?"

"You worked in one of the roughest precincts, did a stint with a few narcotics task forces, trained with SWAT, and the *coup de grace*, you passed your detective exam and worked one year in homicide. So, why come here?"

Because this place gave her the promise of a new start she sorely needed. "Ma'am, if I may, I'm still not comfortable discussing certain private matters."

Steepling her hands, the sheriff folded her fingers together as she rocked back in her chair. Those piercing dark brown eyes, so like her canine companion's, roved over Lila, seeming to pick apart the elements that made her whole and find the parts that were missing. Never one to back down, Lila did her own scrutinizing.

Elizabeth Benoit was a tall woman, standing a good five inches over Lila, with rich brown hair that skimmed her shoulders. A gold star glinted over the left pocket of her desert tan uniform top, declaring to all she was top of the food chain. Except for some bits of leaves clinging to her hair and shirt, she was put together with near military precision. A tidbit of knowledge Lila tucked away for future reference.

"For the sake of an argument, I won't press the matter." The sheriff tapped the dossier file. "Everything I need is right here. I can study your file and read up on all of your past accomplishments 'til the cows come home. What these papers can't tell me is what I want to know by listening to you. You have outstanding credentials, a stellar law enforcement career, and you fast-tracked through the ranks in Chicago PD. Eckardt County is by no means a place to advance a career. Especially for a woman."

"Correct me if I'm wrong, ma'am, but you are the sheriff of this county, are you not? Elected by the people to keep them safe? A woman sitting in a position of power normally controlled by men. I'd say that's a fine career advancement."

Lila enjoyed watching the warm smile appear on Benoit's lips.

"That being said, I need to know one thing from you, Ms. Dayne. I need to know where your focus lies."

"My focus?"

"The deputy whose position you applied for quit. Let's just say there was a major difference in opinion that caused the man to forsake his career. Before I make any final decisions, I want to hear from you what your intentions are for this job and if Eckardt County is a place you can see yourself living in for a good long while. To be frank, I have no intention of appointing someone who will bail on me the moment things go south."

On the spot. No holds barred. Everything the dispatcher had mentioned about Elizabeth Benoit was true. Finally, someone who didn't give a damn about their political rising star and was ready for real police work.

"Ma'am, I firmly believe this position came available at just the right time for you, and for me. I wouldn't have bought a house here if I wasn't certain of where I wanted to live. Being from Chicago, there isn't much I've seen or dealt with that makes me turn tail and run. The final decision is yours, but I don't sense that you're willing to turn me away."

Bowing her head, Sheriff Benoit stared at the open file, then with a bob, she looked up, coming to her feet at the same time. "Ms. Dayne, I'd like to welcome you to Eckardt County. While you're not official until I get the paperwork pushed through on this, I will swear you in today. And consider your position twofold."

"Twofold, meaning what?"

"Meaning, I need an investigator. The deputies I have now aren't capable of handling those details that fall on a detective's shoulders. You have the experience, and it saves me some hassle of having to bring DCI down here every time there's a questionable death."

"Why not ask one of the city departments to provide a detective?"

Sheriff's smile was thin, more of a grimace. "There is only one town in Eckardt that has a police department; the villages rely on the sheriff's office for our services. On top of it, I'm not popular around here. My election into this position brought an end to decades-long crooked dealings by certain officials, and there are about to be some nasty shake-ups. I'm the last person anyone in this county wants to give aid." She crossed her arms, tilting her chin down. "If being an investigator is more than you bargained for"—she pointed behind Lila—"there's the door."

It wasn't an option she had considered, but Lila couldn't disagree with the sheriff. She did have the training, and she was a detective before everything fell apart in Chicago. Why not? As a deputy, Lila still maintained a low profile, and would still do the police work that had been the driving factor in her choosing this career.

"While it's unconventional, I accept it."

"Perfect. Don't worry, I'll be working right alongside you."

"Sheriff, if I might be so bold, but do you have any experience as an investigator?"

A sly smile appeared. "And that right there is why I wanted you. To be frank, I don't have the formal training, so I'll be learning as we go." Rounding her desk, the sheriff approached and thrust out her hand. "Congratulations. Once I've sworn you in, we're putting your skills to the test."

Shaking the woman's hand, Lila frowned. "I'm not following."

"Deputy Dayne, your first day on the job is processing a homicide scene."

CHAPTER THREE

E LIZABETH HAD SPENT a fair chunk of her life in Juniper, except for the years when she was base hopping while Joel rose through the ranks and deployed to the likes of Iraq and Afghanistan. The day her divorce finalized, she returned to Juniper and tried to leave Joel in the past. *Tried* being the operative word. Damn fool wouldn't take a hint.

Bringing her Ford Interceptor to a stop amid the bevy of flashing sheriff's department vehicles, Elizabeth threw the gear shift in park and turned to her newly pinned deputy.

Lila stared at the activity, her gaze narrowing. "You have a medical examiner?"

"Yes. That, we manage to have."

Bentley propped herself on the center console, panting in Elizabeth's ear.

Lila glanced at their ride-along, her gaze sweeping to Elizabeth. "Will she stay in here?"

"Don't worry about Bentley."

Exiting the SUV, both women approached the yellow barrier someone had obsessively strung from one twisted tree limb to another and back again about five times.

"Rookie," Lila muttered, ducking under the taut plastic.

Elizabeth swallowed her chuckle. When she had left to meet with Lila, Meyer'd had the crime scene tape in his hands. The young deputy had taken his training seriously and wasn't about to let anyone ruin what could rightly be Eckardt County's first homicide in over a decade. Speaking of the zealous deputy, he caught sight of their entry and bolted over.

"Sheriff, I'm sorry, but you can't just let anyone in here."

Halting his progress, she slipped an arm around his shoulders and redirected his course. "Deputy Meyer, I'm ever so grateful for your keen attention to protocol, but it's okay. This is our newest addition to the team, Deputy Lila Dayne. She'll be handling investigations like this one from here on out."

Brent Meyer's pale brown eyes darkened. His family hailed from the Rhineland via Ellis Island circa 1898, crossing the country to plant roots here in a little corner of Iowa to farm, bringing with them their dark brown hair, and strong German stature and features. After Elizabeth and Joel had eloped, Brent's father, Pratt, had sold the family farm and was making a go of it in financing and banking. Rumor had it that Pratt was into more than just helping people financially. But his son was far removed from his father's shadow.

After Brent had earned his criminal justice degree at the local community college, he fast-tracked through the law enforcement academy, and had applied for a deputy position under Sheehan. The crooked sheriff would have nothing to do with him, and Elizabeth won the election. It was a no-brainer to bring the kid in, and she didn't regret her decision.

"If you say so, Sheriff." Brent cast a look over his shoulder at Lila.

"I do say so." Elizabeth released him as she caught the wary eye of another one of her deputies. "Next time let's ease the strain on the pocketbook and not string so much tape. 'K?"

"Sure thing, ma'am." He headed back toward his guard duties.

Lila stepped past Elizabeth, turning to face her. "If you don't mind, I'd like to get a better look at the scene and the body if possible."

"You'll have to gear up to rappel down to it. Ask Fitzgerald over there to help you out." Elizabeth pointed at the bearded, blond deputy. "I'll join you in a minute."

Lila gave the approaching Rafe a passing glance as she beelined for Fitzgerald.

Elizabeth stiffened her shoulders as her ex-brother-in-law slowed his stride. Rafe Fontaine was as tall and as dark haired as his brother, except that Rafe was four years younger than Joel and less hotheaded. Coming to stand next to Elizabeth, he watched Lila get Fitzgerald's attention.

"Is that the expected guest Georgia mentioned?" Rafe's voice held a hint of amusement.

"That she is, and she's about to save us time and patience. And maybe earn some trust from our residents."

He turned those blue eyes on her and tapped the corner of his mouth. "You've got a bit of a beard burn going on right there."

"Can it."

His stoic features cracking with humor, he looked away. "I wanted to mention it earlier but decided it wasn't the right time."

Asshat. She redirected her attention to the activity at hand. "Did he even bother to stop to see you?"

"Does he ever." Rafe said it as more of an answer than a question.

The brothers had a love/hate relationship, and Elizabeth was a partial reason for the ongoing tensions between the two.

"Joel is like a drug," she muttered.

Crossing his arms, Rafe grunted his response, keeping his gaze fixed on the newest deputy as she was stepping into the rappelling harness.

"Don't you dare judge me, Rafe Fontaine."

"I didn't say a word." He nodded at the female addition to the department. "So, what's her story?"

"She's keeping the details close to the vest for now. But her credentials are highly impressive. It'll be good to have someone with strong investigative skills on the team."

He shifted to block Elizabeth's view of Dayne clipping on her rigging. "You may think so, but time will tell whether this was a good move on your part or a bad one," he said. "Someone unwilling to divulge their past reeks of trouble."

"Let's not jump to those conclusions so fast."

"Sheriff!"

"Our new investigator calls." She moved to pass Rafe.

His hand shot out and he gripped her elbow. "Ellie."

Staring at their connection, she swallowed hard at the underlying tenderness in his voice.

"I'll stop by your place. If Joel is still there, I'll try to convince him he needs to stay at the farm."

"That's not necessary. I've got it handled, but thanks anyway."

His face scrunched. "You don't have it handled."

She held a finger up, pointing it at him. "No judging." Slipping free of his hold, she strode over to Fitzgerald. "Gear me up, Deputy."

As Fitzgerald assisted Elizabeth with her rappelling harness, two volunteer firemen, trained in search and rescue operations, guided Lila down the side of the ravine. Once Elizabeth was geared up and clipped into the ropes, the men aided her descent where she joined the county medical examiner, Dr. Olivia Remington-Thorpe. Deputy Dayne and the ME were making introductions. Remington-Thorpe's lone assistant had stayed up top to help lower the basket carrier they would use to hoist the body up the ravine. Elizabeth's last remaining deputy, who had not stayed up top with the others, was moving about the crime scene.

Deputy Kyle Lundquist collected anything that could be considered evidence around the unidentified female victim. Lundquist had come in late in Sheehan's term, and had no distinct loyalties to the former sheriff, which in turn made it easier for Elizabeth to keep the man on. His past service record in the navy's criminal investigation unit and a penchant for science made Lundquist a perfect choice for preliminary evidence collection before the crew from DCI arrived. Personally, Elizabeth was aware of Lundquist's reasons for being a cop; they aligned with her own in becoming sheriff. They were both looking for answers in his eldest sister's death.

"Sheriff." Olivia nodded.

"Doctor. Is there anything you can tell me?"

The ME shook her head, stray wisps of her shiny black hair flaring out from the taut ponytail. "Sorry. With the damage done by the roll down the ravine, and traces of animal activity, I can't tell a thing. It's going to take a full autopsy to get any ideas."

"I didn't notice any animal activity."

Olivia smiled. "That's because you're not trained to see it." She pointed at the crows still hovering about. "I found places where they had clawed at the victim's face."

"Anything else?"

"No." Olivia tucked a flyaway behind her ear. "Your newest deputy was just telling me that she has a lot of experience in this area. Chicago homicide, you said?"

"I did," Dayne answered.

"Interesting."

Elizabeth shifted around the two women, studying Deputy Lundquist as he methodically circled the trees behind the victim. "Are you releasing the body?"

"I am," Olivia said. "The basket to get her out of here should be coming down the ravine soon."

Elizabeth looked at the blond-tipped woman. "Deputy Dayne, that is Deputy Lundquist. He's a good man to give you details if you need them."

With a nod, Dayne approached the scene, her steps slow and measured.

Olivia came to stand shoulder to shoulder with Elizabeth. "She's got a story, doesn't she?"

"Don't we all?"

"Ellie, you always seem to attract the strays."

Didn't she know it. One particular stray had an ego the size of Mount Olympus.

"When do you plan to do the autopsy?"

Removing the blue surgical gloves by rolling one inside the other, Olivia tucked the pair into a special evidence bag she withdrew from a velcroid breast pocket of her blue-gray plaid work shirt. "As soon as I can. My morning is booked with appointments, and I have rounds at the hospital this afternoon. I'll call you when I'm ready."

"Mind if I send my new deputy in my stead?"

Olivia frowned. "I don't see why it would be a problem. But isn't this your responsibility?"

It was her responsibility. As part of her duties as sheriff, Elizabeth had to oversee all points of the investigation. But she had other duties as well that couldn't be put off any longer.

"I have a meeting later today that can't be rescheduled. I've already done so the last two times, and the recipient is none too happy with the rainchecks. I was not expecting a homicide today. Deputy Dayne has the experience, and I've got to rely on her expertise."

"I understand that. Once I know when I plan to do the autopsy, I'll pass the word along."

"Thank you. If I can make it, I'll let you know then."

They stood in silence, observing the activities of the two deputies.

"Ellie, I didn't recognize the girl," Olivia said softly.

"I know. We'll need to reach out to the public to see if there are any hits on her identity."

"Who are going to put in charge of fielding all those

phone calls?"

Elizabeth's radio crackled an incoming message. "I have an idea."

LILA CROUCHED NEAR the young woman's body, taking in the scene a piece at a time, every sense alert, doing her damnedest to not flash back to the last homicide, her downfall.

A prickle of awareness crawled up the back of her neck. The other deputy was looking at her.

Rolling her shoulders, she dispelled the sensation. *Focus.*

She pinched the edge of the flannel shirt with gloved fingers and lifted the corner. Lila hadn't asked for the medical examiner's opinion or her observations; she needed a clean slate to assess the body's condition and the state of the scene. Conjecture had no place in this investigation, because conjecture only created problems.

The black tank under the plaid shirt had tears and fabric missing, either from the roll down or prior to it. Through a few of the wider rips, Lila spotted cuts, the blood crusted and browned. A sick sensation roiled through her stomach. Had this poor woman been alive when she was thrown over the edge?

"Who are you?"

Jolting, Lila rotated on the balls of her feet and met the cold blue-green eyes. Like his counterpart above the ravine, Lundquist sported a neatly trimmed beard; unlike Fitzgerald, it looked better on him. But it was the piercing stare that set off Lila's warning alarms. This man could see too far into the soul. She wouldn't dare put her back to him again.

"I'm the new deputy."

With a cock of his head, he sniffed. "The sheriff didn't say anything about a new deputy."

"You'll have to bring that up with her. Now, if you don't mind, I would like to continue my work."

"And what work would that be?"

Giving him a canine-baring grin, she lifted a shoulder. "What every homicide investigator does: assess, process, and proceed."

His features hardened, but he kept his peace and resumed his work.

Assured he would not hinder her duties, Lila returned her attention to the victim. Mentally processing what she could, Lila pushed off her knees to her full height. Blowing the bleached, wavy strands from her face, she rotated to look downhill. The body's descent had been stopped by the squat juniper perched on a level area of the ravine. Had it not, by her guess, the momentum of the rolling the body would have gained going down the side of the cliff. It would have gone right over the flat ground, and on down the hill. To what?

Leaving her post, Lila carefully inched forward to the rounded curve of dirt and grass, planting a booted foot on a fat boulder protruding from the earth. Below was another steep hill of rocks and nearly bare ground that ended in a swollen and fast-moving stream. Had the victim fallen farther, she would have landed in the water, possibly carried away by the current. Most certainly left for the scavenging animals to pick her bones clean, stringing parts of her all over the timbered area for no one to see.

She was not meant to be found.

"Deputy Dayne?"

Lila buried her fists deep into the jacket pockets as the sheriff joined her.

"Your thoughts?"

"Merely impressions at this point. I'd rather gather more details before I say anything."

Sheriff Benoit made a noise of satisfaction low in her throat.

"Might I ask one thing?"

"Fire away."

"Do you know the victim?"

The faded sounds of men talking above and the arrival of yet another vehicle merged with the whisper of wind through the boughs around them. Sheriff Benoit stared down the hill, tense lines deepening her crow's feet.

"We do not," she said after a moment, her darkened eyes turning to Lila. "I'm afraid this case might be far from cut and dried."

Lila's pulse thundered, adrenaline surging through her veins. That old quickening fluttered in her chest, the feeling she missed about being an investigator. The hunt. The thrill of the chase. Finding a killer who wanted to remain in the shadows, free from the law's long arm. All these sensations had been stripped from her in the weeks following the end of her career in Chicago.

"That's fine," she heard herself say. "I like it when they play hard to get."

CHAPTER FOUR

ONCE THEIR JANE Doe had been properly handled and sent to the morgue, and the deputies had finished processing the scene, Elizabeth drove Dayne back to the courthouse. After delegating duties, Elizabeth finished off her cooled morning coffee, and, with Bentley at her side, was about to head out once more. Mrs. McKinnley awaited.

"Sheriff." Deputy Dayne's voice echoed in the hallowed courthouse halls.

Pausing next to the exit, Elizabeth faced her newest addition. "Formality is a bit of a dinosaur here in Juniper. You can call me Elizabeth."

"Not all of your deputies seem to hold to that idea."

Elizabeth smiled. "One day that will change. What can I help you with?"

"I'd like to come with you."

Blinking, she cocked her head and regarded Lila Dayne. The shortened hair was pushed back from her heart-shaped face, and then left to fall in place.

"I know you want me to stay and familiarize myself with the department and how it runs, but I'd get a better feel of things if I just rode with you." She dipped her chin, peering at Elizabeth with her light brown eyes. "The residents of Eckardt County would be more comfortable with me if I am seen with you."

"That's true." Elizabeth took in the quiet street littered with fallen leaves from the three maples dotting the dormant Kentucky bluegrass yard. A blue sedan crawled along the street. "We are a wary lot to outsiders and immigrants."

"And what constitutes as an outsider?"

Elizabeth pointed at Lila. "You. Don't be surprised if the residents around here start off disregarding you in favor of a son or daughter of Eckardt. And I warn you, do not take offense to it."

Opening the door for Bentley to snake-pipe through, Elizabeth gestured for Dayne to follow and exited.

All three settled in Elizabeth's Ford. She backed out of the parking lot, pointed the fat nose of the SUV in the right direction, and drove out of town. Deputy Dayne spent a considerable amount of time studying the streets.

"Why did you decide to run for sheriff?" she asked ten minutes into the trip.

Flicking on her blinker, Elizabeth slowed the Ford to a full stop at the intersection she wanted, waiting for a tractor hauling two grain wagons loaded with soybeans to pass. She waved at the farmer and was rewarded with the obligatory Iowa one-hand lift. Once the second wagon cleared, she turned.

"The crime rate isn't as high as say Chicago's, but in the last twenty years or more there has been an alarming uptick in activity. I spent a lot of time researching this during my campaign."

"Any reason for this?"

"I have my suspicions but no concrete proof. As of late, it

hasn't been my focus. Cleaning up the department budget and squaring off against some egomaniacs who seem to think money can be better spent elsewhere have taken my full attention."

Dayne fell silent.

As she tooled along, Elizabeth met three semis, two coming back from the grain storage facilities and one on its way there. The start to the crop year hadn't gone well for the farmers. Between the late planting due to winter's long grip and the weeklong rains that had drowned the freshly sprouted seedlings, and then replanting when the fields dried out, the farmers were scrambling. They were already into the first of December, and so many of the fields had yet to be harvested. Luckily, the Farmers' Almanac was calling for a delayed winter. As long as that held true, things would work out.

"Where is it you're headed?" Dayne asked as they passed by huge grain storage bins.

"Three Points, the only other town big enough to have an actual mayor."

"And what is your reason for coming out here?"

Elizabeth had certainly chosen the right woman for this position. "A disturbance call."

"This land goes on forever," Dayne muttered after a brief bout of reticence.

"Correct me if I'm wrong, but in my many travels, I seem to remember a lot of crop ground in Illinois."

Dayne frowned, staring at the flat, fertile fields, some bare, some with still-standing, dried yellow stalks. "Yeah, but it's nothing like this."

"No, I guess it isn't, since Iowa is the second leading state in crop production."

The new deputy frowned at her. "And I need to know that why?"

"Because, Deputy Dayne, you are now in the agricultural heartbeat of America and the world, but I digress. If you want to learn and get to know the people who live here, you need to speak their language. Eckardt County is a farming community. Main topics of conversation okay to discuss." Elizabeth held up her hand and counted off. "Weather, how the grands are doing, and what new recipe you discovered. Topics off-limits: politics, religion, and what new ailment your doctor told you about."

At that precise moment they passed a large swine confinement facility that sat about two hundred yards off the main road and was surrounded by a thick stand of fast-growing poplar trees.

"And that right there is the reason Iowa leads the nation in pork."

Dayne sighed. "I think I'll stick to solving murders."

Biting back the humor twitching at her lips, Elizabeth lifted her chin at the large wooden sign painted blue, green, and gold that announced: Welcome to Three Points, Home of the Fighting Militia.

"Here we are."

She bypassed the town's main street and skirted the perimeter to meet with a narrow road that was more seal-coated gravel than pavement. Elizabeth kept the SUV to a slow crawl. A meticulous lawn bordered by a white-painted fence came into view, meeting at the drive with two wrought-iron gates topped with old-fashioned gas lamps. The gates were swung back to allow entry. Off in the distance, through a stand of trees and a tangle of brush dividing the property lines, visitors could make out the outline of what was once a stately Queen Anne home. The ruins were a constant complaint of the resident in the home at the end of the lane Elizabeth drove along.

"Wow," Dayne whispered.

Indeed. The elongated, single-story, brick ranch could be considered a showy house, but the woman living among the bright red walls and white trim was completely the opposite. Mrs. Neva McKinnley, English and British literature teacher-extraordinaire, had never been accused of being flashy or showy. She epitomized her generation as the prim and proper schoolmarm who, after retirement, took up gardening and caring for her ailing husband. Clark McKinnley had passed away eight years ago after a long battle with Parkinson's. Deep in the heart of Germany, Elizabeth had mailed a condolence card to her once-favorite teacher.

Parking her SUV in front of the garage, Elizabeth exited with Bentley hot on her heels. Dayne closed the passenger door with a clap.

"This place looks like it belongs in *Better Homes and Gardens*."

Lifting a shoulder, Elizabeth grinned. "I think a neighbor tried to get her to submit pictures to the magazine, but Mrs. McKinnley isn't in to putting on airs, so she claims." She paused at the bottom of the steps. "Two things. One"—she held up a finger—"she likes to entertain, so do not turn down her hospitality. And two"—second finger went up—

"for a retired English teacher, she can put the best lawyer to shame when she cross-examines, so be on alert."

"Got it."

Bentley waited next to the door, her gaze zeroed in on the handle. Elizabeth pressed the doorbell. Their wait was short. A gauzy curtain fluttered to the left, and then the door swung open.

"Sheriff, so good of you to come. And you brought your sweet pup." Neva McKinnley bowed, her hands cupped Bentley's face, and she lavished the collie with love, then produced the expected treat. Lapping up her reward, Bentley licked the age-spotted hand and then squeezed between Elizabeth's and Dayne's legs to have run of the yard.

Sharp hazel eyes pierced the two women through a pair of spectacles. "Shall we?" She stepped aside.

Elizabeth leading the way, the two entered the McKinnley home, greeted by the aroma of yeast and cinnamon. Dayne closed her eyes, and her chest rose and fell. With a smile, Elizabeth followed the retired teacher down the hall to her kitchen.

"Mrs. McKinnley, I'd like you to meet my newest deputy, Lila Dayne."

Neva McKinnley stopped, turned, and examined the woman at Elizabeth's side. A purse of her lips preceded a nod of approval before Neva continued into the heartbeat of her home.

"Would you like a cup of coffee and a sticky roll?"

"Love to," Dayne interjected before Elizabeth could answer.

Another nod of approval, the elder McKinnley headed

for the coffeepot.

Dayne leaned closer to Elizabeth. "What's a sticky roll?"

"Heaven with pecans." She pointed at the kitchen table. "Have a seat, Deputy. Let me help you with those, Mrs. McKinnley."

Two fat rolls slathered in gooey goodness were plated on the guest china, and two delicate cups of steaming coffee placed on the table. Neva sat along with Elizabeth at the table. The teacher watched the deputy fork in a bite of the roll and smiled that all-knowing smile behind her cup as Dayne's face melted into sheer pleasure.

"Now, Mrs. McKinnley, I received your complaint regarding the noise you heard at the old Barrett place. Can you describe what it was you heard?"

"I can tell you down to the fine details. As you know, it was unusually still last night, and the sounds carried perfectly through the trees."

"How far is your home from this Barrett place?" Dayne asked.

Frowning, Neva glared at the younger woman.

Dayne's gaze flicked to Elizabeth. Giving her new deputy a shake of her head, she gathered Mrs. McKinnley's attention once more.

"Go on."

"For your information, it's a good four hundred yards from here to there. I had my bedroom window open since the weather was so glorious yesterday. The noises I heard coming from that place made my skin crawl. It sounded like someone was trying to scream and laugh at the same time. I also heard sounds like wood splintering. I got up to close my window to stop the awful racket, and the last thing I heard was a low grumble like one of those all-terrain vehicles." She set her cup down and stared right into Elizabeth's eyes. "I'm telling you, those wicked teenagers in town are using that abandoned place for their illicit affairs, and probably destroying that monstrosity in the interim. Mark my words, someone will end up dead in there soon enough."

"Have you heard anything like that before last night?" Dayne interjected.

Elizabeth bit her lip before the smile popped up. The elder McKinnley, however, didn't look so favorable upon the deputy.

"You're new around here."

In an apparent bid to save herself from the scrutinizing stare of a drill instructor teacher, Dayne shoveled another forkful of sticky bun in her mouth.

"Yes, my deputy is new."

"She's got that Chicago nasal going on. Is that where you are from? Chicago?"

Dayne dipped her chin and nodded, her gaze focused on the cup of coffee.

Sighing, Neva met Elizabeth's gaze once more. "Manners, Sheriff, manners."

"Yes, ma'am, we'll get right to it." Enjoying a sip of her coffee, Elizabeth waited.

"This is the twenty-third call I've put into the sheriff's office about those odd, disruptive noises. That Slick Willy excuse of a sheriff from before didn't bother to give me the time of day. Now you, Elizabeth, you have answered every single call."

"Yes, I have."

"And you still can't figure out who is causing all that racket."

"Unfortunately, I have not. I have, however, seen where there have been intruders. I just can't make out if they are of the two-legged or four-legged kind. Maybe Deputy Dayne can help me with that today."

"Let's hope your intuition proves right, Sheriff." Neva picked up their dirty dishes and took them to the sink. "My son believes I'm going senile in my old age. He says that if there is any truth to my claims, it is high time that place be demolished and the ground put to better use." She turned back to the table. "He managed to sway the town and county councils to get the building condemned, which I have no objection to. However, that doesn't stop anyone from running amok through there. The sole living Barrett is livid that he moved on the place without her consent."

Elizabeth cringed. "Who told her?"

"Jason did." Neva resumed her seat with a shake of her head. "That boy of mine has a thick skull when it comes to certain individuals in this county."

Dayne cast Elizabeth an inquiring look, but Elizabeth waved off the inevitable question. "Mrs. McKinnley, I believe my deputy and I will go over to check out the Barrett place. If I find there is something to be alarmed about, I will notify you and your son. In the meantime, keep an ear out for me."

The grand dame gave a courtly nod.

Elizabeth rose, Dayne quickly joining her. "Thank you for the respite. We'll show ourselves out."

"Be sure you take another treat out to Bentley," Neva said.

"I wouldn't dare leave here without one. Bentley would never forgive me."

Elizabeth gave her new deputy a heaping ton of credit as she kept her own council while the two of them strode out of the house, two more doggie treats in hand, snatched from the container left by the door. Releasing a piercing three-tone whistle the minute her boots hit the sidewalk, Elizabeth headed for her SUV. She was at the driver's side the second Bentley raced across the wide yard. The border collie glided to a halt right at her feet and looked up with a smile.

"That's a girl." Elizabeth rewarded her dog and opened the door. Bentley bounded inside and was in her spot before Elizabeth could take her seat. Last treat given, she checked to ensure Dayne was secure and then turned over the engine.

"How many calls have you actually responded to that she's called in?" she asked as Elizabeth backed out of the drive.

"Five since I started. And it's only been a month."

"Eighteen of those went to the previous sheriff. Over the course of how many years?"

"That I couldn't tell you. He didn't track them. Georgia, who has a long-standing memory, recalls at least three years."

The drive was short and sweet, and Elizabeth parked in front of the rotting building. All three spilled out, Bentley staying close to the two women as she sniffed the ground around the gnarled shrubbery.

"Who is the sole living Barrett?"

"Martha Kauffmann. Everyone around here calls her

Ma." Elizabeth picked a path through the tall, brittle grass. "Don't ask me why everyone calls her that, it's just been that way. She was an only child to the last and only Barrett son."

With Dayne following a few steps back, the two circled the house. At one time the residence had been painted a brilliant yellow with blue and green trim, the wraparound porch an inviting place to sit a spell and chat with the family while the kids played on the rope swings hanging from massive oaks now long dead and gone. Elizabeth recalled her parents saying they had met here at an ice cream social when they were a respective eleven and ten years of age.

Now the once grand Queen Anne stood on a sinking, crumbling rock foundation, her three stained glass windows removed, and the remaining windows shattered or missing. The two turret roofs were sinking, while the main roof was tattered and hole-ridden. The still-standing oak trees had been battered and broken by wild midwestern storms, and the prized rosebushes were overgrown and dying.

"Such a sad state for a piece of the town's history," Dayne stated.

Elizabeth stopped next to what had been the carriage house converted into a garage, and looked up at the faded and peeled siding. "Yes. The Barretts' son didn't carry the same pride and joy his parents did over his inheritance. When he died, the place came into Martha's possession. But she'd been estranged from her father for decades, and she never saw fit to redeem her family legacy. By then it was too late to save the house."

"Then why was she so mad that the mayor had it condemned?"

"I don't know. Maybe because it wasn't her idea to do it. Or she's just a cantankerous woman looking for a reason to be mad at anyone and everyone." Sighing, she dragged her gaze from the dilapidated building. "At least there are photos in city hall to remind everyone of what this place once stood for."

She moved toward the back of the collapsed carriage house.

"And what did it stand for?" Dayne asked, following.

"Perseverance and stubborn midwestern pride." Elizabeth halted, staring at a pair of tracks leading away from the site and plunging into the thick woods at the edge of the property. "Someone was here on an ATV."

Dayne crouched next to the closest set, the grass bent and broken by the weight of the machines and rider. "Is there a path through there?"

"There's only one I know of, but it's been decades since I was back there. My ex-husband and his buddies were known to have parties out there. He and his brother know that place like the back of their hand. Though I'm fairly certain things have changed over the years. If memory serves me correct, it's terrain better suited for ATVs or horses."

Coming to her full height, Dayne circumvented the tracks and examined the area around the carriage house. "I see a path through the grass here." She rotated to face the house. "Looks like it leads to the back door."

Elizabeth joined her. Staring at the jagged path, she couldn't tell how many people had trespassed through here. "What are your thoughts, Deputy Dayne?"

"How safe is it to go inside?"

"Let's find out."

CHAPTER FIVE

L ILA WAS NOT prepared for the onslaught of smells when she stepped through the broken screen door. Wincing at the pungent odor of urine and scat mingled with mold and decay, she pressed the sleeve of her coat to her nose. The room she and the sheriff entered looked like the kitchen. All the appliances and hardware were long gone, and the cabinets and counters had been damaged by rain rot or left in splinters.

Before she disturbed any more of the scene, she halted the sheriff and examined the floor. Nature's debris littered the place, piles of dirt and leaves packed into every nook and cranny comingled with crushed beer cans, broken bottles, and other litter. There was too much garbage to tell if anyone had been in here recently.

"As we go through, be careful. The flooring has rotted in some areas to the point you'd fall through into the cellar," the sheriff said as she jabbed a thumb at a darkened closet. "The pantry. Stay out, it's nothing but a hole."

Giving her boss a nod, Lila proceeded forward, her gaze sweeping the room, and finding nothing of significance, she moved onto the next, which proved to have been the dining room. Butted up to the large, open area was another room that had been divided by pocket doors now lying broken on the floor. Lila spotted the weakened places by the dips in the flooring. Carpet had been pulled from the edges and left about in piles. It was more than a shame that this place had gone to rot; it was a crime.

Sheriff Benoit pointed to another room directly in front of them. "The living room or parlor, I guess. Beyond that is the vestibule and a second set of stairs leading to the upper level."

"Would you hazard a guess that it's safe to go up them?"

"It's possible. When they built these houses, they made sure everything was solid and sturdy. We could check it out."

"Got a flashlight?"

"Hang tight." The sheriff left the way they came in.

Lila navigated the debris, trekking to the living area. She noted the lack of dust under the edges of the broken furniture, as if the pieces had been shifted recently. A former table looked freshly splinted—that could possibly explain the sound of breaking wood Mrs. McKinnley heard.

The sheriff calling to her dog and closing the SUV door drifted through the open windows. Lila took stock of the gaping holes where windows should be, every single pane fractured and missing. Without that barrier, as the retired teacher had stated, on a still night any sounds coming from this place would have carried.

Lila gazed up at the grille work that divided the rooms, the broken teeth gaping jack-o'-lantern style, then passed under it. Dust covered railing, but there were disturbed spots. Someone had touched the banister.

The sheriff returned, flashlight in hand.

"There." Lila pointed.

Turning on the light, Sheriff Benoit directed the beam at the banister. "Well, that answers the question of whether it's safe to go up or not."

Together they moved to the staircase. The carpet on the stairs remained, and even with the flashlight's beam, it was hard to distinguish footprints in the mess that covered the steps.

"What do you think, Deputy?"

"Nothing much. Someone was here, but I can't tell you if it was male or female, nor how many." Lila stared up the darkened maw. "We need to go up. Whatever took place here last night had to have happened up there."

"You didn't see anything down here other than the marks here on the banister?"

"It looks like some of the old furniture in the dining area might have been broken. But what's to say a coon didn't sit on it and it broke?"

Sheriff Benoit made a satisfied hmm, and then took the lead up the stairs. Partway up, she halted. "Broken step."

They bypassed the dangerous spot and continued up to a small landing bearing a squat window that miraculously still contained all of its glass panes, then up five more steps to the second floor. Benoit swept the beam along the floor and up the walls, then down the hall.

Lila recoiled at the stench of decay. "Dead animal?"

"Probably. Let's hope so."

The first open door revealed a large bedroom with a rusted iron bedframe centered in the room. Dust, an inch thick, remained undisturbed. Sheriff Benoit shook her head. The two of them edged down the hall to the next doorway.

When the light passed over the wall to their left, Lila grasped the sheriff's shoulder. "Wait." She held out her hand for the flashlight and angled the beam on the marks. "It looks like blood." She straightened. "I just don't know how old it is. This whole place can distort evidence."

"Which makes it a good place to do a dirty deed." Benoit stepped aside and gestured for Lila to take point.

The second room revealed shredded curtains dangling from broken windows. Nothing else. A room devoid of dust. Now that was peculiar. Why this room and not the one with a bed? The sickly sweet odor of decomp emitted from the room directly across from it. A dead possum. Flies buzzed the body.

"Gross," the sheriff muttered and turned away.

Blinking against the moisture building in her eyes, Lila mentally cataloged the otherwise empty room.

"Deputy."

Gladly putting her back to the stench, she followed the sheriff into a small bathroom. What remained in the room was a pedestal sink and a cast-iron, claw-foot bathtub. It was the flecks of brown-red staining the side of the sink that made Lila's pulse race.

She crouched down to get a better look. "I'm convinced this is blood. And that smear in the hallway is too."

"Could be animal blood."

"We can test it." Lila straightened, her gaze landing on the tub. "What are the odds?"

The floorboards creaked under her weight but held. She examined the basin. Between the chipped porcelain, and the exposed and rusting metal, she couldn't make out if there was blood. The whole thing would have to be luminol sprayed and swab tested.

An ominous creak broke through her thoughts.

"Deputy Dayne."

Swallowing against the sudden clench in her throat, Lila peered down at her boots. Another crack followed by a screech made her muscles seize.

"Lila, get back," Benoit warned.

Shaking free of the momentary fear, Lila inched her left foot back. The tub tilted as the floorboards groaned. Panic overriding her senses, she planted her foot down and pushed off. Her vault was hindered by the wood giving way and the tub sinking. She twisted in time to turn the good side of her body and see the sheriff coming at her.

Lila slammed into the splintering floorboards. Pain pierced her momentarily, forgotten the second her body started to slip backward. She glanced over her shoulder to see the tub disappear through the hole she was now falling into. A strong grip on her arms brought her descent to a halt, her legs swung precariously over the edge of the hole. Below the tub smashed into the first floor, and continued its destruction.

"Hold on," Benoit ground out, and hauled back.

Lila scrambled for purchase, feeling her body begin to slide forward. When her hips hit the edge of the hole, she was able to use her elbows to hoist herself out. Flopping onto the floor beside the sheriff, Lila grabbed a quick breath.

"We need to get out of here." Benoit got to her feet and helped Lila up.

Both women backpedaled out of the room as more of the

floor gave way, taking the pedestal sink with it.

"Thanks for the save," Lila gasped out. A stitch in her right side took her breath. At least it was her right and not the left, something she could be grateful for. Had she landed on her left, there would be hell to pay.

"This is not what I planned for your first day on the job, Deputy."

Lila cupped the back of her neck, staring at the shattered remains of the upstairs bathroom. Whatever evidence left in this room was now gone or tainted. She turned to the hallway wall. The mysterious smear was all that was left.

"Well, one thing's for sure." She met the sheriff's gaze. "Mrs. McKinnley wasn't wrong about hearing something coming from this place."

"She never is." Benoit gripped Lila's shoulder. "We should get out of here before more of this place comes down on us."

"Got a pocketknife?"

Frowning, the sheriff reached into her pants pocket and withdrew a knife. Lila took it and patted her coat; her cell phone had remained on her during the fall. Hopefully it had not be crushed. She marched back down the shadowed hall, pulling her phone out, and then stopped. The flashlight had gone down with the tub when she'd tried to save herself.

Benoit seemed to pick up on her thoughts and waved her down. "Don't worry about the light. I've got more in the SUV."

Finding her phone was in good condition, Lila activated the flashlight app and shone it on the smear. She took multiple pictures of it before pulling out a leftover evidence baggie from her pants pocket. With the blade of the knife, she scraped off a good-sized part of the smear into the bag and sealed it. She handed the knife back to the sheriff and pocketed the evidence.

"Now we can get out of here."

CHAPTER SIX

COVERED IN DUST and grime, Elizabeth and Dayne entered the department behind Bentley. Elizabeth noticed spots of blood on her new deputy's shirt around her midriff, but the woman waved it off. Dayne, however, couldn't hide her grimaces and winces as she moved or walked. But Elizabeth wouldn't push the matter. Yet.

They were greeted in the main office with wide-eyed stares.

"Sheriff?" Deputy Meyer jumped up from his seat and hustled over. "What happened?"

Giving the kid a smile she sure didn't feel, Elizabeth tsked. "We're fine. Just a little incident in an old house." She peeked at Dayne, who was holding her midsection and refusing to meet her gaze. "Deputy Lundquist, would you and Deputy Dayne take these samples she gathered to your lab and test them?"

Lundquist strolled out from behind his desk, hooking his thumbs in his duty belt. "What kind of samples?"

"I think it's blood," Dayne answered. "But I'm not sure what kind."

Behind the deputies, Elizabeth caught Georgia tilting her head and jerking it toward Elizabeth's office. The dispatcher's features were tight. A good sign someone was in her office she shouldn't let overhear their discussions.

"You two can discuss that on your way." Elizabeth side-stepped around Dayne. "And while you're at it, have the doc check her over."

"I told you I was fine," Dayne bit out.

"I'm the sheriff, and what I say goes. Hear me, Lundquist?"

"Yes, ma'am." His normally gravelly voice deepened.

Elizabeth hesitated at the change and eyed the veteran deputy. Something was on his mind. When Kyle Lundquist's voice dipped, he was stewing. Right now, she didn't have time to analyze that. When he was ready to offload, she'd hear about it.

"Good. Now if ya'll will excuse me." Elizabeth rounded the corner of Georgia's desk. "She's here already?" she asked under her breath.

"And she isn't the only one," Georgia answered and rolled her eyes heavenward.

Not sure who she referred to by that big gesture, Elizabeth opened the door, allowing Bentley to push inside first. Her expected visitor turned her head as Elizabeth entered, but it was the man sitting beside her that made Elizabeth want to chew nails.

"Ma, nice of you to come early." She closed the door and then glared at her ex-husband. "Joel, why are you in here?"

"I came to talk with you and decided to keep my cousin company while we waited."

"Great, well, now you can leave and allow myself and Ma to have our discussion."

With a chuckle that spoke of years of smoking, Martha

Kauffmann squeezed Joel's knee. "That's all right, Ellie. Joel is family, and this is, after all, family business."

"Ma, he's like your fourth or fifth cousin. I don't think that can be construed as close enough for family business."

Another chuckle and Ma slapped her hands in her lap. "Family is family, no matter the distance. If you were still married to him, you'd still be my family."

And she'd still not care two bits about it. Circling her desk, Elizabeth stepped over Bentley's prone body and slipped into her chair.

"My dear, you look like you got in a fight with a dust bowl," Ma commented.

Elizabeth glanced at Joel. He was studying her, using that damn Delta mojo mental deal he'd perfected on her, trying to get a read on what she was about to say. She hated that.

Meeting Ma's worried eyes, Elizabeth patted her shirt. "Oh, it's nothing but a little dirt and grime from an old house. Your daddy's old house, to be exact."

Ma cocked her head. "What were you doing in that broke down place?"

"Just checking on a disturbance complaint. Ma, we must have a serious discussion about bulldozing that place to the ground. Myself and my newly appointed deputy were about killed when the upstairs bathroom caved in."

Horror filled Ma's face. "My God, girl, what in the world possessed you to walk through it? You know that house is about to come crashing down."

Joel sat unmoved, his features blank and smooth. But his eyes gave away his thoughts. He'd never been able to hide that part of himself from Elizabeth. Once Ma left this office,

Joel was going to lecture her on safety. Where was the whiskey?

"Yes, Ma, I'm well aware of that, and made even more so by the earlier events. Which is grounds for me to push for you to have it torn down. It's either me coming to you on friendly terms or the mayor doing it behind your back. Just having it condemned doesn't stop people from going inside, which is why we were there. Someone is going to get seriously hurt and then you'll be liable."

"We'll discuss that later. What I want to know is what you've been able to learn about my son's death."

Three years ago, shortly before Elizabeth returned to Juniper, Daniel Kauffmann, Ma's second son, was killed in a terrible car accident. The moment Elizabeth had won her seat as sheriff, Ma had pushed her to reopen the investigation. Appeasing the matriarch of the Kauffmann family and easing her own curious nature at the same time, Elizabeth had. What she'd learned was fairly straightforward.

One winter night on a slick, snow-packed gravel road, Daniel Kauffmann lost control of his Chevy Silverado and went off the road at a high rate of speed. The vehicle flipped over an estimated five times, crashing into a highline pole, which ripped the truck in half. Daniel had been ejected from the vehicle and killed on impact with the ground. It was believed he'd fallen asleep, as his body had no signs of alcohol or drug use.

However, Ma maintained foul play was involved. Someone had followed her son and forced him off the road, why else would he have been going so fast? But the investigators on the scene claimed it was possible with the slick conditions for the truck to speed up, or Daniel had pressed the accelerator as he fell asleep. Elizabeth had to agree with the findings.

Clasping her hands together, and with a quick look at her ex, Elizabeth sighed and leaned forward. "Ma, I've gone over all the reports and talked with the first responders who were there. They didn't see any signs someone had forced him off the road."

"They're lying, Ellie, and you know it."

"What would they have to gain from lying about how he died?"

Ma's deep brown eyes sparked. She was known to have a temper but rarely showed it. The woman was the heartbeat of her family, practically raising three boys alone amid the rumors swirling around town about her husband in the years before he died. She'd risen above the poverty Henry Kauffmann had left her in at his passing and regained the dignity that had fallen away from her on the day she said "I do."

"You know damn well my family has gained enemies. I told you so."

"Yes, you did. And believe me, Ma, I don't take anything you say lightly. But there is no evidence to prove your theory."

Ma leaned forward, jutting out her chin in a defiance born of hardships and her stubborn nature. "Ellie, I made no bones about my problems with Kelley Sheehan. I was upfront with you from the start that that man has been out to get me ever since my Henry died. He and his posse were known to lie."

This was an all too common story many people had come to Elizabeth about once she took office. Her predecessor had a mile-long list of complaints from just about everyone in Eckardt County. Problem being, ex-sheriff Sheehan was crafty enough to toe the line with the law so it became next to impossible to prove the allegations against his corruption. And Elizabeth hadn't been on the job long enough to get a chance to dig deeper and prove her own suspicions about the man.

"Ma, let's be frank here, are you insinuating that the former sheriff may be involved with orchestrating Daniel's death?"

Ma's chin lowered. She glanced at Joel, and then relaxed against the chair back. "Mighty big words coming from you, Ellie-girl. All that time following Joel all over the world turned you into someone who is better than your roots?"

"Martha, don't deflect," Joel said softly.

With a humph, Ma stood. "I came to you as an old family friend with a deep concern. I won't sit here and be treated like a crook."

Old family friend, my eye. "That's not what is happening here." Elizabeth rose, feeling the aches from her impromptu rescue. "I need just one solid reason to continue forward with my probing. At this point, my hands are tied. Even the State Patrol troopers who had been on the scene said the evidence just wasn't there to prove he was forced off the road."

"I told you every reason I had." A chill lanced the office.

"When you find another one, come to me about it." Elizabeth stared the older woman dead in the eye. "I mean it. If there is any piece of information that can change the outcome of Daniel's death, I will give it my undivided attention. I can promise you that."

Shaking her head, Ma exited the office, closing the door with a sharp clack. Georgia would know how to handle the situation; she'd dealt with plenty of angry people leaving Sheehan's office over the years.

Elizabeth's attention narrowed to her ex. "Whatever you came here to discuss with me better be quick. I'm in the middle of a homicide investigation."

Joel unfolded his lithe body from the chair and came around the desk to her side. "Rafe mentioned to me that you were going to be tied up for the next few days."

Turning to face him, she became acutely aware of his breech of her personal space. Tired, sore, and fed up with fighting his pull on her, she allowed it. On the flip side, it made her recall why she'd slipped up last night and gave in to her urge to be with him one more time.

He brushed aside the hair tickling her cheek, rubbing the pad of his thumb along her prominent cheekbone. "I didn't come back to Iowa to seduce you back into bed with me."

Rolling her eyes, she huffed. "That's not how it came off last night."

One side of his mouth quirked up. He had not shaven, and the five o'clock shadow reminded her of those days leading up to a mission where he had to look the part. Joel's area of expertise had been Eastern Europe and parts of the Middle East due to his distinct features and the ability to blend in with the populace. And Elizabeth was privy to this only because she had snooped well enough that no one was the wiser.

"One too many drinks." His hand slipped behind her

head, tangling his fingers in her hair. "You do things to me, Ellie."

Craning her head enough to be free of his hand, she put some space between them. "I don't have all day. Come to the point."

Frustration flashed through his baby blues, but he kept his temper in check. "I'm getting out of the field."

Shock pulsated through her. Joel no longer doing missions? Hell had frozen over.

"And why the sudden decision?"

He tilted his head in what could have been a shrug. "The Unit needs younger blood, and there's a candidate list that looks impressive."

There was more to it. So much more.

"Something happened on your last mission."

Joel stared at her, arms crossed, his gaze hard. She knew all too well he couldn't say, but it wouldn't stop her from pushing—a consistent point of contention between them. But she was no longer a Delta Force wife. She had all the right in the world to not put up with his secrets.

"Never mind. Good luck with whatever you decide."

She moved to step past him, but his hand snagged her elbow.

"I'm not getting out. They've asked me to move into an instructor position with Selection."

"And how do Nico and Craig feel about you training new recruits in Selection, instead of running all over hell stopping bad guys with them?" His two closest friends in Delta were also longtime team members. All three had been selected into The Unit at the same time.

Elizabeth liked the men, had enjoyed many a gathering with the guys when they were home. She even dared a bit of flirting with Nico just to get a rise out of Joel. It had never worked.

"They're doing the same."

"Wow. All three of you Selection officers. That should be . . . boring."

Joel maneuvered to face her once more, cupping her face with both hands. "Give up this crazy idea to be sheriff and come back with me. I want us. I want to start fresh and make it work this time."

"This isn't a crazy idea. I like doing this job."

"You've only been at it, what, a month? It's not you, Ellie."

"And who are you to say what is me and what isn't?" She pulled his hands away. "I gave an oath to the people of Eckardt County to protect them. I promised those deputies out there that things would be different, better than they were before. I'm not doing this on some whim."

"No, you're doing it to find out what really happened to Bre."

"So what if I am?"

"For God's sake, Elizabeth, her death was an accident. Let it go."

"You don't get to tell me what to do." She managed to get past him, putting the desk between them. "I gave up a lot for you, Joel. I left this place so you could chase your dreams, while mine were put on hold. I lost friends because I wanted what you wanted. I'm not going back to the status quo."

"Bre's death is why you took all those law classes and got

a criminology degree? Damn it, I should have seen it. This obsession with her death isn't healthy."

Elizabeth shook her head. "Once more you prove just how little you know about me."

Joel held out his hands, a beggar pleading for more. "I know you loved me."

"At one time I did, but I've moved on. I want other things." She snapped her fingers and Bentley moved to her side. "And those things don't include you. Tell the guys I said hi." She headed for the door, pausing as she opened it, and looked back at Joel. "I mean it. I want you out of my house before I get home."

"Or what?"

"Or Rafe comes to remove you. And he's just pissed enough, he won't be nice."

"Still running to my little brother when you don't get your way."

Elizabeth stared at him, swallowing the anger bubbling inside. Sighing, she let the passive smile slip in place. "Jealousy doesn't become you, Joel." With that, she stepped into the open office.

Greeting her with expectants eyes were Meyer and Georgia. She nodded to Georgia.

"Deputy Meyer, why are you not at home getting some sleep?"

"We have an ongoing investigation, Sheriff. Sleep can wait."

"He took a nap at my instance," Georgia said.

Meyer blushed red at the statement. "It wasn't long."

"It's better than no sleep." She looked her dog in the

eyes. "Bentley, stay." The collie sat where she stood. "Georgia, hold down the fort. Deputy Meyer, you're with me."

"Where are we going?"

"The hospital. My afternoon plans have changed, and Dr. Remington-Thorpe is waiting."

Elizabeth chanced a look back at her office to see Joel standing in the doorway. Once upon a time, that had been her, watching him leave with his men to some war-ravaged country, never knowing if he'd return alive or dead. The difference being, she wasn't off to war.

She focused on the hallway before her. It felt good closing that chapter of her life. The new one was a blank page before her. One she was ready to fill with her own story.

CHAPTER SEVEN

THE RIDE IN Lundquist's department-issued truck had been excruciating, and not just because of the pain in her abdomen. Lila couldn't get a good read on the man; her intuition said he was a good cop, but the scowl he cast at the windshield warned of some storm brewing in the man. To avoid any more awkwardness, Lila kept her thoughts to herself, suffering the ride in silence, made more so with the throbbing in her side.

Currently, the pain had eased as she stood in a small lab in a near-empty wing of the hospital, watching Lundquist as he transferred the samples she'd taken from the house to his testing materials. Equipment needed for quick sample testing was scattered about the lab on counters and in foam-padded boxes. Lundquist was prepared for anything, and that felt off to her for a deputy. In Lila's experience forensics was a scientist's realm, not usually a position for an LEO. Yes, she had trained in evidence collection, but most of the actual science was left for the CSIs.

She noted the sealed evidence bags marked DCI with today's date on them. Evidence he'd tagged at the homicide scene this morning. Lila rolled up on her tiptoes and studied the bags better. The items in the bags appeared to be things Lundquist was not capable of handling in his limited lab.

"What do you want me to test for?"

His question rattled Lila out of her snooping. Blinking her face into a mask of indifference, she looked at him. "Is it human or animal blood? You do have the ability to check for that, right?"

Grunting a response, he turned back to his kits and dipped a dropper into a clear vial, then carefully dropped a bead of liquid on a slide with a sample.

Lila abandoned her position and inched closer to the counter, watching for the reaction she hoped she'd see. A moment later the brown fleck separated from the paint and plaster and congealed. Smug satisfaction slithered through her.

"Human," Lundquist said, straightening. He looked at her. "What's the story on this?"

"Not fully sure, but I extracted it from the old Barrett house." She tucked her hands inside her coat pockets, stirring the dust that had settled on the fabric. Her movements earned a scowl from the man across from her.

"That explains your and the sheriff's filthy conditions, but not why you were in there." He set about conserving the samples and labeling them.

"Mrs. McKinnley filed a disturbance complaint and we checked it out. Too bad some of the house collapsed while we were in there, dropping potential evidence into the cellar."

Lundquist's head whipped in her direction, a startled expression momentarily erasing the scowl. "The house collapsed?"

"Part of it did."

Angry lines creased the corners of his eyes, the blue depths sparking. "Neither of you should have been in there. That place is barely standing, the sheriff knows that. What the hell was she thinking? You talked her into it, didn't you?"

Lila flushed from Lundquist's accusation, her spine stiffening. "Why would I? It wasn't my call-out."

Completed with his work, Lundquist snapped the lid on an airtight container and faced Lila, arms crossed and eyes narrowed. "And I see you didn't bother to stop her, either." If she wasn't mistaken, Lila could hear an undertone of protection in his statement.

Who was Deputy Kyle Lundquist to Sheriff Benoit?

"Was this blood sample worth nearly getting killed, *Deputy* Dayne?"

When Lila refused to take his bait, he grunted once again, letting his arms drops. "I rest my case." He strode to the lab door, opening it and pointing at the lighted hall. "Let's go."

She exited the lab ahead of him, heading left and going back the way they had come. With each step, agony rippled through her. Where was the nearest restroom? She had to look at the scrapes and bruises on her abdomen, find out the extent of her injuries from that fall. While she might have avoided further injuring her bad side, things could have jarred the scar tissue.

"Wrong way," Lundquist barked when she passed a hall leading to the main part of the hospital.

Easing to a halt, Lila rotated. "Excuse me?"

He stood at the corner, all six foot three of menacing Viking. "This way to see a doctor." The sign above his head declared that was the direction to a walk-in clinic.

"I don't need to see a doctor."

"You might have a problem with following the sheriff's orders, but I don't."

"That's a rich statement coming from a man who just ripped me a moment ago for following the sheriff's orders."

Lundquist rewarded her comeback with more of that stoic glaring. What was his deal? How was she expected to work with him when he made it plain as the nose on her face he was going to be a hassle and a half every chance he could take?

Glaring back in turn until she felt she'd satisfactorily conveyed her irritation, she changed course and entered the hall. Lundquist fell in step with her as they walked, their booted steps echoing in the sterile corridor. Once they breeched the main registration area, Lundquist led her to a nurses' station.

He tapped the countertop. "Hey, Israel."

The African American male in green scrubs looked up and flashed a smile at Lundquist. "Hey, Kyle. What brings you here?"

"Playing mad scientist again." He jerked his thumb over his shoulder. "And bringing in a wounded deputy per the sheriff's orders."

Israel's dark eyes flicked from Lundquist to Lila. Under his scrutiny, Lila shifted her weight to her left leg, easing the ache in her right hip.

"What seems to be the matter?" he asked, getting up from his seat and rounding the counter.

"Too much concern. I'll be fine with some ice packs and

Band-Aids."

The man, like all the men around this county it seemed, towered over her. But that's what she got for being short.

"Why don't we let the doctor be the judge of that." His gaze zeroed on the blood spots on her once white shirt. "Dr. Thorpe is on call."

"Doesn't she have patients and an autopsy to deal with?" Lila asked.

Israel chuckled. "That's Dr. Remington-Thorpe. Dr. Thorpe is her husband." He turned to Lundquist. "Hang here, I'll get her settled in a room."

"For God's sake . . ."

A lighter-skinned Black man with a neatly trimmed goatee in a white lab coat emerged from behind the station. He strode toward them. "Israel, I've got Mr. Teeter settled. Let's get the lab to fast-track on those tests."

"I'll hound them. We have a new patient for you, sent in by our wonderful new sheriff."

Pale brown eyes focused on Lila. "What's the complaint?"

"She injured herself in the old Barrett place and the sheriff wants her checked out to make sure there isn't anything seriously wrong," Lundquist provided.

"I really appreciate how you like to speak for me," Lila bit out.

A smile lifted one corner of the doctor's mouth. "For the sheriff's sake, and to ease her mind, why don't we rule out anything serious?" He held out a hand and beckoned Lila to follow. "This way, Ms. . . .?"

"Deputy Dayne." She sighed. "Lila Dayne."

Lundquist's gaze tracked her as she passed. Hidden in that mask of stoicism was a hint of concern. The idea that he was worried about her punched Lila in the throat. She looked away, entering the open exam room Dr. Thorpe indicated.

Lila tensed. This sterile environment was the last room on earth—and that also included an operating room—she ever wanted to be confined to again. She'd sworn to avoid it at all costs. And here, against her wishes, she was once more.

The rattle of metal rings on a metal rod brought her heart rate up and sweat pebbled on her skin. *Stifle it.* There were bigger concerns to face than a panic attack.

"I'd rather you close the door," she said, pushing the words through her tight throat.

"I don't usually . . ."

"Dr. Thorpe, either close that door or I leave."

No way was she ever going to let Lundquist hear anything the doctor said when she revealed what was beneath her blouse. These scars were for her and the doctor's eyes only.

"I'll need to get a female nurse in here."

"You don't trust me? Or you don't trust yourself?"

This made him step back. The expression on his features turned skeptical. Without another word, he reached through the curtain and pulled the door shut.

Once that barrier was latched, Lila eased out of her coat. "What I'm about to show you stays in this room. HIPAA laws and all that."

When she'd gone in for a physical for this job, Lila had nearly panicked, ruining her chances of ever doing police work again. The kindly doctor, the exact opposite of all the ones before him, eased her anxious mind and she got through it, lies and all. Lila didn't dare to hope Dr. Thorpe would be that obliging.

He remained silent as she dropped the coat in a chair and began unbuttoning her shirt. When she parted the sides to slip out of the dirty, blood-stained garment his eyes widened.

"Deputy Dayne, I need a full medical history."

CHAPTER EIGHT

ELIZABETH, WITH DEPUTY Meyer hot on her heels, found Lundquist chatting with Israel Jones at the walk-in clinic desk. If he was here, then he'd wrangled Deputy Dayne into seeing a doctor for her injuries.

"Israel, how are things going with my newly appointed deputy?"

"Sheriff." Jones nodded. "Dr. Thorpe is just finishing with her."

"Good."

The phone rang, drawing Israel back to his duties.

Elizabeth focused on Lundquist. "What were the test results?"

"Definitely human. If you want to run more tests, I can."

"Later. Right now, I'm more concerned with that autopsy."

A door opened, and Dr. Dominic Thorpe exited. He stepped aside, allowing Deputy Dayne to leave the exam room. The hesitation in her movements was so slight, Elizabeth was certain her eyes had played tricks on her, but she hadn't been mistaken. The younger woman must not have expected the entourage awaiting her.

Dominic set his tablet on the curved station desk and propped an elbow on the top as he leaned against it. "Sheriff

Benoit, I hear tell you have confiscated my wife for the evening."

"Only for a little bit. I won't keep her long. I promise."

The doctor smiled, giving off that boyish charm that had made a tough-as-nails resident fall madly in love with him. "I pray not. I had big plans for my birthday."

The three deputies glanced at the doctor. Elizabeth snickered.

"Dominic, you're embarrassing the children."

"Indeed." He turned to his patient. "You, Deputy Dayne, do as I say and you'll be back on track by tomorrow."

"And what is she to do?" Elizabeth asked, her gaze holding Dayne's.

"Take it easy, and if she needs to ease the ache, take some over-the-counter pain relief."

"Tylenol it is. Deputy Meyer can stop at the drugstore . . ."

"Sheriff, it's not necessary," Lila interjected. "I'm good. Which way to Dr. Remington-Thorpe's office?"

Elizabeth caught the subtle shake of Dominic's head with the bowed mouth. There was more to this than a few bruises.

"Hold up there, Deputy Dayne."

Pausing, the woman turned, one eyebrow raised.

"I'm having Deputy Meyer take you back to the department. From there, you can hang until I return. Work with Deputy Fontaine, who has been running down leads all day to see who our Jane Doe is. Or head home and rest. But you're not going into that autopsy."

Tension filled the woman's features. "Sheriff, that's a bad

idea. I need to—"

"Take it easy. I won't be swayed on this matter. You've already been hurt the first day on the job, and I've got paperwork to fill out on that to boot. If you wish to disregard the doctor's orders and worsen your injuries, that's on you, but not on my watch."

Dayne looked to Lundquist and then Meyer. Neither man gave her the response she was probably looking for. "You need a trained investigator in there with you."

"I do, but our fantastic ME knows what she's doing. I'm taking Lundquist in. It'll be good training for the both of us."

"Deputy Dayne, heed the sheriff's advice," Dominic added.

A moment passed between the doctor and his patient. The way the woman gnawed on her lip settled it for Elizabeth. Those reasons for leaving Chicago and coming to Juniper her new deputy was loath to mention earlier must have come up during the exam. Rafe might be onto something in his comment about her being trouble if she wasn't willing to reveal her past. But the woman would come around. Elizabeth's faith in her stood firm.

"Fine. Since we need to learn who the girl is, I'll help Deputy Fontaine."

Elizabeth smiled. "Good." She gripped Meyer's shoulder. "Deputy Meyer, please escort Deputy Dayne back to the department. I'll ride with Lundquist." She looked at the young man. "And, Meyer, go home and get some sleep. I'll see you bright and early in the a.m."

"Yes, ma'am."

Elizabeth watched the two leave. At the automatic doors, Dayne looked back, lingering in the exit. Meyer waited, a bit of uncertainty in his face. When she finally left the clinic, Meyer seemed to relax and followed her out. Once the doors slid closed, Elizabeth zeroed in on Dominic.

"Is she going to be okay for duty?"

He pushed off the station desk, gathering his tablet and tucking it under his arm. "My diagnosis stands. Rest and relief. Don't worry too much about her." He looked at Israel. "I'll be with Mr. Teeter." And with that, he sauntered off.

With a nod to Israel, Elizabeth and Lundquist departed for the morgue.

The creaks of their duty belts and the sharp slap of boots against polished floor preceded them along the corridor.

"What's her story?" Lundquist asked as they rounded a corner that would lead them to the main wing of the hospital.

"Not one I can tell, sorry to say. I'm obligated to keep it private. You know that."

"And I also know that if she's hiding things that could land our department in trouble, there will be hell to pay from the county. Not everyone is happy that you're the sheriff."

"Thank you for that reminder."

He shoved his hands in his coat pockets. "Sheehan's been pushing me to give him reports on you."

"And what have you told him?"

"Nothing. I just walk away. I know where my loyalties lie."

Smiling, she bumped his elbow with hers. "Especially

after I gave you free rein to be my forensics specialist."

He ducked his head. Never let it be said that Kyle Lundquist had an ego.

"It surprised me when I came home and learned you were an LEO. I remember you always loved your petri dishes and Bunsen burners. Figured you'd grow up to be some scientist who'd win a Nobel Prize one day."

When Kyle was a child, Elizabeth had been called to babysit him and his baby sister if Brendette was unavailable to watch her younger siblings. Kyle loved it because Elizabeth would actually let him experiment.

"I thought I would too. Life has a way of changing your mind."

He, like Elizabeth, questioned the circumstances around Bre's death. And why his baby sister was left with a crippling fear of the unknown.

A familiar figure in blue scrubs stood next to a pair of wide doors leading to the operating wing. Here came the hardest part of her new job. Elizabeth drew in a breath and glanced at the man who was once her young charge.

"The navy didn't need you, Kyle."

His blue eyes pinned her. "But I needed the navy, Ellie."

They both halted before Dr. Olivia Remington-Thorpe. "Ready?"

"As I'll ever be."

THE UNFORTUNATE YOUNG woman was lying on the metal autopsy table, her clothing removed and placed in sealed evidence containers. Elizabeth's heart ached. If she and Joel had ever been blessed to be parents—and it was a mercy that they had not—this girl could have been their daughter. What this young woman's parents must be going through. Was it anything like worrying if your husband would return on his own two feet or in a flag-draped coffin?

Did they sense that their daughter's life had been snuffed out? Was her mother imagining the horrors that would now be inflicted on her baby girl, who was exposed and prepped for a worse violation to her body? Even in death there wasn't a thread of dignity left. But it must be done in order for Elizabeth and her deputies to find the girl's killer.

Olivia handed them each a pair of gloves and masks. "I won't cut into her until we've gone over every inch of her body. If you would rather not stay for that portion, I have no objections."

Elizabeth nodded. "We'll start and see where we go from there."

Gloved up and masks on, Olivia turned on the large overhead lights. It took the bulbs a moment to get to their full brilliance. Both Elizabeth and Lundquist stayed back as Olivia prepared, setting a pair of autopsy pages on a wheeled tray and turning on a digital recorder.

"Sheriff."

Harkening Olivia's beckoning, Elizabeth joined her beside the table.

"Please take a close look there." Olivia carefully rotated the victim's head to the side, the still damp strands of hair pushed back to reveal the side and back of her neck. The ME pointed at a spot right at the hairline.

Lundquist inched in beside Elizabeth as she bent over and peered at the blemish.

"Is that a bruise?"

"It is," Lundquist answered.

He and Elizabeth backed up as Olivia brought around an adjustable magnifying glass. She positioned it near the young woman's neck and studied the mark, or more accurately, marks as the magnification showed.

"The impressions are round and spaced out. Possibly knuckles."

"The victim was hit there?" Elizabeth asked.

Pushing the instrument aside, Olivia picked up her camera and screwed on a special filtering lens. "Indications would say yes, but I'll need to study it closer and have the ME team at DCI look over it too. Kyle, would you hit the lights, please?"

Once Lundquist had plunged them into semidarkness, Olivia turned on an infrared light. Fascinated, Elizabeth watched as the doctor took multiple photos of the bruising, each flash of her camera changing the woman's pale skin to a darkish purple. As Olivia clicked away, the lens revealed more bruises.

"Could those other bruises be from an attacker?"

"They might have come about when her body went down the ravine." Olivia, with Lundquist's help, rolled the body onto its side. Other than the lividity—where the blood pooled in the body after death—there was a large bruise on the victim's back. Olivia took more photos under the infrared. "This one could have been from hitting a rock, or the tree where she stopped. Sometimes the objects leave impressions, and we'll be able to tell what made what bruise."

Elizabeth's body had turned cold with each revelation. "Are you saying, because she's so bruised up, she was alive when she was tossed over?"

"Kyle, lights, please."

Olivia waited for the room to return to its normal brilliance. Setting her camera down, she picked up a clipboard and rotated it. The diagram of the human body noted each point where she had found notable marks to the victim's flesh. "A fact to keep in mind as you progress through this homicide investigation: even in death, the body will bruise. The depth and size of the bruising will determine if it was hours before death, or right up to and just after. I have to measure and inspect each one of them to know for sure."

"Do you have any idea how she died?"

"Not yet. With everything that has happened to this poor girl, there could be multiple outcomes," Olivia said. "I've got the samples for toxicology, and I'll have them run a few extra screens for drugs outside of the usual."

"Have you checked her blood type?" Lundquist asked.

"I have." Olivia's gaze narrowed on the deputy. "She was AB negative."

Elizabeth quirked her head to the side as her deputy grunted. "Any particular reason this is important to you?"

"Deputy Dayne might be onto something," he answered and turned for the door. "If you'll excuse me, I need to do one more test." And with that, he exited the morgue.

"What did he mean by that?" Olivia asked.

Smiling at her friend. "I'm guessing the injuries Deputy Dayne sustained earlier today might not have been in vain."

CHAPTER NINE

EXCEPT FOR THREE vehicles, one of which was hers, and another being the sheriff's, the courthouse complex was deserted by the time Deputy Meyer dropped Lila off. Despite his insistence to see her inside—these Iowa boys sure had chivalric manners the likes of which Lila had not seen—she assured him it was okay and he could go home to get that much needed sleep the sheriff had ordered. Lila waited for his vehicle to disappear before heading into the department side of the building.

The eerie silence chilled her. If not for the light spilling into the darkened hallway, Lila would have turned around and left.

It was so like the night of the attack.

Coming to the corner of the doorway, she peered inside the open office area. Toward the back of the room, his head bent over a notepad, Rafe Fontaine wrote lefthanded. Curled at his boots, Bentley slept with her nose tucked to her belly. Lila eased her shoulder into the doorframe and studied the man.

His tall, muscular frame filled the chair he sat in. If Lila had to guess, his age was anywhere between thirty-five and forty, but he could be younger. He was chiseled and deeply tanned, the kind of tan that stuck around no matter how gray and cold it got in the winter. But his eyes belonged to a much older man. What had he seen or experienced to age him so?

Bentley stirred, huffing as she lifted her head. Fontaine reached down and scratched her ears while he seemed to reread what he had written. After a sufficient amount of attention, Bentley lowered her head and rested her snout on her paws, her gaze riveted to the doorway where Lila stood. Fontaine resumed his writing.

Unlike Lundquist with his surly, protective nature, and newly badged and eager Meyer, something was different about Fontaine, especially to the sheriff.

The crack of the door seal echoed along the hallway, making Lila stiffen. She wasn't the only one to hear it. Fontaine lifted his head and looked in her direction. Heavy footfalls on the polished floor dragged her attention from the furrowed brow of the man twenty feet from her.

Stomping toward her was the sole remaining deputy she hadn't spent a lot of time with today. He looked fresh and ready for a long night shift.

Lila remained at her post as he approached. He scowled as he passed her but said nothing, entering department quarters.

"Nice of you to finally report for duty, Fitzgerald," Fontaine said, his raspy tone giving the statement more bite.

"The damn car wouldn't start. I had to get Karl to come out to jump it."

Neither man paid any attention to Lila, even as she slipped inside the office.

Fontaine braced his right arm on the desk and leaned

toward Fitzgerald. "Yet, you couldn't be bothered with calling it in."

"She ain't even here. Sheehan didn't care."

The air was sucked right out of the room. Lila's body hummed with the palpable tension flowing off the men. Bentley got the lay of the land and stood, emitting a low rumble in her throat.

"Bentley, off," Fontaine barked.

The border collie gave a full body shake and trotted away from the men, coming to Lila's side to press against her legs. Fitzgerald's gaze never broke from Fontaine's.

Rising to his full height, Fontaine came out from behind his desk and squared up with the other deputy. "Well, I don't give two shits what Sheehan did or didn't do. He's gone, and Sheriff Benoit is running this ship. If you can't stomach that revelation, I suggest you turn in your badge and gun and walk right back out that door."

The ticking hand on the large wall clock tracked the seconds the men stared each other down. With a curse, Fitzgerald moved past Fontaine to grab a clipboard hanging next to the dispatcher's desk, scribbled something on it, and slapped it back on the wall. Hitching his duty belt to settle on his lean waist, he strode through the office.

"I'm heading to the east side and working my way west."

"If the car acts up, call it in," Fontaine fired the parting shot.

As Fitzgerald passed, he ignored Lila. When the deputy was farther down the hall, Fontaine sighed and shook his head, moving to the dispatcher's desk to key in commands on the desktop computer.

"Sorry we have to introduce ourselves under such conditions," he said.

"Correct me if I'm wrong, but I thought anyone who was loyal to the crooked sheriff left."

"Fitzgerald is the last holdout, and to be frank, we have no idea why. My guess is he's Sheehan's spy." Fontaine picked up a mug from the square table set up as the coffee station and poured some coffee. "Want any?"

"No thanks."

With an acquiescing nod, he set the pot back on the warmer and carried his mug to his desk. Bentley returned to her position at his side, where Fontaine stroked her head.

"How long were you going to stand there and watch me before making your presence known?"

Shrugging, Lila took the chair at the opposite desk. "I hadn't decided." She pointed at his notepad. "What are you working on?"

"All the possible leads I'll need to take in finding out who our victim is. She's not from here, and the surrounding counties don't recognize her."

"Have you put out a statewide call?"

"We have. No one has reported back yet. But they've had it for only a few hours. And"—he held up a hand when she was about to speak—"there's a nationwide one too. Same results. So, we wait."

Lila let her body relax into the chair back. Her aches and pains were intensifying. Maybe an aspirin wouldn't hurt. It wasn't as if one pill would set off the madness swirling inside her and suck her willingly back into the vortex of oblivion. Yet her caution over taking even a Tylenol was enough to keep her from popping any pills.

"Any thoughts on what happened?" he asked.

"I'd like the autopsy results before I make my thoughts known."

"Fair enough." Fontaine resumed his writing.

Lila craned her neck to get a better look at the clipboard hooked on the wall. It was the shift schedule. Fitzgerald had scribbled his name next to his allotted time.

"What did you do on the computer?" she asked Fontaine.

"I patched the emergency calls over to Deputy Fitzgerald's unit radio. That way he can respond to them. Georgia only works during the day, and Sheriff Benoit hasn't decided on a night shift dispatcher. If she can convince the men controlling the purse strings to allot her enough funds for one."

"And was there one before Benoit took over?"

"Yep, and he quit as soon as Sheehan was booted out."

"Sounds like he had quite the following."

Fontaine set his pen on the notepad and pushed them aside. "In a way he did. Eckardt County is better off without them."

His laptop, sitting next to his elbow, beeped. "Hmm."

Lila sat forward. "What is it?"

"Sheriff had the X-rays sent over. She says the preliminary autopsy is over. She's heading back here to let Dr. Remington-Thorpe finish up alone."

"Can I see the X-rays?"

Fontaine handed over his computer. Lila set it on the desk and opened the downloaded file.

"Good God."

"Is it bad?"

"It's really bad." She squinted at the image of the young woman's skull and neck. "Something or someone crushed her atlas bone."

"It could have been after death," Fontaine reminded her. "She was tossed down a rocky incline; her head could have struck anything and it would have broken the vertebrae."

"And it could have been the source of her death too." Lila looked at him. "The rest of the X-rays show extensive damage to her skeleton, and most of that was probably caused by her body going down the ravine. There's a sizable fracture in her skull."

Fontaine closed his eyes and bowed his head. "This is not something the sheriff needs right now."

"I have to agree, Rafe."

Lila jolted at the sheriff's voice.

Bentley hopped up from her spot and greeted her owner. Elizabeth knelt and touched her forehead to her dog's.

"What's your next move?" Fontaine asked, rising from his chair.

"Wait for Olivia to finish the autopsy and see what our call-out to other departments brings. Tonight, we get some sleep and start fresh tomorrow. Until we know who this poor soul is, we're not going to be able to make connections to move forward in this case." Sheriff Benoit stood, her gaze meeting Lila's. "There is a plus."

Lila returned Fontaine's laptop. "And that would be?"

"The blood smear you found is a blood-type match to the victim."

A spark flared inside Lila, but she quickly doused it. The odds that the blood did belong to the victim were slim until there was a DNA match. "Lundquist checked?"

The sheriff nodded. "And he's hopeful there is still enough of the sample for a DNA analysis. Olivia is running that right now. We should have the results by morning."

"If that pans out, it means the victim was in the Barrett place at some point before her death. Possibly last night. What does the ME say for estimated time of death?"

Benoit sighed. "Two days ago."

CHAPTER TEN

SLEEP WAS THE last thing on Elizabeth's mind. Instead, after work she swapped out her uniform for more appropriate attire, leaving the badge and weapon behind. A short walk later, she pushed her way inside the establishment known simply as The Watering Hole. Marnie's quirk for the ironic tended to fly in the face of those who would otherwise shun or condemn her for her choices. The crackle of Nancy Sinatra reminding her wayward lover that her boots would walk all over him mingled with the heavy odor of incense. Marnie claimed the incense mellowed her patrons to the point they ordered more alcohol. Elizabeth thought otherwise.

Burning incense tended to mask other odors. Marnie flaunted her "fight the establishment" attitude by allowing smoking in her bar, among other things of questionable legality, despite her big sister being the newly elected sheriff. Marnie was just as notorious for finding loopholes as she was at exploiting them.

Elizabeth loved her sister and, for the sake of family harmony, let it be.

For ten thirty on a Tuesday night, The Watering Hole was busy. Elizabeth didn't recognize quite a few of the men sitting or standing about. They wore clean button-down shirts and jeans, some in Stetsons, others in sweat-stained ball caps advertising popular hunting gear, vehicle brands, or camo American flags. As she skirted past a group, one man turned to excuse himself and paused to flash a smile. But when his eyes, like all men's eyes, darted down to take in her chest, a smirk crossing his face. Bentley bared her canines and snapped her teeth. Going pale, the man backed away from Elizabeth.

Drunken flirtation thwarted. Elizabeth patted the collie's head and moved on.

The antique jukebox exchanged Nancy for The Animals. Marnie was in a mood if she was playing Vietnam-era songs tonight. If Elizabeth had to take a guess, she was certain the uptick in roughneck boys in the bar was most likely the cause of her sister's ire.

Bentley stiffened at a hiss coming from above. Both she and Elizabeth looked up at the exposed rafter beams. A pair of bright yellow eyes haloed in pure black fur glared down at the pair. A swipe of a clawed paw was followed by a second hiss.

"Good evening to you too, Luna."

Bentley barked at the cat, earning a high-pitched squeal.

"Go on with you."

The devil cat gave a parting growl as she sashayed to her usual perch at the top of the stairs leading to Marnie's apartment. Bentley quivered. If given one command, she would take off after the cat.

"Bentley, no."

The red collie looked up, pleading in her beautiful eyes.

"Not even," Elizabeth said and headed for the polished

mahogany bar.

Decked out in her usual goth black top that exposed a mishmash of tattoos, her crown of Cruella de Vil hair a wild mess, Marnie spoke with a disheveled man at the end of the bar. Bentley left Elizabeth's side and trotted around the bar to greet one of her other favorite people in the world. At her bark, Marnie looked down and smiled.

Elizabeth snagged the lone spot left at the bar, bookended by regulars who gave her respectful nods. Her sister gave Bentley a loving rub, and then meandered down the bar. Marnie was such a dichotomy to the young girl Elizabeth remembered, her fingers adorned with rings shaped in the form of tiny dragons or tarnished bands with black onyx stones, her lips painted bloodred, a stark contrast to her pale skin. Elizabeth had always wondered what made her sister seek such drastic changes to her appearance, and she never settled for the pat answer of "a healthy person can be interested in weird things." The changes had happened right after Elizabeth and Joel escaped Juniper and got married. A tiny voice in the back of Elizabeth's mind whispered *maybe you are to blame*, but she didn't give it credence.

Bracing her elbows on the gleaming wood top, Marnie coiled a white lock around her finger. "Here to continue your fun from last night?"

"No. I just needed a place to unwind. Who are all the fresh faces?"

"If my sources are right, and they usually are, it's a group from that new fertilizer plant. Didn't they just open their doors for production like a week ago?"

Elizabeth eyeballed her sister. "You're the eco-friendly

one, and you don't know? I swore you protested the whole thing back when Terra Firma came to bid on the land."

Waving her off, Marnie released the white lock. "I had other things come up. It slipped my mind."

"Right." Elizabeth had hit that nail on the head. Marnie's passive-aggressive music was directed at the men from the fertilizer plant. And they had no clue.

"As sheriff, I would think you would be aware of the newcomers to the county."

"Well, yes, one would think, but there have been more pressing matters as of late. And today I was hit by a bad one."

"I heard the gossip. Sorry you have a murder to deal with right out of the gate." Marnie backed up and snagged a tumbler from the drying rack. Splashing a finger of Johnnie Walker in the glass, she handed it over. "Wash down the day. The doctor is in."

Elizabeth sipped her favored whiskey. "I can't talk about it with you, and you know that."

"It doesn't stop the gossipmongers."

Shaking her head, she set the tumbler down on the bar. "Let them wag their tongues. All they're seeking is attention."

"Tell that to your biggest detractor. He's been in here since four telling one and all his exact thoughts on your lack of experience in this."

"Why do you allow Kelley in here?"

"Paying customers are paying customers."

"The man doesn't have a job, Marnie. How in the hell does he even afford that expensive bourbon?"

Marnie shrugged her right shoulder. Every time Elizabeth brought up Sheehan, Marnie gave cagey answers or none at all. Before she took office, Elizabeth had offered to financially back the bar, but Marnie, in an uncharacteristically angry fit, refused. So she dropped the subject. As sheriff, she did some digging but got nowhere in a hurry. It was a mystery that would remain hidden for the time being.

Marnie leaned closer. "You know, his being here gives me ample opportunity to eavesdrop on him and give you the lowdown. Karl Kauffmann was in here earlier with Stephen."

"He brought Stephen into a bar?" Stephen being the golden child of the Kauffmann clan. Ma had big dreams for her youngest son, and he was living up to them. "That's not going to sit well with Ma."

Stephen was not like his wild brothers. He was quiet and contemplative, a sheer contrast to Karl's brash and loud-mouthed ways. Considerably younger than the middle son, Daniel, Stephen was set to graduate from high school this spring, and Elizabeth heard murmurs that the top three Iowa universities were clamoring for a right to have this bright young mind attend their prestigious school.

"Exactly. Karl had a little confab with Kelley. They sat back in the far corner, bent over their liquor like two men plotting the demise of the world. Karl and Stephen left here a few hours ago."

Elizabeth, taking another sip of her whiskey, rotated to check out the corner her sister spoke of. Still ruling his little parcel of the land, Kelley Sheehan was kicked back, a half full bourbon bottle on the table, and a tumbler dangling from his propped-up hand. He swirled the liquid in the glass, his steely gaze latched on to Elizabeth. With his free hand, he smoothed down his grayed mustache.

"Wonder what they were talking about."

"Who knows."

Feeling antagonistic, Elizabeth lifted her drink in salute and smiled at the crooked ex-sheriff. He scowled, and then tossed back the remainder of the umber liquid.

"Maybe I should go ask." Elizabeth slid to the edge of her stool.

Marnie grabbed her arm. "Don't you dare."

Turning back to her sister, Elizabeth scowled. "Why not?"

"I don't need a dick-measuring contest going on when I have a bunch of yahoos stinking up my joint."

Her tight features slackened into a smile. "Really, Marnie, dick measuring?"

"Face it, Big Sister, when the men start bringing the glass ceiling down closer to your large head, you get the clubs out and start swinging."

She wasn't wrong.

"More?" Marnie asked, taking Elizabeth's empty whiskey glass.

"No. I need to go home. Sober this time."

"He stayed all night?"

Sighing, she nodded. No use in skirting the truth. Marnie had what was best described as a reserved relationship with Joel—at times she could hate him and at others be his staunchest ally. On Joel's end, he liked Marnie well enough to avoid picking a fight with her. His button pushing was better served against Elizabeth.

"Thank you for bringing my car home, by the way."

"Not like it was that far. But you might want to consider keeping your windows closed next time. Hearing my big sister get it on with her ex is not a sound I'll soon forget. Imagine all your neighbors. Come to think of it, I seem to recall the two of you never were the quiet types."

"Enough, Marnie. I get it."

The Cheshire grin on her sister's bloodred lips made Elizabeth want to reach over and smear her face.

"Does Rafe know?"

Shoulders slumping, Elizabeth looked pointedly at the men on each side of her. "Can we not discuss this here?"

"Sure. I just thought since I don't see you during normal hours, this was the best time."

"Never is a good time. How about we never have this discussion?"

Marnie cocked her head to the side. "Not likely to happen." Her face scrunched.

Sensing a new presence at her back, Elizabeth stiffened.

"Back already, Karl?" Marnie asked.

"I need to have a chat with the sheriff."

Elizabeth closed her eyes and drew in a breath. Karl was the last person she wanted a confrontation with tonight. Letting her breath out slowly, she opened her eyes, and faced the owner of the gruff voice.

"Karl, tonight I'm not the sheriff. I'm just plain Elizabeth."

"No, you're the sheriff."

"Fine. What can I do for you?"

Karl Kauffmann favored his long-deceased father in appearance and height, a tall, dishwater blond with brown eyes too small for his block head. He also lacked his mother's and younger sibling's intelligence. A lot of those missing smarts could be contributed to Karl's years of playing football and picking fights with anyone who was bigger and stronger than him—and the suspected drug use. Standing before Elizabeth in filthy, greasy coveralls, he sagged to his left. "I wanna know why you blew off Ma."

"This is not the place nor the time to discuss that subject matter." Elizabeth squared up with the man known to have a decided lack of respect for anyone of authority, except his ma. "Pack yourself up and go home."

He bent over, his face inches from her own. "Not until you answer me." The stench of stale beer on his breath curdled the whiskey in Elizabeth's gut.

"Touch her and you'll be answering to me."

Elizabeth ground her molars together. Why did he have to show up now?

Karl tilted away from her and looked over his shoulder at his distant cousin. "This ain't none 'ur business."

Joel crossed his arms, the bulging muscles straining the seams of his shirt. He had no qualms about a show of force, especially with a man he had no esteem for, family or not. "This became my business when Ma invited me into the conversation. If she finds out you messed with Elizabeth, what do you think she'll do?"

Karl lurched around, glaring at everyone who had suddenly become interested in the free show. "What? You think 'cause you some big-time hero you can jus' butt in wherever?" Karl hocked a wad of tobacco-laced phlegm and spat it on Joel's boots. "That's what I think 'bout you."

"Get this drunk ass out of my bar," Marnie barked.

He swung an arm about. Elizabeth ducked at the last second, taking a glancing blow to the side of her face.

"Damn you, Karl."

Elizabeth straightened, bright spots cavorting across her vision. She danced out of the way as Joel grabbed Karl by the shirt. "Joel, no!"

Too late. He flung Karl across the floor. Anyone in the lumbering man's path bolted. Karl crashed into a table, flipping it and spewing the contents. Joel stalked after him.

"Damn it." Elizabeth scrambled after her ex-husband.

His years as a trained Special Forces operative made him quick and agile. Elizabeth couldn't catch him. And Karl didn't stand a chance. Joel reached down and hooked his hands under Karl's armpits. He hoisted his drunk cousin to his feet. Karl slammed his fists down on Joel's straining forearms, but it only served to anger her ex.

Speed born of necessity, Joel backed Karl right out of the bar and sent him sprawling into the street.

"Marnie, call it in!" Elizabeth threw over her shoulder and followed the men outside.

Joel was getting in more hits than Karl, who was even more unsteady on his feet. Blood dribbled from Karl's nose. Roaring, he tried to rush Joel with a bear hug maneuver. Why did anyone ever think that move would work?

Joel waited for his cousin to come within reach, then swatted his arms aside and tripped him. Elizabeth flinched as Karl face-planted into the pavement.

"Enough!" She interceded, pushing Joel back. "You've

done enough damage."

Karl rolled onto his back and blinked up at the darkened sky. The pavement had left a bloody road rash all along the left half of his face. Breathing heavily, he lay there.

"I warned him," Joel said.

"It was an accident. He wouldn't have touched me otherwise."

"He's too damn drunk to know the difference."

Glaring, she stepped into his personal space and jabbed a fingernail into his nose. "And your skills as a fighter far exceed his own. If you'd killed him, I would have had to arrest you. Then where would you be? As it stands, I should have you arrested for aggravated assault."

"Only if he presses the matter."

"That won't be necessary."

They turned as Ma walked up the sidewalk, Stephen ambling right alongside her.

"Stephen warned me Karl was drunk and stewing for a fight." She looked down at her snoring son, Karl having passed out at some point as Elizabeth lashed out at Joel. "I'll take him home. Sober him up." Her gaze swung to Joel. "We'll consider this a family matter."

He nodded.

"What say you, Sheriff?" Ma pointed at a spot under her right eye.

Elizabeth touched the same spot on her face and winced at the spark of pain. "I don't want to give him any more cause for friction between us. It was an accident."

"I knew you were a sensible woman."

Blue flashing lights announced Fitzgerald's arrival. He

parked next to their little group and took his sweet time getting out of his squad car. "What's going on here?"

Elizabeth took a look around and felt her blood pressure spike. There was a considerable audience hovering in the bar doorway. Right smack in the middle, Sheehan grinned like a fool. Oh, he had to be eating this right up.

"You all have had your eyeful. Step back inside and finish up your night. Now."

Disgruntled, the crowd dispersed. Sheehan lingered, his smirk plastered on his face. When Ma stepped into his line of sight, he lost his humor. Thumbing his nose at them, he entered the bar.

"Ma, where are you parked?"

"I'll be right back." She stepped into the shadows surrounding the building.

A moment later, her ancient Suburban appeared. Leaving the engine running, she exited the vehicle.

"Fitzgerald, would you assist Joel in getting Karl into his mother's car, please?"

A flush to his features, Fitzgerald nodded and helped Joel lift the unconscious Karl into the Suburban. Once she had Stephen retrieve Karl's truck, Ma sighed.

She dipped her head respectfully. "Thank you, Sheriff."

"Good night, Ma."

When they'd gone, Fitzgerald returned to his car. Without a word, he left.

Left alone with her ex, Elizabeth turned to him. "Thank you so much for undermining my authority. I had it handled."

"Karl's a belligerent drunk, Ellie. He would have never

listened to you."

"Guess now we'll never know, will we? My God, Joel, you are not my protector. I don't need saving—I'm the sheriff. By intervening, you just proved Sheehan right and made me look weak in front of my voters. If I'm seen unable to control one drunk, what's that say to them when it comes to more precarious issues?"

"All the more reason you need to give up this asinine idea of being sheriff. Leave it to those who know what they're doing."

The poison of her fury drained from her body, leaving her slack-jawed. What had she expected from her ex? For him to actually support her in this? "Not only do you not know me"—she stabbed a finger into his chest—"you underestimate me and what I'm capable of doing in this job." She turned and headed toward home.

"And what do you hope to accomplish, Elizabeth?" Joel asked.

She paused, catching a glimpse of movement in one of the bar's windows. Sheehan watched her through the beveled glass.

"I'm cleaning up this county. No matter what it takes."

CHAPTER ELEVEN

S TACKED BOXES FILLED with her meager possessions lined the front hall of the small one-bedroom bungalow. Lila kicked out of her boots, leaving them by the front door. Instinct drove her to flip both the dead bolt and the handle locks, ensuring she would never be caught by surprise again.

She had chosen this house because of its recent renovations and updates, high among them the secure windows and doors. Forget the security system. That hadn't saved her last time.

The only other living soul in the house drifted through its brightly lit waters. Green and red fauna waved about, blocking the view of the Easter Island statuette. Lila bent down, peering inside the tank. The blue Betta flicked his gorgeous tail at her and then darted inside the gaping mouth.

"Nice to see you too, Gerry."

Giving the uppity fish a few flakes of food, she checked the thermometer. The water's temp was holding steady. Lila worried during Gerry's precarious trip from Chicago to Juniper that his water would get too cold and put the fish in a state of shock, possibly killing him. It was absurd to be so attached to a fish, but attached she'd become to the Siamese fighting Betta. He'd been an impulse purchase, one that left her grasping for reasons, because she'd never thought she'd ever replace the Koi that perished the night of her attack.

Lila pressed her right hand to the left side of her abdomen. A knife was not the sole thing that had left scars.

A warm glow from the back of the house drew her to the kitchen. More boxes sat haphazardly on counters and the dinette set wedged in the corner. Another reason to take the house: it came fully furnished. Unlocking a hidden drawer under the fish tank, she retrieved the firearm she'd hidden there.

Her certainty of getting the deputy job had been high, but she had refused to bring a sidearm until she took the oath. Lila had felt exposed without a weapon as she'd worked alongside the sheriff, but she was home now. Tomorrow when she reported for her first official shift, she'd have duty belt and gun on.

Shrugging out of her filthy clothing, she chucked them at a pair of slatted, folding doors that hid her laundry facility. Naked, the Glock gripped in her hand, she slipped into the bathroom.

While the Jacuzzi tub filled with hot water, Lila inspected the damage inflicted from her fall in the Barrett house. She hadn't bothered as Dr. Thorpe did his exam. There'd been no use. Without a mirror, she'd not been able to see her sides and back. The abrasions, still lined with tiny dots of blood, were fading to pink. Purple bruising indicated the points where her abdomen had slammed into the broken flooring. All in all, she'd gotten off scot-free.

Steam filmed over the mirror. Backing from the sink, she glanced into the other room. Propped against the wall, the NordicTrack treadmill waited for her to extract it from the box and set it up. She closed the bathroom door. Not tonight.

Easing into the large bathtub, Lila sank beneath the near scalding water and moaned. If it were possible to melt, she'd have done it. After a few moments of letting her body acclimate to the temperature, she ducked under the water and scrubbed her scalp and hair. Coming up for air, she shook her saturated locks. Actual soap and shampooing would come later. She flicked on the jets, setting the timer to turn off in twenty minutes. The water frothed around her, the two jets at her back beating a steady blast against aching muscles. Her hand resting on the butt of the Glock, she reclined against the bathtub's side, closed her eyes, and relaxed.

Two days. The unnamed victim had been dead two days. It certainly explained the lack of rigor and the distinguishable presence of lividity. Despite narrowing down the proximate time of death, they didn't know what had killed her. And why had the victim's rate of decomp not matched the time of death? Two days, she should be bloated and skin beginning to loosen and sag from the skeleton. Oddly for December, it hadn't been chilly enough to slow decomp. Nighttime temps maybe, but for the last two days the daytime temps were in the upper forties and midfifties. Something wasn't right about this.

Shifting her bare bottom on the tub base, she sank farther into the water. No point circling the subject now. There wasn't enough information to make any conclusions, and evidence was lacking. Lila would do what Sheriff Benoit ordered: she'd sleep. Tomorrow there should be more answers.

The thrum of the jets created the perfect backdrop of white noise. Between the heat, and the massage on her body, Lila dozed off.

Her shoulder jerking down as her hand splashed in the water brought her awake. Floundering, Lila shoved her body upright. The jets had stopped, and the bath water cooled. Wiping a dripping hand over her face, she groaned. A nap in the tub was never a good idea. Stiff from sitting on the hard surface, she rose gingerly. After running the shower for a quick rinse, she stepped out. Towel wrapped around her, she reached over the tub, grabbed the Glock, and left the bathroom.

Hesitating at the curtain separating her sleeping quarters from the rest of the room, she tilted her head to the side. Glock gripped firmly in hand, she rotated. There it was again. Gun cradled in her hands, she crept to the doorway. The buzz came from her pile of clothing.

Right. Her phone. Lowering her weapon, she padded over to the pile. Digging her buzzing cell from her coat pocket, she checked caller ID. Cecil. Answer it, or let it go to voice mail? There was a right answer to that question. Sighing, she tapped the green phone icon.

"I'm not coming back."

"That's not how you answer a call. Now let's try this again. Hello, is Lila there?"

Biting the inside of her cheek, she stopped the grin. "Hello, Cecil."

Detective Cecil Waterford, retired, was the sole man she trusted to know her whereabouts. Her partner for the brief time she was a detective, Cecil had been the unfortunate soul to find Lila after the attack, barely clinging to life and shattered. He'd vowed to find the bastard that had put an end to their partnership. But Lila couldn't wait forever.

"I'm still not coming back," she said.

"I never said you would."

She headed back into the bedroom. "Every time you talk to me you insist I rethink my decision, and tell me the force still needs me."

"Well, it does." He sighed. "But I understand why you left."

"Do you? Really?" She hit the speaker icon and dropped the phone on the bed, next to the Glock.

"Yes. Really."

Lila dug out a pair of yoga pants and an oversized sweatshirt from her suitcase. "So, what brought you to this enlightenment?" Screw putting on undergarments. She slid into her comfy clothing.

Cecil cleared his throat, and let silence permeate the fiber optics.

"Wow, those must be some heavy thoughts brewing in your head." Silence remained on his end of the connection. "Cecil?"

"I'm here." His voice cracked.

Her chest tightened, as if a hand had reached inside and squeezed her heart. They hadn't been partners for long, but Cecil had managed to fill a Dad-shaped void in Lila that had been empty for the majority of her life. Biting her quivering lip, she drove back the emotions.

"Hey, you know, this isn't why I called," Cecil said.

"They made a positive ID on one of the victims."

The room spun. Squeezing her eyes shut, Lila brought a halt to the vertigo. She picked up the phone, stiffening as her hand shook. Her legs unable to keep her upright, she collapsed onto the edge of the haphazardly made bed.

"Which one?" she whispered.

"John Doe number five, the one found off the Eisenhower. His name was Brian Waters."

Lila swallowed against the tidal wave of bile in the back of her throat. "How many does that make that have been ID'd?"

"Brian makes six now."

Six known victims, and four left unaccounted for. And those were only the ones discovered in the greater Chicago area, all along major interstates. God knew how many were still out there, waiting for someone to stumble upon their graves.

"Where was Brian from?" Why was she asking this? She shouldn't be asking. Not her problem.

"Arizona, a suburb of Phoenix called Surprise." Cecil sighed. "He's been missing for nine years."

"Why was he in Chicago?" She should end this conversation. Now.

"His family doesn't know. He was twenty when he went missing. So far, that makes him the youngest of the victims."

Lila cradled her forehead in her palm, digging her fingernails into her scalp. "Why are you telling me all this?"

"This was your case, Lila."

"*Was*, Cecil, was my case. It isn't any longer. It stopped being my case the moment that psychopath broke into my home and attacked me."

"You can move as far away as possible. Try to separate yourself from the inevitable, but you'll never outrun it. You have to face that fact. You aren't the investigator working the case—you are now the case because you encountered this guy and lived. He's still out there."

"And every time you bring me back into the fold, you give him a chance to get that much closer to finishing what he started."

"It's not my intention. I want you informed so you know what your next move is."

Slapping her thigh, she jerked her head up. "My next move is to get over it. Move on with my life and let the guys do their job back there. I'm not bringing it here. I won't be a victim again."

Dead air met her outburst. For a solid eight ticks of the second hand, Lila held her breath. Had he hung up?

"I don't want that, either." The strain in his voice brought a quiver to her lip.

Moisture built in her eyes. "I appreciate you watching out for me. But I've got a good thing started here, and I want to focus on that."

"You're sure?"

Wiping her eyes, she cleared her throat. "I'm sure. But that doesn't mean you're forbidden from calling to check on me."

"Just from talking shop with you."

"To a certain extent."

"I can live with that." He let the normal pause in their conversation carry on longer than usual. "Are all aspects of your former life off-limits?"

Lila frowned. "Depends." She pushed off the bed. Her growling stomach begged for relief. "What part of my former life are we talking about?" She ambled out to the kitchen.

"A few nights back I ran into Tate."

Halting, she stared at the fridge door. "That part is off-limits."

"I figured as much. But if you ever get the urge to know—"

"Not happening. He made his decision, end of story." She yanked the door open and bent over to look inside. Empty. Like it had been this morning and last night.

"You sound tired," Cecil said. "A long day?"

"Aren't the first days on the job usually long?"

He chuckled, the warm sound lifting Lila out of her funk, even if for a brief moment.

"I'll let you go."

Propping her elbow on the fridge door, she leaned into it. "Despite the news you dropped on me, I'm glad you called."

"You could repay in kind."

"I'll think about it. Night, Cecil."

He grunted his response and the connection went dead.

Lila looked at the screen as it faded to a photo of Gerry peeking between red fronds. As she lowered the phone, her gaze drifted to her reflection in the darkened windows above the dining table. The woman using the fridge as a prop was not the woman Cecil wanted.

Tearing away her gaze, she shut the door with a slap and stalked to the pantry. A grocery sack sat on the middle shelf, its contents spilled out of the bag. Dry cereal for supper. She dug a hand inside, pulled out of fistful of Lucky Charms, and kicked the pantry door shut.

As she turned to return to her bedroom, a flicker of motion outside made her freeze. Gulping a mouthful of marshmallow rainbows, she scanned the area. Empty.

Heart rate back to normal, she exhaled. It was her reflection in the windows. That was it.

"Damn you, Cecil."

One day she'd get past this. But that day was not today.

CHAPTER TWELVE

Day 2: Thursday

THE RHYTHMIC KNOCK rattled the screen door against the frame. Elizabeth peeked around the counter/cabinet room divider, then returned to garnishing her bowl of oatmeal. "Door's open," she called out.

Hinges squealed and his boots clapped lightly on the hardwood floors. "He's still mad at you."

"Good for him." She poured full-fat milk over the oatmeal. "He's damn lucky I didn't arrest him on principle."

Rafe cocked a hip against the divider's counter. "Why didn't you?"

"Because the wounded party refused to press charges on the grounds it was a family matter."

One light brown eyebrow lifted. "More like the matriarch said so."

Elizabeth spooned a mound of oatmeal laced with honeyed cinnamon pecans into her mouth then held the bowl and spoon aloft.

Rafe shook his head at her offer and then shifted to lean his back into the support wall. "Ellie, you can't be the sheriff this county needs if you cater to Ma at her insistence."

"I'm not. To follow the letter of the law, she needed to press charges. She didn't. Let's face it, even if she or Karl had, we would have government types flocking here. And that's the last thing we need."

Rafe didn't argue. Smart man. He, like she, was mindful of the pull backing his eldest brother. Make no mistake, Joel was an honorable man, and he wouldn't let the lawyers railroad the system nor make his ex-wife out to be a spiteful woman. But the publicity was not wanted.

"Did you follow up on that lead I gave you last night?" she asked between bites.

"Yes. I wasn't able to catch everyone before they went home."

Elizabeth scraped the bottom of the bowl. When Rafe didn't continue, she set the dish in the sink. "And?"

He smiled, then rubbing that smile away with a hand, he pushed off the wall. "Those I spoke with didn't recognize the girl. One man mentioned that quite a few of the employees brought their families. I'm planning to head out to the plant around the lunch hour and see what I can learn."

"Take Deputy Dayne with you." Elizabeth handed Rafe a mug.

He watched her pour the coffee. "Are you sure about her?"

"Still questioning my choices, Rafe Fontaine?" She blew on her energy fueler.

"Shoot straight with me. There's no one here to worry about overhearing. What is Lila Dayne trying to keep under wraps?"

"Who said she was?"

His eyes narrowed. "Ellie."

Sighing, she placed her mug on the counter and pulled

out a drawer. She set the extracted folder on the counter next to him. "Her story isn't exactly secret. I say that with this caveat: she's going through something none of us will ever be able to understand."

Rafe opened the file. "Good God," he rasped.

She retrieved her coffee and let him read.

Minutes later, he looked up. "Is she aware you have this?"

"Yes and no. Some of that came from her, the rest I gathered on my own or from what her former superiors gave me."

Flipping the folder closed, he faced Elizabeth. "You knew this and still you hired her?"

She stuck the folder back in the drawer and hip-bumped it closed.

"That kind of trauma makes for an explosive cop. We'll never know when she will either erupt or freeze and get someone killed. This hire was not a smart move. If she implodes, it will be your head the voters will be after."

"It warms my heart to know that you worry about me so." She pat his scruff-covered cheek. "In case you've forgotten, I'm quite capable of holding my own. As I reminded your brother last night."

He grasped her wrist, holding fast. "You're underestimating the severity of the situation this county is in." He invaded her personal space, lowering his face within inches of hers. "Exposing a vulnerability like Lila Dayne is opening yourself up to attack. The scent of blood is all Sheehan needs to strike."

Meeting those tumultuous depths head on, Elizabeth

snapped her spine to attention. "I'm underestimating nothing. The people of Eckardt are fed up with the status quo, and if having a damaged woman protecting them is what it takes to end the cycle of corruption"—she leaned closer—"then so be it."

They stood there, locked in an age-old battle that hearkened back to when Adam first realized Eve tricked him and Eve refused to be his scapegoat. Neither would convince the other. It was a fact as true as the fact that she regretted the day she'd chosen the wrong brother.

She freed her wrist and stepped back, keeping her gaze locked with his. "Go home and sleep."

Taking his sweet time, he left the kitchen. She tracked his movements to the door, stiffening when he turned.

"Joel isn't leaving until the end of the month."

If he'd expected a reaction from her, Elizabeth didn't give him one. Rafe left.

She stared at the empty doorway. Both of those men were determined to turn her into a stark, raving madwoman.

A warm, wet snout nosed her hand. Without looking down, she stroked Bentley's silky head, fluffing her ears.

"Some days I believe I would have been better off as a nun."

Her phone vibrated and skipped along the countertop. Picking it up, she slid the answer icon across the screen. "Sheriff Benoit."

"Sheriff, I hate to start your day on a bad note."

"I think you're ten minutes too late, Georgia."

"Let me make it worse."

GOOD TO KNOW her newest deputy was on the ball.

Elizabeth stepped out of the SUV at the same moment Deputy Dayne, wearing her uniform, exited her car. The sun thawed the December morning, the promise of another unseasonably warm day to ward off the chill of winter. Rolling the front and back windows down, Elizabeth commanded Bentley to stay and went to join the detective.

Dayne donned a pair of aviator sunglasses. "Sheriff."

"Deputy Dayne. Did you sleep well last night?"

"I slept."

Elizabeth lifted an eyebrow.

Dayne placed her hands on her duty belt. "Looks like another all-hands-on-deck scene."

That was a line item in the department budget Elizabeth needed to go full-court press on with the county. The night shift deputies needed to be at home sleeping before their next shift. Manpower was at a premium.

Together, she and Dayne walked to the taped-off scene, Deputy Dayne moving a bit stiffly, her injuries from the day before clearly proving to be bothersome. Deputy Meyer, apparently taking Elizabeth's suggestion to go easy with the yellow tape, had planted iron rods in a square, forty feet away from the massive oak and the body. The young man stood off to the left, Deputy Lundquist next to him.

A lone crow, perched on a twisted limb midway up the tree, cocked its head and squawked. Where were his partners in crime?

Rafe was speaking with Fitzgerald, halting his conversation when Elizabeth came into view. Rafe's gaze held hers for a moment, then flicked to Dayne. The flesh around his mouth thinned. He could disapprove all he wanted. Elizabeth's decision stood.

Meyer broke rank and held up the tape for them. "Mornin', Sheriff."

"Good morning, Deputy Meyer. I trust you are rested for the day?"

"That I am, ma'am."

"Deputy Lundquist, what is the ETA on our ME?"

"She's en route, should be here in ten."

Nodding, Elizabeth cautiously approached the body, pulling out gloves from her back pocket.

"Why are you so worried about how we sleep?" Dayne asked, snapping on her gloves.

"Must be the mothering instinct in me."

What lay before them made Elizabeth's heart ache. Another young woman, fully clothed, sat propped against the tree trunk. Where her eyes should have been were blackened, bloody holes. Her head tilted at an awkward angle, resting on her right shoulder.

Dayne squatted to the victim's level. "Her killer broke her neck."

"You sound certain."

"I've seen this before. But the X-rays will have to prove it. Does she look familiar?"

"No."

"Doe number two. Not good," Dayne muttered. She swiveled around, wincing. "Fitzgerald? Is she in rigor?"

The taciturn deputy ceased preening his three-day-old

stubble. He had found the woman on his last round before clocking out. He shook his head.

"Did you touch her?" Dayne asked.

"I'm not an idiot, *deputy*. I saw the birds, checked it out, and called it in. I'm not getting within ten feet of that."

Sighing, Dayne leveraged her body upright, and inched closer to the victim. She gripped the forearm and lifted it. The arm bent easily at the elbow. No rigor.

Another caw. Elizabeth's attention diverted from her detective to the yellow and brown foliage. The lone watchman had doubled. Two pairs of beady black eyes stared down at her.

What do you know, scavengers?

"Sheriff?"

Her gaze dropped to the woman standing next to her.

"We need to process this scene now. Those birds have done enough damage as it is."

Nodding, Elizabeth motioned for Lundquist to get going. She took hold of Dayne's elbow and escorted her off to the far-right edge of the tape.

"I want your honest assessment. Was she dumped last night?"

Dayne glanced back at the body and then stared out across the fallow hay field. How and why Fitzgerald decided to come this direction was an honest answer Elizabeth highly doubted she'd get. After a few moments, Dayne's gaze returned to Elizabeth.

"It's possible she was dumped last night. If there are enough of them, it doesn't take the birds long to consume the eyes."

"Which brings me to my next question: if they ate the eyes here, why not the first victim's?"

Her features pinched, Dayne rotated to face the body. "Good question." She wandered over to Lundquist.

Elizabeth followed. The first victim's time of death still made no sense. There were minimal signs of decomp, which, if the young woman was tossed down the ravine at the time of her death, should have been prevalent.

"Lundquist, wait," Dayne said, holding up a hand.

He frowned at Elizabeth. She gestured for him to give their detective a minute. Again, Deputy Dayne squatted in front of the body. A moment of studying and she duck-walked closer, pressing a finger into the victim's cheek.

Gravel crunched under rubber. Swinging her attention from her deputy to the area beyond the tape, Elizabeth spotted Olivia as she emerged from the ME van.

She met Olivia halfway.

"What's going on?"

"Before you attend to your duties, I need your thoughts on something."

Peeking over her shoulder and then back to Elizabeth, Olivia scowled. "About what?"

"Is it possible the victim from yesterday was kept cold, or even frozen, before she was dropped into the ravine?"

Her gaze flicking to the men around them, Olivia grasped Elizabeth's arm and tugged her closer. "It's possible."

Elizabeth's muscles seized. "Wouldn't that throw off your timeline for death?"

"It can, especially if the body was frozen, but in this case, she was not. Otherwise, when I did the autopsy on the body,

I would have found frozen tissue. She hadn't been in that ravine long enough to cause thawing if that were the case."

"Is it possible she could have been kept cool enough to stop decomposition but not freeze her?"

"Again, yes, it's possible," Olivia said. "If her body had been exposed to normal air temps for a long period of time, say overnight, it could change her core body temperature. If I recall, the low for Tuesday night was twenty-nine, and it warmed up yesterday to the fifties."

"This girl has been here longer than just last night."

Elizabeth turned to her detective. Dayne held up a plastic evidence bag—inside were tiny yellow dots.

"Eggs," Olivia said, taking the bag.

"Two nights?" Elizabeth asked.

Dayne shrugged. "It's hard to say for certain. The killer could have placed her body here in the early morning hours yesterday. But it's been long enough for insect activity and the birds to get at her. Decomp is in process."

"She may have been kept cool like the other. Yesterday's warmer temps got the process going. She's had at least a full twenty-four hours of exposure," Olivia stated.

Elizabeth held up her hands. "What you both are saying goes to a pattern. Which means it was the same person who could have done this."

"Maybe," Dayne said.

Which begged an interesting question. Elizabeth marched over to the two men who lingered on the fringes of the crime scene tape.

"Fitzgerald."

He twitched at her bark, masking the jolt with his customary scowl. "What?"

Letting the attitude slide, she parked herself in front of him, the yellow line a thin barrier between them. "This route isn't part of our normal patrol. Why did you come out here?"

"It might not be part of the route, but we shouldn't forget about it."

"What do you mean?"

"You're the sheriff, you should get what I mean."

Elizabeth leaned closer to Fitzgerald. "I am the sheriff. And I hold the keys to your continued presence in this department. Sheehan might have liked to play games, but you will note that I do not."

Their stare down ended when Fitzgerald fidgeted and looked away.

"I had heard scuttlebutt that people—teenagers—like to use this field for their little rendezvous or beer parties." His attention returned to Elizabeth. "The farmer who rents this field has complained that he's found burn spots from bonfires on the edge of the field near the woods. Every other night or so, I come this way to check it out."

"But you found the body two hours ago. That's too late to catch kids."

"Not too late to catch an addict getting a fix from their dealer." Fitzgerald jutted his chin at the tree. "Her body was placed right on top of the drug cache."

Elizabeth leaned away from the sullen deputy. "You've seen this?"

The resentment bled from the man's features, and for a brief tick in time, Elizabeth witnessed a side of the man he had yet to show her: honor. "It's how I caught Daniel Kauffmann."

"What?" she and Rafe said as one.

"I don't remember you bringing Daniel in on drug charges," Rafe said.

Fitzgerald smirked, his swagger returning. "That's because you were on a need to know status, and Sheehan deemed you not to know."

Elizabeth snapped her fingers in front of his face, earning a fresh scowl. "Let's bring this to the here and now. Why was I never informed of this? And why are there no records of the arrest?"

Heat radiating from another body warmed her side. Dayne, of course, arms crossed and at full attention.

Fitzgerald had to be feeling cornered if the flash of panic in his eyes was an indicator. "I don't know."

"Don't lie," Rafe said.

"I'm not," Fitzgerald snapped. "Sheehan took care of the situation and kicked me to the curb on the deal. All I know is, I never caught Kauffmann out here again before he died."

Elizabeth leaned back from the deputy. Each step she took in these murders, more pieces came into play. And if Sheehan was involved in any way, all the more needles to pierce his leathery hide with.

CHAPTER THIRTEEN

"IS IT ME, or does she look a little like the first girl?" Lila brushed aside the brown-and-purple-dyed strands, holding them aloft to expose the poor girl's features. Prominent cheekbones, either by design or a lack of nutrition, were made more prominent with the missing eyeballs. The birds had pecked at the flesh, scoring her skin with jagged, red marks.

Crouching next to Lila, Lundquist settled back on his haunches. "Maybe a little in her facial structure, but that could be from being young. Neither are the same height or same hair color. Without her eyes, we can't determine if they were the same color."

"True." Lila let the hair fall back. Then she gently pressed on the victim's chin and pried her mouth open. Metal blinked at her. "She's wearing braces."

"Shit. She doesn't look that young."

Lila released the chin. "It's hard to tell in this day and age. A lot of people wait until they're older to get them." She rested her forearms on her thighs.

The victim's stomach pushed against the confines of her clothing. Clothing that matched the first victim in style: jeans, a green button-down shirt over a brown tee, and retro combat boots. This girl had a thing for jewelry. Each swollen appendage was adorned with rings, and a tiny stud pierced her right nostril. The killer obviously had not taken any trophies. Not his kind of thing.

Chilling them appeared to be his MO. If the killer had put this girl on ice, so to speak, that skewed the timeline. And it would make for one hellacious investigation.

"What were you alluding to on the similarity?" Lundquist asked after a few moments of quiet. "Serial killer?"

Her body spasmed. *Shut it down.* Once the tremors subsided, she forced her battered and bruised body to unfold; standing upright alleviated the pressure on her tender midsection. "No. Something different."

Lundquist rose, towering over her. He appeared to have had a better night off than she. He was refreshed, beard neatly trimmed and his uniform crisp except for the few wrinkles gathered from his constant crouched movements as he collected potential evidence.

Turning to him, Lila caught a whiff of cedar. The woodsy scent suited him, playing into the whole Viking persona. Her nose tingled. Combating the sensation, she rubbed the cuff of her jacket against her nose.

"So," he said as if unaware of his effect on her. "What is this 'something'?"

"I don't like to speculate until I have some kind of confirmation."

"Which makes it harder for us to look for this something if you don't tell us."

She smiled. "Maybe. But what good does it do if we run off half-cocked over a suspicion? Coloring the evidence to match what we could come to believe. Always better to refrain, get all the information, and then piece it together to get the correct evidence."

Frowning, Lundquist squinted at her. "Are you always this pragmatic?"

No. Quite honestly, she had been that half-cocked rookie chasing after the White Rabbit on a trail to danger and death.

"Ask the doc if we can get a blood sample from the vic so we can run a comparison on the ones we have from our other samples."

"Already done," he said. "And I have the DNA results on the sample you took from the Barrett place."

"Do you have them with you?"

Lundquist shook his head. "After I do the tests from this one, I'll bring the results to the office later."

Nodding, she left him to continue his processing. Lila wandered to the backside of the tree, scanning the ground. Grass covered the entire area, eliminating the chance of tracks. And the road leading to this field was gravel. If this truly had been, or still was, a drop point for drug deals, it was a perfect spot. The only way to get caught was to leave behind evidence or have the misfortune of a cop coming this way, as Fitzgerald had years back.

A chorus of caws tracked Lila's movements. She looked up. The dead foliage that hadn't relinquished its grip on the limbs fluttered around the ten or so crows. What was it they called those opportunistic birds when they gathered?

"A murder."

Jerking, Lila blinked at the sheriff. Benoit was eyeballing the sleek, black birds.

"Come again?"

"A congregation of crows is called a murder, not a flock." Benoit's gaze swung to Lila. "The irony is not lost on me."

"Is there any way we can get them out of here without defiling the scene any more than it has been?" Lila asked, pointing at the white glops.

"Short of shooting them, we'll have to let them be. It's just a shame we don't know which or how many of these scavengers consumed the eyes. I'd like to trap them and do a necropsy."

"Not an effective measure. Like you said, we have no idea who did the deed."

"Then we do this old-fashioned way." Benoit checked her watch. "Since Deputy Fontaine refuses to go home, I'm sending him out on his next assignment." Benoit looked at Lila. "And you're going with."

"To do what, exactly?"

"Interview people at the fertilizer plant. We got a tip last night that the first victim might have ties to that place. This one"—she nodded at the second victim—"might as well. Just give her description. I don't want people seeing her like this."

"Yes, ma'am. Do you want us to leave now?"

Benoit faced Lila. "You read my mind."

SUPERVISING THE EXTRADITION of the unnamed victim left Elizabeth's nerves frayed. Two bodies within two days. No motives for their deaths. The reasons would remain elusive as long as they were unidentified. And a whole host of characters were dividing her attention. What a mess. How did she ever dream she could manage this position?

"Sheriff, I'm of the same mindset as Deputy Dayne on the cause of death."

Elizabeth pursed her lips and gave Olivia a nod.

"I'll begin the autopsy as soon as I get to the hospital. I asked for my appointments to be rescheduled so I can give these two cases my full focus today."

"Thank you, Olivia."

The ME gripped Elizabeth's bicep and squeezed. "Don't be too hard on yourself. Wicked people do wicked things, no matter who wears the badge." Olivia stepped outside the tape. "I'll give you a call once I have my findings."

"Before you go, can you give me an age estimation on this victim?"

Olivia sighed. "She's young, Ellie. Too young. But if it's a number you want, I'd give the range anywhere between sixteen and twenty."

"Too young," Elizabeth repeated.

After the dark paneled van pulled away and rumbled down the road, leaving a gravel dust cloud in its wake, Elizabeth turned to her men.

"Fitzgerald, show me the spot."

He did not hesitate or give her any grief. Lundquist and Meyer followed on her heels.

Squatting in front of the old oak, Fitzgerald used a glove to sweep aside the debris at the base of the trunk, in the exact spot the victim had sat. He pushed his hand into the glove and then picked at a particular spot inches from the toes of his boots. A lid sprang up.

"They have it camouflaged?" Meyer sounded incredulous.

"What better way to keep people in the dark," Elizabeth said.

Reaching inside the shallow burrow, Fitzgerald extracted a metal box and held it aloft. Elizabeth took it, prying open the lid. Inside were three baggies of crystal meth, beneath those an empty envelope.

"It appears someone missed their drop. Or has not been by to get it yet." She slapped the lid shut and held it out to Lundquist. "Bag and tag."

Fitzgerald rose, dusting off his pant legs.

"The time you caught Daniel, what was he getting?"

He squinted. "If I recall right, he wasn't getting it. I think he was dropping it off. I caught him with heroin."

Elizabeth gnawed on her lip. "Dropping it off, you say?"

Nodding, the deputy removed his gloves. "I have no idea why they're still using this location after it was discovered."

"We have no idea how long that meth has been in there," Meyer pointed out.

"Fitzgerald, are you aware of any other locations?" Elizabeth asked.

"I don't specifically know of any other locations, but my gut says there are more in this county. This is the only one I've found."

Tapping a finger alongside her chin, Elizabeth stared at the hole. A caw. A solitary crow ruffled its feathers, the others having vacated the area once the body had been removed. They brought such an ominous vibe to crime scenes.

Here were two young women so very close in age to Bre when she'd died. And just like then, Sheehan's name found a way into the conversation. Drugs had been thrown around as a reason behind Bre's death—an accidental overdose. At the time, Sheehan had been a deputy, and there at the scene, a fact that was left out of all accounts. His predecessor found no fault in his star deputy. The king viper coddling his eventual successor.

Too bad the old sheriff was moldering in his grave and the truth rotting along with him.

Elizabeth still lacked the proof to pull the trigger. And these recent deaths demanded her full attention. Bre's death had waited this long; it would have to wait a bit longer.

"Sheriff?"

Deputy Benjamin Fitzgerald. The solitary holdout from Sheehan's days. A man who, at every turn, tried to be a hard-ass and contrarian to her orders and service. But his admission of Sheehan's lack of trust in him opened her eyes.

"Thank you for relaying what you know. I know it's hard to swallow the fact I'm now the sheriff. It was quite a leap from Sheehan and his policies to me."

He gaped.

"Go home and sleep so you're ready for your shift tonight." She moved closer to him. "I do have one request of you. Go through your memories and try to recall times when Sheehan skirted the law with Daniel Kauffmann."

Fitzgerald opened his mouth, and she stopped him with an upright finger.

"Before you protest, let me finish. I'm aware that you feel

a sense of loyalty to the former sheriff, and I don't fault you that. But you must ask yourself, why is that so? If this one example of Sheehan railroading you with Daniel Kauffmann is any indication, I'm sure you had many situations where he usurped the law and your work to do his own thing. How many times were you told to look the other way or ignore something? And how many times did that bother the heck out of you to do it?"

Unable to hold her gaze, he stared at the wadded gloves.

"You're a good cop, Ben. Don't let another man's agenda ruin you."

Red brightened his blond beard. Elizabeth wasn't going to lie; she was proud to see her words had gotten to him.

"I'll just head home." He headed for his squad car.

"Would you take the car to the shop and get it looked at? I would rather you not get stranded."

"Uh, sure thing, Sheriff."

Once he was backing out, Elizabeth turned to her youngest deputy. "Deputy Meyer, it hasn't escaped my notice where we are nor how far we are from the old quarry road and our first victim."

"You want to go see her?"

"I need to speak to her about this. Better it come from me than the rumor mill. Also, we need permission to do further searches of the area. My gut is telling me this isn't the only place for a drug cache."

"He's not going to like it."

She placed her hand on his shoulder. "She's your mother. If you're with me, there's not much he can say against that."

"You have high hopes, ma'am." He shrugged. "I guess

it's not a bad thing. I haven't seen her since I took this position."

"All the more reason to come."

If there was one thing Elizabeth knew all too well, it was how dysfunctional families were in this county. She had married into one.

CHAPTER FOURTEEN

L ILA PARKED NEXT to Fontaine's Dodge Charger. How
was it that, out of all the deputies, he got the muscle car?
Sheriff playing favorites?

Terra Firma Inc. loomed before them. A hint of ammo-
nia hung in the air.

"Holy hell." And here she'd thought some of the facto-
ries in the burbs of Chicago were huge.

Fontaine rounded the front of his vehicle. "You coming?"

Dropping her arm, she caught up with him. "This looks
new."

"It just opened about a week ago. They have a new hous-
ing development going up west of Three Points for the
workers who moved here from other states."

Lila scowled. "Correct me if I'm wrong, but wouldn't
they have built this with the intent to use local people
already living here?"

He huffed. "You'd think. Not enough locals, apparently." Removing his reflective sunglasses, he peered at the sign
on the metal door directing visitors to the office around the
corner.

They headed in that direction.

Lila twitched, glanced over, and discovered the man

squinting at her. Was he pitying her? "Something on your mind, Deputy Fontaine?"

"Nope."

Right. She'd press the matter later.

More of that Iowa chivalry came out as Fontaine grabbed the door before she could and pulled it open, holding it for her to enter first. This would take some getting used to.

Behind a curved receptionist desk sat a stunning brunette in black-rimmed glasses, wearing a dark blue polo with the Terra Firma company logo on her left shoulder. She gave them a smile, her gaze lingering on the beefy deputy at Lila's side. This was going to be an issue with this man, no matter where they went.

"Welcome to Terra Firma, how can I help you . . . deputies?"

Lila leaned an elbow on the counter and let her impromptu partner take the lead. After all, she wasn't all too sure what his plan of attack was for this.

"Could we speak with the manager?" Fontaine asked.

"Just a minute." The woman picked up the phone and punched an extension button.

Lila's gaze roamed the walls, taking in the framed photos backing the receptionist. The largest one, front and center, showed off the ribbon cutting with a lot of suits. One would surmise that some of those suits were politicos.

"He'll be right up." Blue eyes batted at Fontaine.

He dipped his chin and put his back to the desk, hooking his thumbs in his duty belt. The receptionist seemed stymied by his lack of interest.

This amused Lila to no end. Crossing both arms on the

counter, she leaned on them. "A fertilizer plant out in the middle of nowhere."

The receptionist looked at her. "Yes, it was a condition with the state to not bring complaints from residential areas. The chemicals can get . . . overwhelming."

Lila propped her chin on an upraised fist. "Is that so? Hmm."

A line lit up and the phone rang. Her attention still on Lila, the receptionist picked up the handset. "Good morning, Terra Firma. How may I direct your call?"

A light tap to her arm pulled Lila away. Fontaine beckoned her closer to the door.

Ducking his head, he scrunched his face. "What are you doing?" he rasped.

"Getting a lay of the land. Is there a problem with that?"

"It could be. We're about to ask some sobering questions, and the last thing we need is someone with a bee up their . . . rear."

Lila smirked at his adjustment. "Chill out, Fontaine. I'm not here to hurt anyone's feelings."

Sharp clack of leather against polished flooring ended their little confab. A whipcord-thin man wearing snug-fitting dark blue jeans, a tan blazer over a light blue button-down, and square-toed boots rounded the desk.

"Rafe, how are you?" He thrust out his hand.

Shaking the offered hand, Fontaine smiled. "Jimmy, I didn't know you were managing this place."

"Putting that ag degree to good use." Jimmy's eyes flicked to Lila, his hand following suit. "Jimmy Rhoads."

Lila gave him a firm squeeze. "Deputy Lila Dayne."

Jimmy's attention returned to Fontaine. "What brings you clear out here?"

Her partner looked back at the receptionist. "Is there someplace we could speak in private?"

"Uh, sure. Let's head to my office." As he led them past the desk, Jimmy caught the brunette's attention. "Send my calls to voice mail."

The men adopted a leisure pace, which suited Lila's aching body just fine, and it gave her time to assess the wall adornments.

"How long you been back, Jimmy?"

"Since they poured the concrete." Jimmy slapped Fontaine's Kevlar-strapped shoulder. "I'm surprised we haven't run into each other before now."

A throaty grunt was the answer.

"Hear from your brother much? I heard he and Elizabeth split up and now she's the sheriff."

"Yeah, something like that."

Lila shivered at Fontaine's frosty tone. Apparently, conversation about his brother was off-limits.

"How long did it take to build this place?" she asked.

"Two and half years. Seems like a long time, but the business plan is to recoup the costs in less time. The owners have a good track record of doing as they promise." Jimmy paused outside an open door. "Here we are."

Once again, Lila was allowed first entry into the immaculate space. The room was painted a dove gray with midnight-blue trim, leather and wood furniture, and above Jimmy's chair anchored to the wall, a stuffed pheasant midflight.

"Nice bird."

Jimmy grinned, closing the door. "Bagged him last season." He took position behind his desk but didn't sit. "Okay, Rafe. We have privacy."

Fontaine weaved between the two visitors' chairs and rooted himself next to the desk. "My visit here isn't a pleasant one. What I'm about to ask you stays in this office. Do you understand?"

Blinking, Jimmy grasped the edges of his blazer. "Good God, Rafe, it sounds like you're about to deliver some bad news."

Fontaine met Lila's gaze. The look in his eyes troubled her. Was he regretting his decision? His focus returned to Jimmy.

"Is this place running at full capacity?"

"No. We still need about twenty more employees, some of those have yet to arrive. I'm expecting them by the end of the month."

Lila shifted to attract Jimmy's notice. "When this place is fully operational, what is the expected employee population?"

"Two hundred to two-fifty. Is this going somewhere?"

Fontaine ripped the Velcro flap from his left side pocket on his pants. Reaching inside, he withdrew his cell phone. "Of the ones working here now, how many are locals?"

"Barely a third. The rest are from Illinois, Missouri, and I've had a few come down from Minnesota. There's a group from western Iowa."

"Of the out-of-staters, what percentage of them are families?" Lila asked.

"Lower than the singles population. Not many people are willing to uproot their families and move, despite the pay incentives these jobs bring." Jimmy's worried look turned skeptical. "I still don't see what this has to do with your reasons for being here."

Setting his phone on the desktop, Fontaine slid it across the calendar, pulling his hand back to reveal a photo of the first victim. "Do you recognize this girl?"

It took him a moment, but the curious look Jimmy gave the photo turned to shock. "Is she dead?"

"Yes."

Jimmy's head whiplashed back.

"Oh my God." He took a step back from the phone. "I don't know that girl, and I didn't have anything to do with her death. Never seen her in my life."

Lila moved closer to the desk, holding up her hands. Jimmy looked on the verge of a panic attack. "Mr. Rhoads, look at me." His gaze snapped to her. "We aren't insinuating that you had anything to do with her death. We're just trying to learn who she is."

The panic didn't abate, but Jimmy seemed a little more in a listening mood. "I'm serious. I haven't seen her before."

"Maybe you saw another girl, she's about five-eight, dark brown hair with purple ends, a nose piercing, wearing braces?" Lila asked.

Jimmy shook his head. "Hair color like that I would remember, but no. That doesn't mean they don't have family here."

"That's why we came," Fontaine said. "Has anyone not shown up for work for any reason in the last three days?"

"You would have to ask the plant foremen. I haven't seen the reports for this week yet."

"Would you call them in here? I'd like to speak with them."

Shaking his head, Jimmy held up his hand, looking more in control of himself. "Rafe, I can't bring the foremen in here away from the duty stations. If I did that, I'd have to shut down their whole section, and that's not going to happen."

"Would it be all right if we went out there?" Lila asked. "We could split up and cut the time in half."

"I can authorize that." Jimmy reached for his phone.

"Before you alert them"—Lila held her hand over the phone keypad—"is there a way to get an employee roster?"

"Uh, yeah. I can have payroll print out one. Give me a sec."

As he made his calls, Fontaine gestured for her to step outside the office with him. In the hall, he looked up and down.

"Nice work. I don't remember him being flighty."

"Most people aren't, but when they're faced with a DB they tend to revert to the primal urge to run. How many homicide investigations have you done in your time, Deputy?"

"Including this one, two. And the first one, which turned out to be an accident, I was relegated to security detail."

Lila patted his vested chest. "Good to know." She entered the office just as Jimmy hung up the phone.

"They'll meet you in the plants. Alice is bringing the employee list."

"When she gets it here, would you go through it with us

and mark the ones you know are here with their families?" Lila said.

"Anything." Jimmy stared at Fontaine's phone, still sitting on his desk. "She looks really young."

Fontaine picked up his phone and closed the photo. "Unfortunately, she does."

THE TWO FOREMEN Lila spoke with managed the liquid storage tanks and one of the mixing units respectively. Neither men recognized the young women, and neither had anyone from their workforce who'd missed any work in the last three days. Lila was waylaid by a call as she headed to her next destination.

"Deputy Dayne, meet me at the north storage building," Fontaine said by way of greeting.

Rotating to get her whereabouts, Lila spotted the building he referred to. "On my way."

Her neck prickled from the blatant stares. Gossip would spread like wildfire the moment one of those foremen broke their sworn promise. And the sheriff would have a whole ball of yarn to unravel with that one.

Entering the facility through the main door, Lila stepped into an enclosed office area with walls made of thick glass. Fontaine stood with Jimmy and a burly, bearded man in white protective coveralls and yellow helmet.

"What's up?" Lila asked, hooking her hands on her hips, relieved to learn that the more she moved, the less her body hurt.

"We might have our connection." Fontaine nodded at the foreman. "Earl here says a husband and wife who work his unit called in sick today."

"So soon?" Lila asked.

Earl shook his head. "Got me. They haven't been here long enough to come down with anything."

"They could have picked up something before they moved here," Jimmy pointed out.

"This is beside the point," Fontaine interrupted. "The point is, they have a family, a girl. And they're not here."

"Mr. Rhoads, we're going to need their address or a way to contact them," Lila said.

"I'll give you both." He looked at Earl. "Remember what Deputy Fontaine said."

"Yes, sir."

Jimmy led them out of the facility and back across the compound to his office. Fontaine sent rapid-fire texts to someone the entire way.

"Sheriff is tied up," he said after three more texts.

"She wants us to handle it?"

He tucked away his phone. "That would be the orders."

"You lead, I'll follow."

He looked her way, the bright blue sky reflecting in his sunglasses. "I thought as the designated detective, you'd want lead on this."

"Oh, I will once we get there. I just meant that you lead the way to the home. I don't know where I'm going. Brand new and all."

"Uh, yeah."

Jimmy left them in his office to gather the vital information. Lila stared at the stuffed pheasant. She didn't have much exposure to the bird, as they weren't known to walk the streets of Chicago.

"How long do you think it'll take one of those men to start talking?" she asked Fontaine.

"I know Earl. He's a good man, served during the Iraq War as a navy man. He's all too aware of 'loose lips sink ships.' As for the ones you talked to, you've got a fifty-fifty chance one of them will spill the beans, so to speak."

"We've got three hours, tops, before the whole county knows, then."

"Pretty much," Fontaine said as Jimmy returned with a sheet of paper.

"If you need anything else, Rafe, let me know."

Folding up the sheet, Fontaine slipped it inside a pocket. "Please relay to the two foremen Deputy Dayne saw how important it is they don't spread unnecessary gossip."

"I'll get right on it." Jimmy shook both of their hands.

The brunette didn't bother to give them the time of day as they passed the front desk. Once outside, Lila chuckled at the snub.

"What's that for?" Fontaine asked, slipping his sunglasses on.

"Between you giving her flirting the cold shoulder and my inquisition, she was none too happy with us."

"I didn't give her the cold shoulder. And she wasn't flirting."

Lila shook her head. "If you say so." She reached her car and popped the handle.

"Whether she did or she didn't, it's none of my concern.

There's a job to do." The tension in his voice gave Lila pause.

She studied him. His relaxed stance seemed forced to her. Maybe there was more than knowing looks passed between the sheriff and the deputy.

"Let's go," she said, climbing into her car.

CHAPTER FIFTEEN

E LIZABETH RETURNED HER cell to its case on her duty
belt. A few feet ahead of her, Deputy Meyer stood on
the front stoop of a brick two-story, waiting. She joined him
under the grand colonnade holding sentry.

"It's nearly lunch. He'll be home soon," he said.

"Hope he had a lunch meeting."

He gave her a perturbed sideways look, and punched the
doorbell. "This is my father we're talking about. If he so
much as sniffs a problem, he'll be here in two seconds flat."

"If that's the case, I'll handle him."

"Good luck."

The door swung open on well-oiled hinges, revealing a
put-together woman with dusty brown hair skimming the
shoulders of an emerald-green blouse and wearing a pair of
wrinkleless black slacks. Her warm brown eyes took the two
of them in, and a heartbreaking smile creased her features.
"Brent, honey, what brings you here?"

He glanced over at Elizabeth. "The sheriff needs to speak
with you, Mom."

Sophie Meyer stepped back and gestured for the two of
them to enter. "Pratt is not home at the moment, Sheriff. I
do expect him anytime now."

"It's you I've come to speak with." Elizabeth stepped onto the polished wood flooring and hesitated, looking down at her dirty boots then Meyer's. They were going to leave a mess.

But Sophie took Elizabeth by the elbow and linked their arms like they were old chums. "It's what Swiffer dusters are for. Follow me." She escorted them into a bright, sunny room, bursting at the seams for Christmas. Standing tall and proud in front of the bay windows, the red-and-silver-decorated balsam fir fragranced the room. "Have a seat. Would you like some coffee?"

"Mom, no. That's okay."

"That would be wonderful, thank you."

Giving her youngest child a half smile, Sophie patted a rich red-brown leather chair. "Brent, relax. Give me a minute." She vacated the room.

Meyer stared at the chair, looking like he would bolt the instant it snapped at him.

"Your mother's right. You need to relax." Elizabeth eased onto a cream-colored, plush leather chair, careful to keep her sidearm from hooking into the folds.

"Sheriff, I can't. The second he shows up, it's going to get very ugly."

"As I said, let me handle it."

"This is my father we're speaking of, no one but *him* handles things."

Elizabeth gave her young deputy a smile. He had much to learn about what his sheriff could and could not handle. Men like Pratt Meyer were cast from the same mold, a mold Elizabeth had encountered more times than she cared for over the years she'd been an army wife.

Sophie returned carrying an intricately detailed wooden tray. Setting it down on a sidebar, she first handed Elizabeth a turquoise cup, and then served her son, who moved to stand next to the beautifully decorated fireplace. Taking a cup herself, Sophie settled on a mate to Elizabeth's chair.

The former office manager tilted her head to the side. "Now, Sheriff, what is it that you needed to discuss with me?"

"We've had a misfortunate occurrence on your family's property this morning."

"Which property would that be?"

Pratt may have brought social status and new wealth to the Meyer family name, but Sophie came with a wealth of her own. Her family had owned a sizable chunk of Eckardt County's rich, fertile crop ground for more than a century. When her father passed on and her mother had gone into a nursing home, the estate became Sophie's to manage, and so she did, despite her husband's protests. Sophie was the sole heir, having no siblings. Her elder daughters were steeped in their father's way of thinking that farming was an archaic practice and no way to make a comfortable living. Her youngest child was her last hope of continuing the family legacy.

"It's Grandad's east hayfield."

Sophie's cup clattered on the table beside her chair. "Was there an accident of some kind? That field is so far out of the way. I know my tenant has complained of young people being out there, drinking and carousing, but there hasn't been an accident before."

Elizabeth scooted to the edge of her seat, halting Sophie.

"It's not an accident." She glanced at Meyer, who was facing the fireplace. He was holding her to her word. "Sophie, a homicide victim was left in the field."

Gasping, a hand flying to her mouth, Sophie gaped at Elizabeth. "My God, how awful."

"I wanted to be the one to tell you before the rumors began flying and you, or Pratt, heard the wrong things."

Sophie grasped Elizabeth's hand. "Thank you for that, Sheriff. I appreciate the thoughtfulness."

A door at the back of the house clapped shut. Meyer stiffened, backing from the fireplace as the rat-a-tat footfalls came their direction. Releasing Elizabeth's hand, Sophie stood as her husband entered the room.

The man looming large in the doorway epitomized the ideal of what a successful businessman from a large city looked like. Dressed to the nines in a dove-gray suit and shiny black wingtips that would have taken all of Elizabeth's meager paycheck, Pratt Meyer was the complete opposite of his son, standing feet away.

"Sheriff, this is an unexpected visit." His midwestern accent had long been eradicated while attending Loyola University Chicago.

"Yes." Elizabeth set her cup down and stood. "It is, Pratt. I came to speak with Sophie about a matter."

His cool gray eyes slid to his son, then back to Elizabeth. "This wouldn't happen to be about the body found on her family's property this morning, now would it?"

That he knew did not surprise her in the least. The man had a finger in all the pies in the county. A bonus when he was the financial manager for nearly every business owner and was a board member of one of the county's largest banks.

"As a matter of fact, it is."

Pratt made a dissatisfied sound. Another unsurprising move. Though her suspicions were, as of yet, unfounded, Elizabeth believed Sheehan and Pratt had an "understanding" of sorts. Pratt had vocalized his opposition of her winning the election—remarks about women unable to handle running a governmental office—but toed the line when she'd taken over. After all, he was as welcome to his First Amendment rights as the next person.

"Dear, the sheriff was about to explain to me her next steps in the matter."

He crossed his arms, his attention swinging to his son. "What, pray tell, would those steps be?"

The tension in the room pressed on Elizabeth. She shifted to the right, getting closer to her deputy. "We are investigating the matter at hand. It is a homicide and is, therefore, being treated as such. However, in the course of our search this morning we came across a drug cache in the field."

Pratt's attention snapped to Elizabeth and his scowl deepened. "What are you insinuating?"

"She insinuates nothing, Pratt," Sophie cut in. "Are you sure about that, Sheriff? Drugs?"

"I'm afraid so. As a courtesy, I've come to ask that we have uninhibited access to the field and its surrounding properties to search for more caches."

"Absolutely not," Pratt barked.

"Being able to search the properties can aid in our homicide investigation."

"And I forbid it. Searching for drug caches has nothing to do with a homicide. You want access to that property, you bring a warrant and you ensure that warrant covers exactly what you need."

"Pratt. That is not your decision to make." Sophie glared at her husband.

"Sophie, when you asked me to ensure the financial stability of those properties by coming onto the corporation board, you gave me a full say in what happens." His cold, cutting words seemed to break Sophie's resolve. "The sheriff's department will be granted access only to the part that pertains to the homicide investigation until a warrant is presented."

"Why does that not surprise me."

Brent's cutting remark made the tension snap like a taut guitar string.

Pratt's ire turned on his son. "And how is this boy taking part in this affair?"

"It's not an 'affair.' I'm a deputy, and I'll be doing my job as the sheriff sees fit."

Red spots peppered Pratt's cheeks. A few days after she'd returned to Juniper, Marnie had brought Elizabeth up to speed on the Meyer family saga. No matter how much Brent achieved, his father would find fault and criticize. There had been, according to Marnie, some highly publicized screaming matches between the two as Brent had gone through high school, and a memorable moment where he had wrecked his father's brand-new Lexus on purpose. No one knew the exact reason for the falling out between son and father—they could only speculate. But it was a wound so deep, it drove Brent to train to be a law officer instead of following in his father's footsteps as a financial mogul.

"Sheriff, I believe you have completed the task you set out to do here. It's time you go."

Hurt flashed through Sophie's eyes. Elizabeth could only imagine the pain Sophie must be going through as this rift continued between the two men she loved.

"Throwing us out like we're some petulant children. Get a real hard-on exercising your authority, *Father*."

"Brent," Sophie gasped.

Red filled Pratt's features. His arms dropped and he moved toward his son. Elizabeth darted between the two men, her hand slapping against Pratt's chest.

"While he is your son, Pratt, need I remind you, if you strike a sworn officer of the law, I will have to arrest you."

His furious gaze fell to her. "Get that insolent child out of my house." He backed away from her hand and adjusted his slightly rumpled suit jacket. "My decision on this stands: no access without a warrant. Now, both of you, leave."

Elizabeth pointed to the front door. "Deputy Meyer, return to the unit."

He did as ordered, his eyes staying on his father until he rounded the corner and disappeared down the hall.

"It is one thing for you to come to my home, Sheriff, but to bring him along is a personal insult to me."

"Pratt, please."

He gave his wife a withering look, and then exited the room. When his footsteps faded down the hallway, Sophie bowed her head.

"Sophie, I meant no disrespect. I only hoped for Brent to be able to see you again."

Giving Elizabeth a quivering smile, Sophie nodded. "I appreciate the gesture. I hold out hope that one day those two will reconcile."

Elizabeth squeezed the woman's thin shoulder. "Don't give up on it."

"Thank you."

Elizabeth exited the house, leaving the poor woman torn between her obligations to her husband and her love for her son. Deputy Meyer was standing next to the SUV, staring at the expansive yard with its meticulous landscaping. As she crossed the paved driveway, he took his spot on the passenger side. Bentley hopped onto the center console and settled her chin on his shoulder.

Elizabeth's steps faltered at the sight. The young deputy had an ax to grind with his father, but it did not mean that each encounter with the man didn't rip away a piece of him. She would go easy on him this time. Who was she to criticize a man when he was wounded?

If Pratt wanted a warrant, then a warrant Pratt would get.

CHAPTER SIXTEEN

T HE APARTMENT COMPLEX took Lila by surprise. The one-story units reminded her more of the single-family homes typically built in the suburbs sprawling westward from Chicago. My God, the yards were bigger than a postage stamp.

Consulting the paper given to him, Fontaine pointed left, following the sidewalk to a unit with blue-gray siding. He stepped aside and allowed her to mount the lone step under a small stoop. She rapped on the door, then took position on the opposite side.

They didn't have long to wait. The door flung open and man in rumpled clothing squinted out at them. "Mary, it's the cops," he called back into the apartment.

"Peter Wagner?" Lila asked.

A thin brunette in equally rumpled clothing with her hair pulled back in a ponytail emerged from a side room and came to stand next to him. Pulse thrumming in her ears, Lila swallowed hard.

"Yes," he said. "Is there something we can help you with, officers?"

"It's deputies, actually. I'm Deputy Fontaine, and this is Deputy Dayne. May we ask you a few questions?" Fontaine had to see it too.

"About what?" Mary asked, gripping her husband's arm.

Lila swept the perimeter, catching movement in a window in the building next door. "This might be best done inside."

The Wagners' attention darted around the complex. Paling, they backed from the doorway and gestured for Lila and Fontaine to enter. Peter closed the door with a parting look outside, but the couple remained in the foyer.

"Mr. and Mrs. Wagner, I can't help but notice you seem on edge. Is something wrong?" Lila asked.

"It's never a good sign when the law shows up at our door," Peter said. "It usually means that Maya has done something again."

"Maya?"

"Our daughter," Mary supplied.

Tremors took control of Lila's hands. Clenching her fists, she covertly tucked them behind her back. Fontaine glanced at her; she avoided direct eye contact with him. Frowning, he focused on the Wagners.

"Maya has a history of legal troubles?" Fontaine continued.

"It's why we took jobs here and moved from Illinois," Peter said. "She needed a fresh start away from all the bad influences."

Forcing her brain to function, Lila cleared her throat. "The bad influences being?"

"Her cousin. My worthless sister's daughter," Mary said, adjusting her hold on her husband's arm. "We haven't seen Maya in a while, but that's normal."

"When was the last time you saw her?" The words tore

from Lila. She couldn't do this. *Not my job.* Lila coughed and turned her back on the couple.

"Deputy Dayne, are you okay?" Fontaine asked.

"I'm done," she whispered and reached for the door.

He caught her hand. "What?"

She jerked free, glaring at him. "Don't touch me." She grabbed the handle and managed to get the door open.

"Excuse us a moment," she heard Fontaine say as she stumbled out of the house.

Drawing in deep breaths, she stood on the sidewalk, exhaling out of her mouth. Fontaine stomped up beside her.

"What the hell is this all about?" he growled.

"Back off."

"No. We're in the middle of this; you don't get to bail on me."

"You be in the middle of this. I'm not."

He shook his head. "I knew it. I warned her this would happen. It got real and you're freezing."

Lila scowled. "Warned her? What are you talking about?"

"Deputies?"

Fontaine stared at the Wagners for a few seconds, then turned back to Lila. "Go back to the department. GPS will show you the way. I'll handle this."

"It's not your job."

"Apparently, you're making it mine."

The fragile hold on her emotions was slipping. He was giving her an out. And all she wanted to do was argue. Slapping her thigh, she rotated on the balls of her feet and marched to her car. Cradled in the leather seat, she happened to look up as she reached to start the engine, and hesitated.

Fontaine was speaking with the couple, but Mary was staring past him, watching Lila. The fear permeating from the other woman breached the distance and hit Lila. Mary knew. She didn't have to be told. She knew her daughter was gone.

A sob choked Lila. Death notices were not part of her job description. She should have made that clear to Benoit.

Starting the car, she strapped in and threw the car in reverse. There would be no need for GPS. As she turned the car to leave, she chanced one last look at the trio. Fontaine's gaze tracked with the car's movements.

Lila had hoped for a few days' reprieve before explaining her past.

There was no hiding anymore.

ELIZABETH LET BENTLEY into her office and stalked over to Georgia's desk.

"I don't like that look." Georgia handed her a stack of papers.

A desk drawer clapped shut. "Sheriff, I'm sorry."

Cupping the back of her neck, Elizabeth squeezed. As she drove back to the department, she'd called the judge, asking for a warrant, and was soundly rejected. Probably Pratt maneuvering his rook in some dirty backroom deal to ensure his demands stood firm. A power play all too common in this county overburdened with sexist, corrupt, dickless twits. Meanwhile, Meyer had made it a point to grovel for his misstep.

Releasing her ire in a steady exhale, Elizabeth turned to her youngest deputy. He was not the object of her anger. He had reacted as a son would when faced with abject rejection. "Deputy Meyer, please stop apologizing."

"I just can't believe I let him get to me like that."

Elizabeth met Georgia's uh-oh look and shook her head, heading for her office. "For the last time, don't beat yourself up. We all have moments we'd like to take back and have a do-over."

The sharp smack of the door echoing in the hallway made Elizabeth hesitate. Who had returned? Voices murmured followed by heavy footfalls. Rafe rounded the corner, features pinched. He came to an abrupt halt when he found their little group lingering.

"Sheriff," he growled the title. "We need to talk."

"Okay," Elizabeth said gently. "Meyer, please return to patrol."

"Yes, ma'am." Her younger deputy left the bullpen, giving Rafe a wide berth.

"Georgia, hold my calls. And when the food arrives, knock three times."

"Ten-four."

Rafe followed Elizabeth into her office, closing the door with a clap. She threw a frown over her shoulder.

"Where is Deputy Dayne?"

"I have no damn idea."

This brought her to a halt. Rotating, she scowled. "Run that past me again."

Rafe pointed at her nose. "I warned you she was a loose cannon. I wanted to give you the benefit of the doubt, but she proved you wrong and me right."

Catching his finger, she pushed his hand down. "How so?"

"Down the hall in the waiting room are a husband and wife whose daughter is lying on the slab in the ME's morgue."

A tightness spread through Elizabeth's chest. Closing her eyes, she bowed her head.

"They don't know yet. I knew it from the moment I saw the wife, and apparently so did Dayne. But instead of doing her job, she bolted like a scared colt."

Elizabeth met Rafe's furious gaze. "You brought the couple here?"

"What else would you have me do? They need to be told, and I'm not the best person to do it."

Shaking her head, Elizabeth sat on the edge of her desk. "It was too soon for her."

"Dayne shouldn't be doing this at all."

"That's not for you to decide."

Rafe reached across their professional boundaries, cupped her cheek, and rubbed a callused thumb along her jaw. "There are just some things you can't fix, Ellie."

They stayed that way. She was loath to break the connection, wishing they were not boss and underling. Let them be anywhere else but here, where their every movement was not under scrutiny and she was allowed the chance to blur the lines. Give in to her desire to be closer to him, kiss him, strip away all the what-ifs and just be Rafe's woman. Not Joel's ex-wife. Just Rafe's.

He pulled back, hooking his hand on the butt of his

weapon. "We shouldn't keep them waiting any longer."

Pushing off the desk, she snapped her fingers. "Do you think they suspect?" Bentley hopped down from her throne and ambled over to Elizabeth's side.

"I think the wife has a clue. When Dayne left, Mary, the wife, got real quiet. Like she sensed what we were there for."

"Which young woman you think is their daughter?"

Rafe grasped her hand. "It's the girl we found this morning. You don't need a picture to figure it out. She's the spitting image of her mother. The girl's name was Maya."

"Take Bentley into the room. I need to call Olivia and see where she's at with the autopsy. I'll be in after I'm done."

Giving her a squeeze, Rafe gestured for Bentley to follow him, and together they exited her office. Through the open door Elizabeth caught Georgia's upraised chin, and the single finger she held up. Once the door clicked shut, Elizabeth rounded her desk. Line one blinked red on her phone.

"Sheriff Benoit."

"Ellie, it's Olivia. I've completed the autopsy on the second Jane Doe."

"Good. Do you have her closed up and presentable?"

"Being done now as we speak. Why?"

This would be the hardest part for Elizabeth with this job. Death notices always had been. For a few years, she had been the den mother of sorts for the wives in The Unit, and when the chaplain showed up at her doorstep, she knew what she had to do. Too many widows had screamed their grief and rage out on her chest.

"Rafe is certain we have the parents of that young girl here in the department. I'll be bringing them over. How long do you need to prepare her for an identification?"

"Give me a half hour."

"Done."

Setting the handset on its cradle, Elizabeth pursed her mouth. God help her.

She exited the office.

Georgia pointed at the bags contained in a narrow cardboard flat on the dorm room fridge beside the coffee station table. "I'll put it in the fridge," she said.

Elizabeth nodded her thanks as she left the bullpen.

In the waiting room, she found Rafe standing sentry, Bentley lying in the middle of the room, watching the couple, who sat next to each other on chairs facing the doorway. The noonday sunlight pouring in the four windows backlit the man and woman. As Rafe had warned, the woman's features struck Elizabeth.

She was indeed the mother of Jane Doe number two.

"Sheriff Benoit, this is Peter and Mary Wagner."

The Wagners stood, Mary clinging to her husband with a resigned expression. Mary suspected her daughter was dead; what she waited for was how she'd died.

Sighing, Elizabeth sat in a chair across from them, gesturing for the two to resume their seats. Bentley remained in her position, her gaze riveted to the two.

"Sheriff, we know this has something to do with our daughter, Maya," Peter said. "Do you know where she is?"

The thread of hope in his voice shattered Elizabeth.

"Mr. and Mrs. Wagner, I need to ask you a few questions. When was the last time you saw Maya?"

Mary met Elizabeth's gaze. "I was the last one to see her.

It was Monday. She was leaving for school, told me I didn't need to drop her off. She had a ride. She didn't come home that day or any of the days after."

"Did the school alert you of her absence?"

Mary sighed. "According to their records, she attended all her morning classes Monday but didn't show up after her lunch period. We gave her a few days to return because this was her usual pattern when she decided she'd had enough of us. I didn't think anything of it until yesterday. She's never gone longer than a day or two."

"Who was this ride with?"

"I don't know. She wouldn't say. But I have my suspicions. Last week I caught her chatting with her cousin, Regan. Maya has been banned from hanging out with her cousin."

"But," Peter interjected, "Regan is supposed to be in a rehab center in Naperville."

"Naperville, Illinois?" Elizabeth asked.

"Yes. Regan is my sister's daughter," Mary said. "Mother and daughter are kith and kin, one drug addict spawning another."

Elizabeth held her hand out for Rafe's phone. He took it out and located the picture, then handed her the phone. Elizabeth stared at the image of the young woman with her eyes closed.

"Mrs. Wagner, how old is Regan?"

"She's twenty-one."

"And Maya?"

"Sixteen."

Rafe shifted his stance and then excused himself. Elizabeth did not fault his decision.

Rotating the phone, Elizabeth held it up. "Is this Regan?"

Peter grabbed the phone from her hand and gaped. Mary closed her eyes, turning her head away.

"Why does she look like that?" Peter whispered.

Elizabeth stood and gently pried the phone from his death grip.

He looked up at her. "Why, Sheriff?"

"This is going to be very difficult for you, but I need you to understand that it is for all our benefits if you do this. Mrs. Wagner, what was Maya wearing the day you last saw her?"

Peter clamped his mouth shut, looking at his wife. Carefully, as if pulling at loose threads of memory, Mary described in detail the exact clothing they had found Maya wearing. Once she finished, Mary buried her face in her hands. "She's dead," she sobbed.

Peter's features crumpled and he wrapped his arms around his wife's shoulders, pressing his forehead against her bowed one.

Bentley came to her feet and padded over to the grieving couple. She sat, waiting for a sign that they would accept her comfort. The Wagners leaned into each other, filling the silence with their strangled crying.

Elizabeth sat down, letting them have their moment. There would be plenty of time to bleed their hearts dry with the news that Maya had been murdered. Right now, they needed to draw on what little fortitude they had for the coming storm.

The scuff of boots against the floor drew her attention to the doorway. Rafe, his back to the room, reached around the doorframe and gripped Elizabeth's shoulder. She resisted the urge to press her cheek against his hand, instead letting his liquid strength seep into her bones. She needed it, because what she had to do next would cut her legs out from under her.

CHAPTER SEVENTEEN

HUNGER GOT THE better of her two hours after she'd ditched Fontaine. Lila located a fast food joint and took her burger and fries order to a local park. Sitting in her car, watching kids on the playground equipment, she let her ravenous side wipe out the panic.

They all looked so happy out there, running, swinging, and squealing as they chased each other. One girl seemed to be the ringleader and a bit of a daredevil as she jumped from the end of one playset, grabbed on to the monkey bars, and catapulted her body onto another playset, landing with the ease of an acrobat. That had been Lila in her youth.

She'd always wanted a girl. Wanted to teach her all the things she knew. Show her daughter how to be a woman in a man's world. Lila's hand cupped her abdomen. That was all gone.

The straw rattled against the bottom of the cup. Jerking out of her stupor, Lila set the cup aside. Her food was gone, and she didn't recall eating a bite of it, only that the hunger pangs had subsided. But the haze of her panic attack lingered. Dumping her trash on the passenger side floorboard, she drove away.

She was cruising Broadway Street when she spotted it. Swinging the nose of the car into a parking spot in front of the building, she peered through the windshield at the neon sign: The Watering Hole. Aptly named. Killing the engine, she palmed her keys and stepped out.

Three thirty in the afternoon and the place was open. It should be empty of customers. Lila pushed inside and was greeted with the heavy strains of country rock, a song she was familiar with. Owner had good taste.

A guy wearing a lumberjack shirt with rolled sleeves exposing a mishmash of tats worked behind the bar. Two men nursing their drinks of choice occupied tables on opposite ends of the room. An antique jukebox belted out the next song, another honky-tonk-style hit.

From above her head, a yowl startled Lila. She looked up. Gazing at her from the edge of an exposed support beam, a black cat flicked its tail with the speed of a metronome.

"She's saying hello."

The tattooed bartender had been joined by an equally tattooed woman with nearly black hair and a bold white streak through the middle. Dark red lips smiled at Lila. The woman looked more at home in one of Chicago's trendy goth bars than here in small town, USA.

"You must be Ellie's new deputy."

Lila glanced down. Oh, yeah, she was in uniform. Wandering over to the bar, she sensed a pair of eyes tracking her. Ignoring the ripples of awareness, she stepped up to the polished redwood.

"Ellie being the sheriff?" she asked.

Chuckling, the woman held out a hand adorned in black and silver wrap rings, one a coiled snake with red stones for eyes, fangs bared. "Marnie Benoit, I own this establishment.

Ellie is my sister."

Lila shook her hand. "Lila Dayne."

"Chicago." Marnie winked a cat eye. "I've always loved that nasally accent." She reached for a glass. "What can I get ya? Since you're on duty, it won't be alcohol."

"Uh, water would be fine."

Sticking her tongue out, a ball stud flashing in the light, Marnie shook her head. "Naw, we don't give away that plain crap. Deke, grab me the Italian stuff."

Deke passed his boss a green glass bottle. Marnie broke the seal and poured the fizzy water over a mountain of ice. She handed over the tall glass.

"*Alla tua salute!*"

Lila blinked. "Thanks?"

Marnie laughed. "You cross me as Italian. True?"

"I have absolutely no idea." Did she just admit that?

The goth eyed Lila, then shrugged. "Familial ancestry fascinates me. So, what brings you wandering in here in the middle of the afternoon?"

"Needed a break, I guess."

"Good enough reason."

"Marnie, where are you!?"

"Douse those hot pants, Fred. I'm comin'," she yelled over her shoulder. "Take a load off. My beer guy is here." Off she went.

Turning with the bubbling glass, Lila ogled the room. Cloves, orange, and something woodsy hung heavy in the air. She spotted the culprit on a slim shelf pressed against the staircase where a trio of incense sticks smoked from a glass tube. Wrinkling her nose, she focused her attention toward the front of the bar and moved to a table near the jukebox that put her back to the wall. Settled on a hardback chair, she sipped the fizzy water. Not bad. It beat the alternative. Not that she'd been much of a drinker. Growing up with a wino for a mother, who on occasion would hook up with a man who liked his liquor, Lila never took to it.

Pills, on the other hand, were her personal demons. During her recovery, those white devils had called to her, promising oblivion from the memories and the pain. The surgeries that saved her life and ended all her dreams had done more to hurt her mental well-being than the attack itself.

Cupping the glass between her curved hands, she rotated it. She could lie to herself all she wanted, but the truth was, the man who had invaded her home and tried to kill her had altered her life course and left her with nothing but a gnawing emptiness. Her panicked reaction at the Wagners' was just a sign that she would never be the cop she once was. Warmth filled her face. She had all but handed Fontaine the key to her weakness. That Sheriff Benoit knew enough about Lila's past to tell Fontaine made her want to throw up.

What a damn mess.

Coming back as a law officer had been a mistake. All during her recovery, she'd fought for the right to wear a badge again. *Don't let the attacker win*, was her mantra. He might have waylaid her plans, but he wouldn't take her livelihood. But the memories, still so fresh and raw, had proved too much. And the narcotics, a convenient and plentiful abyss. Until she woke one day, bleeding from a new wound on her abdomen, a wound she couldn't explain or remember how she got.

It scared her sober.

She had to leave Chicago. Cecil and her former sergeant agreed to the change, in part because her attacker, the serial killer they'd been after, was still out there, waiting to finish the job. It would infuriate him that Lila had survived. Six hours away didn't seem like far enough, but it was all she was comfortable with.

Maybe leaving Chicago also meant leaving the profession she'd loved. That cut deeper than the knife blade.

Lifting the slick glass tugged on her still-sore abdomen, sending ripples of fire down her leg and around her back. Wincing, she set the cup down and breathed through the pain. An urgent voice in the back of her mind broke through the barriers, cajoling her to give in. It would ease the suffering. Give her a chance to forget about her humiliation. It couldn't be that hard to find someone with access to those circular pieces of heaven.

A shot glass clinked on the tabletop, jolting her and shutting down that evil voice. She glared at the tiny cup as it was joined by a bottle of bourbon.

"That pussy water won't fix what ails you."

Her gaze traveled up the denim-clad arm and locked with whiskey-colored eyes. The gray-bearded man dipped his head.

"I'm not looking for company."

He sucked on the toothpick dangling between his lips. "Maybe so, but perhaps you would listen to some advice."

Lila leaned forward and scooted the glass and bottle toward her uninvited visitor. "Advice is the last thing on earth

I'd ever want from man who can't take a hint."

Smiling, he removed the toothpick, studying it. "It appears she picked someone to do this job who has more balls than the ones already working for her." Those whiskey eyes flicked back to Lila. "Chicago, right?"

Grinding her molars, she kept her face neutral.

"Most of the transplants we get from there are gangbanger wannabes. Always bringing their shit here, thinking we're backwoods and ignorant." He set the toothpick in the shot glass. "Until we prove them wrong."

Bracing his hands on the tabletop, he bent forward. "You being new here and all, I'll let your sass slide. And leave you with this little tidbit. Trust is a two-edged blade, and not all are who they seem."

The spell he was weaving around her was broken as the bar door squeaked open. Looking to his right, he grunted. Pushing off the table, he grabbed up his bottle and glass.

"Those behind that one especially shouldn't be trusted." With that parting shot, he walked away to his table at the back of the bar.

Lila glanced over as Deputy Meyer drifted in her direction, his attention on the man who had left her. What did the old man mean by "those behind" Deputy Meyer?

"Deputy Dayne, what are you doing here?" Meyer asked, shoving his hands in his pockets.

"Taking a break." She placed a boot on the edge of a chair and pushed it out. "Rest your feet."

"I'm fine."

"Hey, Brent."

"Afternoon, Marnie." He focused on Lila. "What did he

say to you before he walked away?"

"I don't see how that's any business of yours."

"That's the ex-sheriff, Dayne. Everything he does or says is the business of this department when he's undermining it."

So, that was Sheehan. Interesting. That man right there was all the reason she needed to remain an LEO, even a flawed one.

Lila lifted her glass of fizzy water, grateful that the pain was dulled, and threw back a mouthful. Slapping the empty tumbler on the table, she rose. "Thanks for the drink."

"Anytime," Marnie said.

Hitching her duty belt higher, she strode past Meyer. "Back to work."

As she held the door open for her fellow deputy, she chanced a look at the far table. Sheehan lifted his full shot glass to her. Putting her back to the man, she let the door smack shut.

SITTING ON THE courthouse steps, Bentley between her legs, Elizabeth watched the world creep by. The Wagners' grief at the sight of their murdered daughter still rang in Elizabeth's ears. She tangled her hands in Bentley's silky coat and buried her face in her companion's neck, receiving an affectionate nuzzle against her cheek.

"I want this day to be over."

Bentley whined.

Tires crunching autumn's leftover debris brought Elizabeth's head up. The dark blue sedan parked, and the driver remained in their vehicle. She braced her forearms on her thighs and waited.

A few minutes passed, and then Deputy Dayne exited her car. She strolled up the sidewalk, her hands buried deep in her jacket pockets.

Bentley shifted her position to watch Dayne. Elizabeth straightened her spine as her deputy came to a stop before her. They studied each other a moment, letting the sounds of the end of day traffic take place instead of words.

Dayne jiggled her uniform jacket, looking away. "He tell you what I did?"

"He mentioned it, yes."

"Am I in trouble?" Her gaze swung back.

"Should you be?"

The deputy's shoulders slumped.

Elizabeth patted the spot next to her. "Sit."

Once Dayne was seated, Bentley traded loyalties, plopping her chin on Dayne's leg. The younger woman's hand hovered over Bentley's head, and then she hesitantly stroked the dog.

"I got Bentley a year before I divorced. She liked my ex-husband, they both got along, but her loyalties have always been to me. She's an old soul." Elizabeth clasped her hands. "My ex is Rafe's older brother. There's some resentment that flows through my ex-brother-in-law regarding his feelings on how his brother abandoned me."

"Did he abandon you?"

Smiling, she shook her head. "Joel is a Delta Force operative." She looked toward the street. "His marriage was to his job. I grew up and moved on. There was no abandonment."

After a few moments of silence, Dayne said, "The man I thought I loved abandoned me."

That was a piece of her soul Elizabeth wasn't prepared to hear. She gripped the younger woman's arm.

"Men can be real pricks sometimes."

"Amen." Dayne sighed. "What happened with the Wagners?"

"Jane Doe number two is Maya Wagner. Doe number one was her cousin Regan Flynn."

"I noticed similarities in the two."

Elizabeth soaked in that bit of information. "Regan was a drug addict, like her mother before her. Maya may have been too, but we won't know for sure until the toxicology report is in. Maya died when her neck was broken. Regan's cause of death is still undetermined."

Dayne bowed her head and focused on petting Bentley.

"Deputy Dayne. Lila, I need to know. Are you prepared to continue in your duties? Or is this it?"

A leaf fluttered down from above and settled on the step below their feet. It teetered on the breeze, then flipped over and off it went.

"I came to Juniper to start over fresh. I also came to ensure my safety from a serial killer who failed to add me to his menagerie of corpses." Lila lifted her head. "My failures will come to head as I navigate this. I nearly died, and doing so again scares the hell out of me." She looked at Elizabeth. "But I want to continue my duties."

Giving her a weak smile, Elizabeth gripped Lila's shoulder. "That's what I like to hear."

Bentley huffed, earning a smile from Lila.

"Hungry?"

"Actually, I'm starving. Again."

"Come on." Elizabeth stood, dusting off her rear.

"I met your sister," Lila said as they walked the department hallway.

"Something else, isn't she?"

"I'd say so." They came to the office. "I had a run-in with Sheehan too."

Elizabeth looked at the younger woman. "He try to screw with your head?"

"Something like that."

"Be very careful around him, Lila. He didn't get to where he is without reason. If he so much as smells a weak link, he'll hound it until he achieves whatever goal he has in mind."

"And what of your suspicions about Fitzgerald's loyalties?"

"I'm pulling at the thread little by little. He's a good cop—he just has to realize it."

"Let's just hope you're not being naïve about him."

Elizabeth smiled. "I'll eat to that."

CHAPTER EIGHTEEN

THE CONSTANT TICK of the clock was joined by the soft turn of a page. A solitary lamp held the dark of the December evening at bay. Elizabeth read the autopsies, along with Lundquist's test results and each of the deputies' detailed reports from both crime scenes.

Bentley lay on her chair, tucked in a ball, snoring away.

Pausing in her reading, Elizabeth gazed at her dog. Maybe it was time to call it a night.

She'd seen Fitzgerald off as he started his shift. He had insisted that he could not recall any moments in his memory where Sheehan had used his authority to cover up a crime. Elizabeth asked him to think harder.

Later, she chastised Fontaine for wanting to honor his shift, ordering him home, and she had Lundquist take Rafe's rotation, since he'd had an easy day. Then she'd sent Meyer and Dayne home. Frankly, there wasn't much Elizabeth could do now, as exhaustion was setting in.

Gathering the reports together, she tucked them into their respective files. A sharp rap on her doorframe brought her to a halt. Bentley bolted to her feet and stared at the intruder. Clasping her hands, Elizabeth settled them on top of the reports.

"Ma."

The Kauffmann matriarch wore a Native American print coat over a plaid button-down and faded jeans, her graying hair pulled up in a messy knot at the top of her head. She shuffled farther inside the office, glancing at Bentley. "Keeping late hours, I see."

"The nature of the job."

"The former sheriff didn't feel no such desire." The piercing hazel eyes swung back to Elizabeth.

"I am not he, and he not me."

Settling in a chair opposite of the desk, Ma made herself comfortable. "No, you're not, Ellie."

Apparently, this was not going to be a quick conversation. Sitting back in her chair, Elizabeth gestured for Ma to move it along.

"Karl sends his apologizes for the bruise."

"Water under the bridge."

Ma acquiesced with a head bob. "When we spoke yesterday, you insisted I come to you with a more substantial allegation to back up my belief that Daniel was murdered."

"You have not once said anything about him being murdered. It has always been he was forced off the road."

"But if that were true, would it not be murder?"

"That depends on the law. I'm not a lawyer."

Drumming her fingers on the armrest, Ma tilted her head. "You found another body today?"

While her group did a fine job of keeping the news low-key, it did not stop someone from leaking it. Elizabeth had to believe that leak came from the hospital, as people were coming and going there and probably paid too close attention to what they shouldn't have. Midafternoon, she got a call from the newspaper and then a reporter from the local news station. While she did her best to downplay any hysterics the reporters could exploit—the newspaper journalist being one of Juniper's own—it didn't stop the news station reporter from rousing up some excitement. The whole of Eckardt County now knew that there had been a double homicide.

"That second body was found on the property of a particular family. True?"

Elizabeth had been brought up in the art of not saying. If you kept your mouth shut, people were not apt to learn what was true or false, whether you were guilty or innocent. The art served her well.

"By not answering me, you confirm my suspicions." Ma sat upright. "Ellie, dear, I don't have to tell you about the long-standing problems between Pratt Meyer and my Henry, and now myself."

"I don't see how Sophie's family property has anything to do with your and Pratt's feud."

Her gaze narrowing, Ma leaned forward, pointing a finger. "I know you know about what happened there with Danny."

"What is it that I'd know?"

Ma chuckled, shaking that pointed finger. "Ben was never the loyal type. Let that be a reminder to you."

Elizabeth rotated her shoulders. "Stop beating around the bush and get to the point."

"My point is, Pratt Meyer is not the upstanding savior of this town as he wants us all to believe. He's got a deal with the devil, and he'll do anything to keep his throne."

"By having your son run off the road and killed? To what end?"

"To remind us all not to interfere."

"With what?"

At this, Ma sat back, going silent.

Frustration warring with patience, Elizabeth rocked forward and rested her hands on the desktop once more. "I need viable evidence to prove what you're alluding to is enough to stir that pot. Do you have anything for me other than conjecture?"

Lips pursed in a stern line, Ma huffed.

"Well, then, this conversation is over. As I said yesterday, if you have actual concrete evidence to prove to me that Daniel's accident was more than that, bring it, and I will investigate it fully. Until then, I can't disprove what those who came before me have said."

After a moment of stinging silence, Ma stood. "I dare say that perhaps you got into the wrong line of work, Elizabeth."

"Perhaps I did. But as of this instance, I am the sheriff, and as such, I will do my duties to the best of my abilities until the voters of this county say otherwise."

A cruel smile played up the corners of Ma's mouth. "There are two things that every sheriff has learned while doing this job. The first is that they always come in the first day with high hopes of being better than the previous sheriff. The second is that reality strips them of that optimism. Eckardt County is what it is, Elizabeth, and no one will change that."

"I'll keep that in mind."

"You do that."

Elizabeth didn't move until she heard the distinct suction of the closing door echo through the hallway.

"Bentley, I do believe that woman needs a harder look-see."

THE MILD NIGHT beckoned. Clad in a hoodie, sweats, and thick wool socks, Lila sat on the front porch steps nursing a steaming cup of herbal tea. As she sipped, she listened to the night sounds, tensing as the occasional vehicle passed.

This unease was problematic. The sheriff might not have judged her for her actions today, but Lila couldn't forgive herself. The Wagners were harmless—how would she react when actually faced with a life-threatening situation? Fontaine was justified in his distrust. At this point she didn't trust herself.

Placing the warm mug against her chin, she inhaled the scent of lemon and mint. A former patrol partner had turned her onto the tea. When faced with a difficult night or matter, Lila steeped the brew and let the combo do whatever magic it held. The tea soothed her. No one could tell her otherwise.

"What are you going to do?" she whispered.

The million-dollar question.

Squeaking brakes carried on the silent night. A pickup truck with a heavy-duty cow kicker parked along the curb, the headlights turned down to the low setting. Seconds passed and the engine quieted. Lila's grip on the mug tightened, her right hand inching down to her side, settling on the Glock lying next to her thigh. The driver's side door groaned open. Through the dimmed lighting, Lila made out the striking figure.

Viking.

Lundquist shut the truck's door, and rounded the front, his long body slashing through the light beams. He approached at a snail's pace.

Her hand remaining on the Glock, she sipped her tea.

"I come in peace." His gruff voice danced over her nerves.

"Shouldn't you be on patrol?"

Lundquist halted at the base of the steps, placing one booted foot on the bottom stair. He carried that whole country boy persona well. "It's quiet for the time being. We didn't get a chance to regroup today."

Their conversation at Maya Wagner's scene trickled through Lila's brain. "No, we didn't." She set the mug down beside the Glock, then pulled the sleeves of the hoodie over her hands, tucking them against her body. "At this point, the blood sample results are just confirmation to what Fontaine and the sheriff learned today."

"In a way, yes." There was a hitch in his tone.

"Meaning?"

"Meaning, DCI needs to run their tests to confirm what we know. That'll take a while."

Waiting for the scientist to do their thing was nothing new for Lila. Where Iowa, as a state, differed to that of Chicago, a city, was the rate of homicides per year. Iowa DCI certainly didn't have that type of a backlog.

"Lundquist, why are you really here? It can't be to talk shop."

He dragged his upraised boot across the wooden step and placed it on the ground. Squaring up, he ducked his head. Lila swore she could almost hear him say "shucks, ma'am" in that moment.

"Is it too forward of me to ask you a personal question?"

"I wouldn't respect you as an officer of the law if you didn't."

Clearing his throat, he thumbed the side of his nose. Must be some serious kind of question.

"Why Eckardt?" He looked off to his left, and then back at her. "Why come here at all? There had to be places closer to home for you."

It appeared Lundquist wasn't in on the loop. And were Meyer and Fitzgerald left in the dark as well? The sheriff could have left it up to Lila to reveal as much as she wanted, if at all, to her fellow deputies. Not knowing Lila's secrets must be grating on Lundquist for him to directly broach the subject.

"If you were to know why, what do you get out of it?"

"The truth."

"Truth is subjective. What may be truth to you could be a lie to me."

"Lying about your reasons for being here is justifiable?"

Lila rolled her shoulders inside the hoodie, burrowing deeper into it. "I'd have no reason to lie about my being here. It'd serve no purpose."

"Then suspend with the mind games and explain yourself."

Whatever relaxing measures the tea provided were undone at the authoritative tone coming from a man who had yet to scratch the surface of her years as a police officer. Pushing her hands back through the cuffs, she rose, leaving the Glock on the porch, a level of trust she dare not give any other person, but for some reason she gave him.

"Deputy Lundquist, I keep my own counsel. Whatever my reasons, they remain mine and mine alone. Those in the know are informed. You, however, are not. Now that we've cleared the air on this matter, haul your ass back to your unit and leave."

"If I refuse?"

She descended the steps, stopping on the middle one that put her at eye level with him. "Refuse." She shrugged. "Fine." Turning on her heel, she marched back up the steps, grabbed up the Glock and mug, and headed for the door.

His radio crackled. Fitzgerald was hailing him.

"Your job beckons, Deputy Lundquist." She let the door clap shut behind her.

Lila lingered in the entryway, palming the pebbled grip of her service weapon. Lundquist's rumbled reply to his night shift partner filtered through the door. A moment later, the truck's engine came alive, and then pulled away.

Gerry, the blue Betta, hovered at the edge of his tank.

"What're you staring at?"

Blue fins rippled in the water.

"I don't need any judgment from a fish."

Lila did enough of that on her own.

CHAPTER NINETEEN

Day 3: Friday

MARNIE WAITED FOR her on the old dam lock. Elizabeth took the proffered cup of witch's morning brew her sister was known for and sat next to her on the refurbished wood bench. Bentley tucked her body between the two women's legs. Together, as they had many Friday mornings for the last year and half since Elizabeth's return, they enjoyed their coffee and watched the river surge and roll over the bedrock. Their breath mingled with the slip of steam escaping through the cup lid. A cold front had moved in overnight, dropping the temps into the upper thirties. The air tasted crisp, fresh, a promise of snow on the horizon. Across the river and along the bank, eagles floated above the treetops.

"Fine mess you've got developing," Marnie commented before tipping up her cup for another drag.

Elizabeth clenched her gloved fist. "Be specific. I've got a lot of messes developing."

"Fine mess number one." Marnie flicked up a gloved finger. "Kiss and make up with your ex so I can stop listening to his bitching and moaning."

"Solution number one, not happening."

"Mess number two: screw that brother of his and get it

over with."

Elizabeth groaned.

"Number three: your double homicide. Now that it has hit the papers, you're going to have lots of unwanted scrutiny. Keep everything close to your vest and let that new detective deputy run with it."

"If she stays up to the task."

Marnie's three fingers retreated. "Not working out, is she?"

"It's complicated."

Grunting, her sister crossed her legs. "Like everything else with you. For once, just make it simple. Like scratching the itch that's Rafe Fontaine."

"When I want relationship advice, I'll get it from someone who isn't a known free love proponent."

"Just saying."

Elizabeth sighed. "Are you quite done with lecturing me on the messes in my life and career?"

"Fourth and final mess: you getting caught up in the Meyer and Kauffmann version of the Hatfields and McCoys."

"I have no intention of doing any such thing."

Marnie laughed, reaching over to pinch Elizabeth's cold cheek. "Aren't you just the cutest in all your denial."

She swatted her sister's hand aside. "I deny nothing. It hasn't broken any laws, therefore, I have no reason to interfere."

"Ah, but Ma Kauffmann is going to make damn sure you side with her no matter which way she swings that big dick of hers. In the years you were gone, she's become quite the

Marm Mandelbaum."

Marnie and her veritable encyclopedia brain of useless historical facts was always good for an eye roll.

"I doubt that she's become a nineteenth-century crime boss."

"Would Ma Barker suit you?"

Pressing her fingers to her forehead, Elizabeth moaned. "Sister, dearest, you digress."

"Ah, that I do, but you have to admit I'm right."

"I have no proof Ma has become anything other than a woman looking after her family."

Marnie squinted at her. "Right." Sarcasm dripped off that single word like hot tar on a post.

"Is there a point to all of this?"

Tapping the side of her empty cup, Marnie stood and looked down at Elizabeth. "There is. You are in the trial by fire stage, Big Sis, and if you fail this level, you're out. And the coach will send Sheehan back out." Bending over, she kissed her sister on the forehead. "Watch your back."

Elizabeth watched her younger sibling strut across the park. She remained on their bench. Bentley hopped up, and nosed her way under Elizabeth's elbow, resting her head on her lap.

"Screwing Rafe is the easiest out of the four."

Bentley huffed, bumping her snout into Elizabeth's midsection.

"Yeah, I think so too."

LILA NOTED THE number of vehicles in the parking lot when she arrived at the department as the sun breached the horizon. Two. Since Fitzgerald and Meyer drove the old Crown Vics, Lila couldn't be sure which of the men were here. Missing was Fontaine's Charger. Good. She had a little more time to pull together a believable "sorry, I'm not sorry." The non-squad car had to be the dispatcher's, one Lila hadn't quite made herself familiar with. So, that left the sheriff and Lundquist MIA.

Slipping through the door, Lila walked as quietly as she could down the hall. Low voices drifted from the main office area, halting as she emerged.

"Good morning, Deputy Detective." Georgia smiled.

"Mornin'." Lila refused to meet Lundquist's gaze. If he was here, where did he park that truck? "When do you expect the sheriff to get in?"

"Since it's Friday, she'll be a bit behind schedule. She always has coffee with her sister." Georgia picked up an Eckardt County mug and a coffee carafe. "Black?"

"Uh, yeah."

Fitzgerald stood with a groan. "Since she's here, I'll shove off."

"I'll let you know when the car will be ready, Ben."

"Thanks, Georgia." He shoved his arms inside his deputy's jacket as he headed for the door. He momentarily locked eyes with Lila.

Did Lundquist voice his concerns about her to Fitzgerald last night? Or was the man always a scowling pain in the ass?

"I'll be waiting in the truck," he said over his shoulder in Lundquist's direction, and moved on.

Lila smiled her thanks and took the offered mug. "You have those reports?" she asked Lundquist.

Sighing, he stood and ambled over to a desk littered with papers, yellow and pink sticky notes, a few stray paper clips, and pens scattered from here to eternity. He snatched a folder from the top of the mess and held it up. "The sheriff has everything else."

Lila took the file and tucked it under her arm. "Thanks."

She looked around at the scattered desks. The one she'd seen Fontaine sitting at the other night had to be his; it appeared neat and organized, sort of like the man himself. Three desks remained, and two looked unoccupied. Which one was supposed to be hers?

"Georgia, tell the sheriff I went home. I'll check in later."

The dispatcher acknowledged the deputy and answered the ringing phone.

Lundquist gathered his things, and with a parting look at Lila, headed for the exit.

"Because I found it safer than where I was," she said in a low voice as he passed.

Lundquist came to a halt. Confusion marred his features. Had he forgotten that he'd asked her why she came to Juniper? As if a light bulb had gone off upstairs, the scrunched lines in his forehead smoothed out. If he expected more of an answer from her, he wasn't going to get it. With a nod, he departed.

Alone with Georgia, Lila tested the coffee and considered the file under her arm.

"If I were you, I'd take that desk." Georgia pointed at the one butted up to Lundquist's. "It's free, and my gut tells me the two of you are going to be working together a lot."

"I don't know about that."

An all-knowing smile crossed the dispatcher's lips. "Uh-huh." She lifted a pair of files rubber banded together and held them out. "The sheriff left these for you."

Lila took the bundle, catching the names and a case number on the labels. These belonged to the two young women.

Carrying them, and her coffee, to the designated desk, Lila set her stack down but didn't sit. "Georgia, how long have you been the dispatcher for the department?"

The curly blonde tilted her head and contemplated Lila. "Twenty-three years."

"You worked under Sheehan?"

Georgia's face puckered. That answered that.

Lila settled on the edge of the desk. "Fill me in."

Georgia glanced at the empty room. "I don't like to gossip."

"This isn't gossip—this is informing. I'm running blind here when it comes to him and his history with this department. His history with the sheriff."

"Shouldn't you be discussing this with the sheriff?"

"The only thing I got about him from her was to watch myself. There's more to it than that. And who better to know the intricate details than the dispatcher?"

Picking up a pen, Georgia scribbled on a notepad. "Yes, I do know details. But most of what I know is suspicion."

"Suspicion works for me."

The dispatcher looked at Lila like a mother would when she'd caught her child in a lie. "Let me be frank with you,

Deputy Dayne. You're in Eckardt County now. People in Iowa are friendly and giving, some would call it nice. That veneer is what we want the outside world to believe."

"I see." Lila leaned back. "As an *outsider*, I won't get anywhere with these fine folks. As the sheriff so readily pointed out my first day here."

"She's not wrong. Word of advice. Keep one of the boys with you at all times if you're not with Ellie."

Lila held up a finger and shook it. "But the sheriff was gone from here for years. How does that not make her an outsider?"

"Ever hear the saying, no matter how far you run, you'll always be welcomed home with open arms?"

Sheriff Elizabeth Benoit was a daughter of Eckardt County. No matter where in the world she had traveled or how long she'd been gone, she was one of them. Same with her ex-husband, and anyone else who grew up here, went away, and returned.

Then what about her? How did she shake free of that stigma? "Let's say I spend the next ten to twenty years here, working for the sheriff's department. What makes people see me as anything other than an outsider?"

Georgia tucked her pen behind her ear. "Deputy Dayne, that is a question that may never be answered."

The phone rang, putting an end to that conversation.

If Lila did decide Juniper, Eckardt County, was her final stop in life, then she had her work cut out for her. Circling the desk, she settled into the creaky office chair. Sipping the coffee, she glanced at the large wall clock. Time to get this day started.

While she waited for the sheriff, Lila read through the autopsies and reports. The cause of death for Maya Wagner was noted: fractured spine between the C3 and C4 vertebra resulting in instant death, manner was decided as homicide due to the bruising along the victim's jaw and on her neck, indicating where her killer gripped her head to force the snap.

The ME had noted that there were no signs at all that Maya's body had been cooled down to slow or stop decomposition. No indicators of frost or freezing. Was that just a passing idea from the sheriff?

No signs of sexual assault, but there were indications that Maya had been sexually active, though maybe not recently. She had faint tracks on the inside of her right elbow. Heroin user? Not good. Such nasty stuff, heroin was a drug that users ended up hooked for life, and it eventually killed them. Worse, it was cheap to buy.

Lila licked her lips and clamped down on her tongue. The ME hadn't seen any new needle marks, but that didn't stop a user from finding ways to take it without leaving behind visible clues. Lila flipped to the Wagners' statement, noting that the sheriff had taken the information. The couple revealed Maya had been known to smoke pot and abuse prescription opioids. Guess she decided the harder stuff was the way to go when the pills weren't enough. Her tox panel would determine if she truly had used heroin in her last days.

Lila dragged Regan Flynn's autopsy on top of Maya's. The medical examiner had no clear cause of death, but the manner was listed as homicide. Copies of the X-rays Lila and

Fontaine had observed the other night were in the file, and Lila's gut told her that weird break in the back of Regan's neck was probably the actual cause. If Lila was right, both women had been the victims of a neck-breaking fiend.

There were blatant signs of drug use indicated in the perforations in her nostrils from snorting and the dark tracks found inside her left elbow. A vaginal swab found semen; Regan had had sex before she died. The ME noted there were no signs of this being a rape, but the sex could have been with her killer, and DNA could help them get closer to finding out who killed them and why.

Elbow planted on the desktop, Lila plowed her fingers through her hair and braced her head against her hand. Had the girls gone foul with a dealer? Supplier? Could Regan have paid for the drugs with sex, but when it came time for Maya, she refused? But why break her neck? Seemed too personal when a bullet would have done the trick. Messier, but effective.

Clamping down on her tongue once more, Lila stared holes into the reports. Trace blood evidence pointed to one of the girls being in the old Barrett place, the DNA testing had not yet come back to prove which girl. But if Lila went by Mrs. McKinnley's timeline, the two young women should have been killed the night before Regan's body was discovered. Her autopsy said otherwise. Had the killer put the girls on ice? Chilling or freezing the bodies made no sense. Then again, chilling the bodies had some merit, because somewhere in all of this, the killer didn't want them to know something about the girls' deaths.

Maybe Mrs. Neva McKinnley had her nights mixed up?

A flash of auburn and white startled her out of her meanderings. Bentley sat next to the desk, staring up at Lila. Her gaze left the dog, wandered to Georgia's desk, and landed on the woman with a glittering star on her chest.

"Must be some deep thoughts you have there, Deputy Dayne."

"Sheriff." Lila stood. "We need to discuss some things."

"I'm sure we do." Benoit took the offered pink slips from Georgia, eyeing the top note. "Oh goodie," she muttered and turned to her office. "Let's go, Deputy Dayne."

Both Lila and Bentley followed their leader into her domain, Bentley peeling off to jump up in her favored chair and flopping down on the battered cushion.

"Wouldn't a new dog bed be better for her than that old thing?"

Benoit rounded her desk. "She has beds at home she barely uses. Why bother?" She set the slips on her desk calendar and took her chair. "What's on your mind?"

"I want to have another talk with Mrs. McKinnley. Preferably this morning."

"Any particular reason why?"

"You and I both know something is screwy between her lodged complaint of trespassers and the ME's time of death. I want to double down on her timeline."

Steepling her hands in front of her, Benoit eyed Lila above her fingertips. "Because you sense what?"

"That she might not be wrong on the night in question and what she heard. And there could be a potential third victim we're not aware of."

Benoit made a noise in her throat, drumming her fingers

together. "I think you're onto something there, Dayne." She dropped her hands and sat back in her chair. "I would like to come with you, but I have other pressing matters that require my attention. Go with Deputy Fontaine."

Lila winced.

"Too soon?"

"Sheriff, if I may, send Meyer with me. He needs the experience, and . . ."

"And Fontaine probably isn't over how you ditched him yesterday. I completely understand. You're right, Deputy Meyer is a good choice." Benoit reached for the slips. "Are the reports sufficient for you?"

"More than enough." Lila stepped closer to the desk. "One more thing."

Looking up, Benoit met her gaze, a single eyebrow lifted.

"Do we have access to ATVs?"

The sheriff cocked her head. "ATVs? Why do you need one?"

"To follow that trail behind the Barrett place."

"I see. I'm not aware that we have access to any for department use, but I'm sure Fontaine can rustle up something to use. Give me the morning to get that figured out."

"That'll do."

There was a light rap on the doorframe.

Deputy Meyer hooked his thumbs in this duty belt. "Orders for the day, Sheriff?"

"You'll be with Deputy Dayne today. If things change, I'll have Georgia radio you."

Meyer nodded, his eyes flicking to Lila. She flashed him a grin. "You drive, rookie."

He frowned, following her. "You're the new deputy. That makes you the rookie."

Benoit's laughter echoed behind them. Meyer's candor was much appreciated, elevating Lila's mood. He sounded like a younger version of Cecil.

"Meyer, I've got ten-plus years of law enforcement over you. I did my rookie tour on the mean streets of the Windy City while you were chasing girls in middle school."

"You're not that much older than me," he grumbled.

"Fine, high school." She gripped his shoulder. "Don't worry, the shiny chrome will tarnish and no one will notice."

CHAPTER TWENTY

ELIZABETH EYEBALLED THE top phone message. Pratt Meyer wanted to set up an appointment to meet with her. Today. She didn't want an appointment with Pratt. In fact, she wasn't all too thrilled with the town council meeting this evening—she had not been able to fine-tune the budget due to the uptick in unexplainable homicides.

Ahh, the joys of politics and administrative duties as sheriff. Well, Elizabeth had handled the internal workings of the army's good ole boy network and the spouses who wielded their soldiers' rank as a battering ram. Small-town politics were a cakewalk in comparison. Yet, she recalled many a Juniper church potluck that would make even the highest-ranking officer duck for cover from the barrage of verbal mortar rounds.

Too bad she didn't have a believable excuse to get her out of talking with Pratt.

But wait. Maybe she did. Elizabeth rocked back in her chair and lifted her gaze to the ceiling. Someone should talk with the Wagners again, see if they had any clues that could point the investigation into their daughter's death toward her killer. And Elizabeth should get permission from the school principal and or the superintendent about speaking with students. Over the years in her capacity as a family liaison and as a teenager herself, Elizabeth had learned one solid lesson: if you wanted the truth about the goings-on in any community, rural or military, you asked the teenagers. There was always more truth than rumor in the things students whispered among themselves. Despite what most adults thought, kids were on the front lines, and they saw more than any parent wished they would.

A firm rap on her door rocked Elizabeth forward. Just the man she wanted to see.

Rafe crossed his arms and leaned into the doorframe. "She didn't throw in the towel?"

Elizabeth shook her head and tossed aside the pink message slips. "Don't be hard on her. She's got the bull by the horn on this one and isn't sure how to start the dance."

"Still think it's a bad idea."

"And that's why you're a deputy and I'm the sheriff."

Snorting, he pushed off the frame, entering her domain. "Have any special orders for me today?"

She gestured for him to close the door. Once they were sequestered, she relaxed in her chair. "Know anyone who would be willing to let us borrow some four-wheelers or side-by-sides?"

Rafe narrowed his eyes. "Maybe. Why?"

"Dayne wants to check out those trails behind the Barrett place. We noticed tracks leading from the house into the timber, probably the escape route of whoever took those girls there."

"Horses would be better back there than ATVs."

"Do you see our intrepid investigator from Chicago on the back of a horse?"

"Then maybe you and I should go, not her."

"I can't today."

Rafe tilted his head to the side. "I'll take Lundquist."

Elizabeth shook her head. "Since the two of you switched shifts, he's sleeping."

"I know that place like the back of my hand. You can't get everywhere by four wheels."

"But someone or two someones did." She vacated her chair and wandered to the front of her desk. "Rafe, she's not comfortable with you after what happened yesterday. Brent knows the timber well enough for the two of them to check it out. Just get access to the vehicles, and we'll go from there."

"I should be there."

"Why is it so important for you to be there?"

"That's family property, remember."

"Do you have the authority to give permission for us to look?"

His eyes narrowed. "You know the answer to that."

"Then don't act like you're the keeper of all things Barrett. Ma will be informed, and I'm certain she'll give access."

"And if she doesn't?"

Elizabeth reached behind her and grabbed up a notepad and pen. "She'll give access." Scrawling instructions on the top sheet, she ripped it off the pad and held it out to Rafe. "I have a special assignment for you."

He took the notepaper and read her orders. "What the hell?" He shook the page. "You want me to poke around in Ma's affairs? My own cousin and her family?"

"You've never liked her." Elizabeth returned to her place

behind her desk. "That should make it easy for you to pry."

"Whether I like her or not, it doesn't seem right. What do you hope to accomplish with this, other than putting me on her bad side?"

"She paid me a visit last night, and some of the things she said and didn't say have me wondering. Fitzgerald told us Daniel had run afoul of the law and Sheehan did nothing about it. Why?" She pointed at Rafe. "You and I both know Sheehan has always been up to no good, but what we don't know is with whom and what it is. Maybe Ma and he have a pact, a little 'you scratch my back I scratch yours.'"

"That's reaching, Ellie. I don't deny that Sheehan has things to hide. But Ma? Really? What could she possibly be involved with that would let her have any sway over Sheehan to get him to look the other way?"

Elizabeth stared at Rafe, hoping he'd catch the scent of the trail she was leaving. He did.

"You think she knew about the drugs and what Daniel was up to?"

"I think it was more than knew. I think she's the one pulling the strings behind it."

"Are you drunk? Because that's the only explanation I have for you to even *think* that."

She crossed her arms. "You're starting to sound like Joel."

Rafe glared, crumpling the note. "Low blow."

"I call it like I see it. This isn't a mission behind enemy lines. All you need to do is dig through any files and reports Sheehan had and further back if you must to see if there are things that line up with Ma, Henry, or anyone in the

Kauffmann family. Go as far back as you can."

"And if I find something?"

"Then you tell me right away. Not a word of this gets to anyone else. You work alone on this. Understood?"

Rafe cupped the back of his neck and sighed. "I don't see what this has to do with our murders."

"We've got blood evidence in the Barrett place that points to one or both of those girls being there. Maya Wagner was left at a place where Daniel Kauffmann was caught with drugs. And the field belongs to Sophie Meyer, the wife of a longtime antagonist to the Kauffmann clan. A feud of which Ma reminded me of last night, and a thing I thought had long burned out." Elizabeth let her arms fall to her sides. "Something is up with these murders and her family. What? I want to know."

"You think Sheehan is connected somehow?"

"That one, I'm not sure about."

"What about Ma's insistence that Daniel's death wasn't accidental?" Rafe asked.

"Two birds, one stone. While you're dusting off the archives, see if Sheehan was careless enough to leave something behind about that. From what I've been able to learn, everything was done properly and all involved came to the same conclusion. I need to give her a dog bone because I'm tired of her riding my ass about it."

He gave her a nod and turned to the door. Elizabeth watched him exit, leaving the door open. Georgia spun her chair, phone pressed to her ear, and held up two fingers. Acknowledging the message, Elizabeth grabbed up her phone and punched the red blinking line two.

"Sheriff Benoit."

"Sheriff, Pratt Meyer."

Elizabeth tensed. Looked like she wasn't going to get away with not calling him back.

DARK GRAY, HEAVY clouds built in the sky, towering over the sporadic farm buildings. Snow, the radio weatherman predicted.

Beside her, Meyer tapped out a rhythm on the steering wheel only he seemed to understand. Lila dragged her gaze from the glass and peered at her new partner. He twitched, ceased his drumming, and glanced at her.

"Am I bothering you?"

Lila shifted in her seat to face him better. "Brent, right?"

"Yeah."

"Brent, I'm not bothered. I just have one question for you. Why?"

He frowned, slowing the squad car for the turn onto the road leading to Three Points. "Why what?"

"Why are you doing this? Why be a deputy?"

The talk radio host filled the silence as Meyer completed the turn. Lila let him think over her question. Adjusting his grip on the steering wheel, he tilted his head to the side.

"I always had a desire to help. It just grew into this urge to be something different than what I was raised in."

"And how was that?"

The Three Points sign flashed past. Meyer chanced another glance at her.

"The sheriff didn't tell you?"

"Sheriff Benoit isn't the type to just blurt out the gossip on all of her deputies."

He shrugged. "True."

The car slowed as they breached the first row of residential homes. Having been here only once before, Lila was glad things were looking familiar to her.

"My father is Pratt Meyer. If you do a quick internet search, you'll learn all you need to about that man. My mother is Sophie Fontaine-Barrett-Meyer."

Lila jerked. "No shit?"

"Yeah. She doesn't like to broadcast it much."

Sitting back in her seat, Lila let his revelation sink in. "Is everyone related to everyone around here?"

"Kinda sorta. If your family or families lived here long enough it gets to be a thing. And in some cases, a problem."

"In what ways?"

"I'll use my family for example. The Meyers and the Kauffmanns have hated each other since the moment they settled here. I think it started out as a Catholic versus Protestant ordeal. No one can really remember why, but why give up a good feud?"

"What about the sheriff's family?"

"Outsiders." Brent smiled. "Geesh! The Benoit family has lived here since before World War I, I think, and people still act like they just moved here."

Lila frowned. "Outsiders? That's not what Georgia was telling me this morning, she said the sheriff isn't an outsider, that's why she was so easily elected and people accept her."

"There are exceptions to the rule. She married into a

long-standing family and that's how everyone sees her."

"But they're divorced."

"And she and Rafe have been dancing around each other for years. She's one of our own. That and people really do like her."

Lila huffed. "Explains why Mrs. McKinnley barely tolerated me, yet Sheriff Benoit had her feeding out of her hand."

Shrugging, Brent turned onto the street leading to the McKinnley home. "You have to understand one thing about Eckardt County and the towns of Juniper and Three Points. There are those who can trace their ancestry back to the founding of this state. And then there are those who came after."

"And yet, you're related in one way or another," Lila said. "How close is your mother to Deputy Fontaine?"

"They're second or third cousins, I forget how. Mom is actually closer in relation to Martha 'Ma' Kauffmann."

"Isn't she the last living Barrett, the one who owns that place where I found the blood?"

"Not the last living Barrett, just the last of her particular family line. When she married Henry Kauffmann, her father disowned her."

Brent slowed the squad car and nosed into the driveway.

"You said your family and the Kauffmanns hate each other. Isn't it better now that there is a relation married to one?"

He grunted. "It's worse now. I think it has more to do with the fact that my father is wealthy and the Kauffmanns aren't any better off than when they bought their first plot of farmland."

Parking the car, he cut the engine. Lila found a handheld radio and prepared to exit the car, while Meyer called in their location.

"Why are we here?" he asked, opening his door.

"I have some lingering questions for Mrs. McKinnley I need cleared up. Just catch me on any social faux pas I have. Me being an outsider and all."

"She's not as bad as most. It's that strict rule of thumb she had as a teacher to not tolerate ignorance."

"I'll keep that in mind."

Lila quietly groaned as she exited the car. Her body had healed from her crash through the floor days before, but her muscles were still not happy with her. She hooked the radio to her duty belt and zipped her coat.

Together, they closed the unit's doors and headed up the drive. A cutting wind plowed through the yard, pelting Lila with shards of ice. The snow had arrived. She hunkered inside her coat, glad she'd chosen to wear this instead of the jacket like the day before. Welcome to the Midwest, the land of "If you don't like the weather, wait five minutes. It'll change."

The wind rushed headlong before them, buffeting the house with force. Lila froze when she spotted movement coming from the front entrance. Her hand shot out and grabbed Brent's elbow, her other hand going to her sidearm, unsnapping the holster strap.

"Something's not right," she hissed. Unholstering her weapon, she lowered the gun against her thigh and stepped ahead of him. "Call it in."

As he radioed Georgia, Lila inched up the remainder of

the driveway, watching the door creep back into a position that made it look closed. The wind whipped her hair into her eyes. Swiping it back from her face, a futile effort, she hesitated at the bottom step.

She would not fail. Not this time.

He touched her arm. "Backup is on the way."

"Who?"

"Fontaine."

"What did you call it in as?"

The door glided open.

"I didn't call it anything," Meyer said, his voice tense. "Just said to have someone come out."

It would take Fontaine every bit of fifteen or more minutes to get here. Lila didn't know if there was time to wait.

"Go around back. She had a patio door. Look for any forced entry or if someone is here." Lila pointed the opposite direction. "I'll check out the garage and the right side of the house, then come back."

Nodding, he started to walk off.

"Meyer, give me some kind of heads-up either way."

"Copy." Off he went.

Drawing in a breath, Lila headed in the opposite direction, sidestepping the lawn ornaments and dormant gardens, every few steps glancing back over her shoulder to make sure no one came to the front door. The garage had no windows or a way to see inside, but for the most part it appeared to be shut up tight. Once she cleared the side of the house, seeing nothing suspicious, she returned to the entrance.

"Dayne," Meyer hailed her.

She grabbed the radio from her hip and, hauling it up, she pressed the button. "Got anything?"

"Nothing. The drapes are drawn, but there's a light on over the sink. Window is too high up for me to see in."

Maybe Mrs. McKinnley was still in bed? Why would she leave her front door open?

"Are the patio doors locked?"

"Yes," Meyer said after a moment.

Best way to enter this odd situation was to leave him back there protecting the exits. Lila didn't like that idea when she was only one person at the front. She gnawed on her lip. No way was she entering an uncertain situation without someone covering her backside.

She keyed the radio. "Meyer, come back."

Waiting for him to return, she called on the calming techniques she'd learned to keep from losing it completely. When Meyer joined her, she had a handle on her state of mind, ready to face the situation before her.

Lila stared hard at the free-swinging door. No sign of forced entry. But Neva McKinnley did not cross Lila as someone who just left her doors open.

"What do you want to do?" Meyer asked.

Throw up, that's what she wanted to do. Instincts screamed something was wrong here. But an unlatched door didn't prove what her frayed nerves were warning.

She peeked at Meyer. He had not drawn his gun. She looked down at her hand, her grip tight on the butt, so tight her knuckles were white. What was she doing? This situation did not warrant for her to have her gun out. Damn it, yes it did. What was wrong with her? She could not be second-guessing every situation.

"Dayne?"

Jerking, she slammed the door on her self-doubt. "Maybe she didn't get the door shut all the way as she left to go somewhere."

"The garage has access inside the house. Why would she leave by the front door if she drove off?"

"I don't know," Lila barked. This wasn't getting them anywhere. "Her door is open, and it doesn't look like anyone is home."

Meyer stared at her like she'd turned into some kind of dragon or a harpy.

Get a grip.

"We knock and call out," she said.

He nodded and headed up the steps. Lila swallowed hard and followed him. Positioning herself on the left side of the door, she let Meyer knock.

"Hello? Mrs. McKinnley, it's the sheriff's department," Lila called out in a firm voice. Intestinal fortitude ruled the day.

Silence. Lila met Meyer's gaze, then nodded down at his still-holstered gun. After drawing his weapon, he pushed on the white-painted door. It swung back on quiet hinges. Stepping forward, Lila entered the open doorway.

"Mrs. McKinnley, it's Deputy Dayne. I'm coming inside." Her announcement echoed against the tiled entryway.

Meyer slipped in behind her, taking position at her left shoulder. Her years of experience and the long-ingrained training were taking over her mental shortcomings.

"Check the ground floor first," she told him. "Meet up

in the kitchen."

They stepped forward. Lila did a quick check down the hall before Meyer headed to the bedrooms. All the doors were open. She swung right, entering the living room. Crossing the room to a walled-off area, she checked the dining room. The table was primly set with place mats, and all the chairs in their place under the table. No signs that Neva McKinnley had disturbed anything or eaten at her table this morning. Lila looked back over her shoulder, glimpsing Meyer moving from one room to the next. Stepping into another tiled area, she discovered the garage access and followed her sidearm into a combined laun-dry/mudroom.

An empty clothes basket sat on the dryer. Lila pressed her hand on the metal top—cold. She popped the door and peeked inside, clothes lay in a tangled pile inside. Closing the dryer door, she checked the garage door. Locked. Unlocking it, she eased into the darkened interior. She found the switch to her left and flipped it.

A newer Buick sedan sat in the middle of the one-car garage. Neva was home. But where? Lila scanned the facility, noting a back door she'd missed on her initial assessment. She should kick herself for not spotting it. Such a rookie mistake.

The garage appeared untouched, no sign anyone had been in here for a while. Turning back to the mudroom, Lila shut and locked the door, then made her way to the kitchen through the dining room. As before, everything had a place and was in its place. No coffee made, no breakfast cooked, no dishes in the dish drainer. Meyer announced his entry into the room.

"Anything?" she asked.

"The bed doesn't look like anyone slept in it."

Lila's whole body hurt. "Basement."

Had the poor woman tripped and fallen down the steps?

Meyer seemed to read her thoughts and rushed to the door, flinging it open. Lila, hot on his heels, blinked as the stairway lights flared to life.

"Oh my God," Meyer croaked before running down the carpeted steps.

Over his head, Lila saw the sight. Closing her eyes, she bowed her head.

Neva McKinnley's body lay twisted and broken at the bottom of the steps, a darkened spot haloing her gray hair.

CHAPTER TWENTY-ONE

ELIZABETH STOOD SENTRY at the top of the basement steps as the medical examiner did a field examination.

"She's in full rigor." Olivia stood. "This happened some-time last night."

"Accident or intentional?"

The doc shook her head. "That's not an answer I can give you yet."

"Sheriff."

Elizabeth turned to Lundquist, whom she had to drag out of bed so he could dust the house for prints. "Did you find anything, Deputy?"

The strained lines on his face gave a hard mule kick to Elizabeth's chest.

"Other than the places Deputy Dayne and Meyer indicated they touched, I'm not finding any prints."

"In this entire house?"

"I've been thorough with the path from the front door to the kitchen, doorknobs, handles, windows, appliances, kitchen facet, light switches, everything." Lundquist sighed. "Sheriff, someone wiped every surface down. I know Mrs. McKinnley was fastidious about cleaning, but this is above and beyond even her."

"Check the other rooms and the bathroom, go through

the cellar entrance and go over the basement rooms. If someone truly did come through this house and erased their presence, it'll show."

With a nod, Lundquist followed orders.

"If he's right," Olivia said from the bottom of the staircase, "I might have to consider ruling this a homicide."

"Might?"

"It still could have been accidental and someone doesn't want you to think badly of them for not reporting it."

"Olivia, I want to believe she tripped and fell. Or had a heart attack. I really do. But the last three days are making me think otherwise. Find evidence to prove it one way or another. Just don't say homicide until you know for sure."

With grim features, the ME returned to her examination. Elizabeth's attention was drawn to the two deputies hovering in the middle of the living room.

Dayne's right hand rested on Meyer's shoulder. The younger deputy was hunched over, distress and shock wreaking havoc on his youthful face. Neva McKinnley had been a favorite teacher to a lot of people in this community, and Brent Meyer was no exception.

Dayne frowned at Elizabeth and turned back to her partner for the day. She said something to him. Meyer nodded and found a seat on the sofa.

Deputy Dayne sidled up to Elizabeth's side. "This has certainly not turned out the way I wanted."

"Run through with me again what you did when you got here."

Dayne flinched and her hands ceased their motion. She shoved them into her coat pockets. Her struggle to regain her confidence in this job would continue to plague her until she either gave it up or found a way to defeat it. Elizabeth gave her credit for making a solid effort to do the latter.

"The door was left open?" Elizabeth prompted.

"Swinging in the wind. After I got Meyer calmed down and away from the body, I double-checked all other entry points. They were all locked except the front."

Elizabeth frowned. "Did you see any notations anywhere that would suggest she had planned visitors?"

"I hadn't gotten to that stage."

"I think she keeps an appointment-like calendar in the kitchen." Elizabeth turned to head that direction.

But she heard raised voices outside and made a one-eighty for the door, Dayne following.

"Jason, it's not a good idea," Rafe said as he grabbed Mayor McKinnley by the coat and blocked his movement.

"Rafe, let go of me. I need to see my mom." He swatted at Rafe's hold on him.

Elizabeth hurried down the steps, gritting her teeth against the cold sting of flurries that resumed their relentless battering.

Jason caught sight of her. "Sheriff! Tell him to release me."

Laying a hand on Rafe's bulging arm, she gave him a nod. He relaxed his hold but shifted in step with Jason as the other man tried one more time to get around him.

Elizabeth snagged the Three Points mayor's arm and gently rerouted him toward the garage. "Mayor McKinnley, I'd like you to walk with me a bit first." She looked to the road and the line of vehicles that had gathered in the short time since she'd arrived.

This incident was going to make headlines on tonight's evening news reports.

Jason kept looking over their shoulders, his body tight and coiled, ready to bolt the moment she gave him a chance. Elizabeth refused to allow him to see his mother in her current state. The memories he had of her alive and vibrant were what he needed. Not of her untimely death.

"Mayor McKinnley." She brought him to halt on the far side of the driveway, next to one of Neva's prized flowerbeds. "I don't need to tell you what you most likely have surmised from our presence here at your mother's home."

He looked at her, face pale, moisture pooling in his eyes. "She's dead." The attempt at being matter-of-fact crumbled on the word *dead*.

"Unfortunately, yes."

A tortured moan ripped past his lips. Then he manned up, stiffening his body and lifting his chin.

"Jason," Elizabeth said with a softer touch. "I don't want you to see her like that."

"She's my mother, Sheriff."

"And we're taking extra special care with her." She took his hand and clasped it between both of hers. "Is it all right if I ask you a few questions?"

"Sure. Whatever."

"Let me introduce you to our newest investigator." She beckoned for Dayne to join them.

He blinked at her. "Investigator?"

Lila held out her hand. "Deputy Detective Lila Dayne. I'm sorry about your mother, Mayor."

Dazed, the young mayor shook her hand. His gaze slid back to Elizabeth. "What did you want to ask me?"

"Jason, when was the last time you saw or spoke to your mother?" she asked.

His features scrunched. "Uh, I talked to her last night."

"Do you know what time that was?"

"I don't know. It was around supper time, I suppose. Six thirtyish."

She gave his hand a gentle squeeze. "Did she mention that she was expecting any guests?"

"No. She never has anyone visit her at night."

Lila remained silent, cocking her head as she listened. Elizabeth would have to ask her deputy's thoughts once they were done talking with him.

"When was the last time you saw her?"

"Yesterday after her luncheon with some of her fellow retirees. She stopped to chat with Amy."

"Did she seem out of sorts?"

He shook his head. "Just peeved that someone had been breaking into the Barrett place again."

Elizabeth's and Lila's gazes met. Raising her eyebrows a notch, Lila returned her attention to the man.

Patting his hand, Elizabeth caught his eye. "One last question. Do you know if anyone has spoken a bad word against your mother?"

"No. Everyone loved her. Even the students who had given her the most grief didn't have a bad thing to say about her."

"I think that's enough for now. Where's Amy?"

"At work."

Steering him around and pointing him in the direction of his dark blue Enclave, Elizabeth escorted him farther from the house. "Call your wife. Tell her to meet you at the hospital. Okay?"

Woodenly, he obeyed, pulling his phone from a pocket. When she had him far enough away from the house and a safe distance from the morbid onlookers, she waved Rafe over.

"Don't leave his side until he's in his car and driving away. And keep that bunch"—she pointed at the crowd—"away from him."

Rafe touched his forehead.

Elizabeth started back to the house, ignoring the shouts for her attention. It was bad enough she had to blow off Pratt Meyer to be here—she would not hear the end of that from him—there wasn't room in her patience to deal with a barrage of questions she had no answers for.

Lila met her at the base of the front steps. "He seems genuinely stunned by her death. But we can't rule him out as a person of interest. Or his wife."

"I can't see either of them harming her, much less leaving her at the bottom of the steps to die."

"Sheriff, that's a mentality you need to get rid of when doing this job."

Jolting, Elizabeth shook her head. "I disagree. I'm well aware of the need to always look closely at the family first. But Jason is an only child; he loved his mother. When his father died, he was a zombie for days. His mother dragged him out of it. And Jason's wife has never been able to kill a gnat without crying her eyes out."

"If they're innocent, they'll be ruled out. Let me do my job before you make any final decisions."

Sighing, Elizabeth nodded. "Right. You're right. Do your thing."

Re-entering the house, she paused in the entryway. Meyer had remained in his position on the sofa and had graduated to watching those around him. Lundquist dusted for prints in the bathroom. Olivia discussed with her assistant the best way to get the stretcher in and out of the house without doing any further damage to the scene. Elizabeth checked her watch. She'd called in DCI for this, and their estimated arrival wasn't for another hour.

"Sheriff."

Dayne beckoned to join her in the kitchen—the one room that had entertained more guests than she could count. Would this house ever be the same?

Taking stock of the kitchen, she located the calendar she'd mentioned. Moving over to the corkboard hanging next to the refrigerator, Elizabeth checked the dates. Minus yesterday's luncheon, the dates were empty until Christmas, when Neva expected to celebrate the holiday with her son. This would not be a cheerful season for Jason and Amy.

Lila stood next to the sink, brushing loose, black dust into a pile.

"This had to be an accident. Or a medical emergency," Elizabeth said.

Lila shook her head. "I don't like how this whole situation is set up. She lives out here alone, the nearest neighbor being an empty, run-down house. Her front door was left unlocked, and the screen door swinging. I know you don't want to consider it, but we need to treat this as a homicide."

"Deputy Dayne, right now there's no solid evidence to prove it."

The hardened stare made Elizabeth's spine snap upright.

"At this given point, we don't have the luxury of time for solid evidence. Doesn't it cross you as suspicious that on the very night the news breaks about the girls' deaths, the one woman who could potentially have been a witness dies?"

"Coincidence?"

Lila shook her head. "Before you and the others arrived, I took the liberty of checking her bathroom cabinet and bedroom for medications. Not a thing. Either this woman was fit and fighting, or whoever decided to end her life absconded with her prescriptions. I doubt she had a medical emergency to cause her to fall on those stairs."

"We'll ask Jason if he was aware of whether she was on any prescriptions."

"No need." Olivia joined them. "I was her doctor. She was taking thyroid medication. That was it."

"Would you check and see if she still has a bottle?" Lila asked.

Reaching behind the investigator, Olivia opened the cabinet and pulled out the orange bottle. "She kept it right here, as she told me, so she would remember to take it every day."

"But nothing else?" Elizabeth pressed.

"Ellie, other than missing her thyroid, she was healthy."

Elizabeth avoided Lila's pointed look. "That still doesn't rule out a sudden condition like a heart attack."

"As you pointed out, let's not jump to the homicide conclusion yet," Olivia said. "The autopsy will tell me more.

Did you get Jason to agree to one?"

Elizabeth winced. "I didn't ask him yet. I told him to go to the hospital."

"That might be better. I'll speak with him," Olivia said.

"But if the sheriff convinces him that it could be a homicide, we won't need his approval."

Elizabeth gaped at Lila. "I will not presume anything just to circumvent a grieving man."

Huffing, Lila rammed her hands under her arms.

Someone cleared their throat, and then Lundquist entered the kitchen. Meyer shuffled up behind his fellow deputy.

"Sheriff, this house was wiped clean," Lundquist said. "There are no prints on any surface. I found some on a few bathroom items, but I'm certain those will come back as Mrs. McKinnley."

Elizabeth felt Lila's eyes boring into her.

"What more do you need?" she asked.

Giving each person in that room a full-on stare, Elizabeth bowed to their wisdom. "We will treat this as a homicide until such time as an actual ruling can be determined. For now, that piece of information stays within this department and with the ME. Understood?"

They all gave her a solemn head nod.

"I'll deal with the press."

"You're going to need to tell Fitzgerald about this and to keep his mouth shut," Lundquist stated.

Elizabeth wrinkled her nose at this. "Is there any way he'll listen to you?"

He shrugged. "Maybe. But we both know he's more apt

to listen to authority over a peer. Even if he doesn't like you."

"Let me talk with him," Lila interjected.

"Deputy Dayne, you barely know the man, and he's not too keen on you."

One corner of the woman's mouth kicked up. "Maybe it's time I change that."

"I'm not opposed to the idea. Do what you can, but wait until later today. He's got night shift again, and I don't want him working on minimal sleep.

"In the meantime, DCI is on the way to process the house. Lundquist, you stay here and work with them. Deputy Meyer, you and Deputy Fontaine are on guard. Dayne, you're with me. Doc, do your thing. We'll make sure you can get the van out of here."

As her team dispersed to do her bidding, Elizabeth headed for the door. Dayne fell in step with her.

"What are we doing?"

"I'm facing the horde and giving them something to chew on that will get them off our backs here. And when I've sufficiently whet their voracious appetite, we're going to the high school. We need to establish a timeline for Maya Wagner."

CHAPTER TWENTY-TWO

L ILA HOVERED BEHIND the other deputies who stood with the sheriff as she addressed the press. Studying the small flock of inquisitive reporters, Lila noted with relief, no one appeared interested in her. All it took was one overzealous person to go digging where they shouldn't to expose Lila, and she'd have to seriously consider moving. A task she wasn't keen on doing again so soon.

Once Sheriff Benoit had dismissed the crowd, she and Lila sequestered themselves inside the sheriff's SUV. Each woman kept to her own counsel as the sheriff drove to the school Maya Wagner had briefly attended.

Lila's shoulders sagged. Had she not insisted on seeing Neva McKinnley again, how long would the poor woman's body been left at the bottom of the stairs? Worse, who would have found her? Obviously, the sheriff was right in keeping the son at arm's length to protect him from the gruesome sight, but there was a good chance Jason McKinnley would have found his mother like that. If he wasn't the one who'd done the dirty deed.

Lila could agree with the sheriff on a certain level. Jason McKinnley's reaction to the news of his mother's death looked legit. On the other hand, far as Lila could tell, he had everything to gain from her death. Greed turned even the most loving of families into monsters.

Still, intuition whispered in Lila's ear. The mayor of Three Points was not the man she needed to look for. Someone else had been in Neva McKinnley's home last night. Someone with murder on their mind. And their motive could be as simple as shutting her up.

This family feud Deputy Meyer spoke about between his family and the Kauffmanns, a name that kept popping up in the last few days, intrigued Lila. The Kauffmann matriarch owned the Barrett property next to McKinnley. A deceased son was part of a drug situation in the same spot as a homicide victim. And now the revelation from Meyer. If Lila were honest with herself, she had hoped that by getting out of Chicago she'd see less of a mafia-type mentality. Obviously, she'd been wrong.

The sheriff interrupted the stillness. "How are your injuries from the other day?"

Lila rubbed her midsection. "I haven't felt a thing the last few days."

"Sounds like we followed the doctor's orders." Benoit slowed the Interceptor at a four-way stop. "I had Deputy Fontaine call in a few favors and locate some ATVs for you and Meyer to use in the woods behind the Barrett place."

"You want me to take Meyer?" Somehow, Lila didn't see the rookie being much of the backwoods type of male. Especially if his comments about his family held true, Meyer probably hadn't spent much time riding around on four-wheelers. Fontaine, on the other hand, practically swam in good ole boy testosterone, and it made more sense for him to take her behind the Barrett place. Except they were not on good terms at the moment.

Turning left after the stop sign, Benoit frowned. "Are you finding the young deputy lacking in some way, Deputy?"

"No, it's not that." Lila cleared her throat. "What I meant was, with the long-standing animosity between his family and this Ma Kauffmann, should he be even near the property?"

"Told you about that feud, did he?"

"Among other things, yes, he did."

The sheriff made a noise in her throat. She said nothing, parking her vehicle in an overflowing lot across the street from a sprawling two-story, red-brick school. Cutting the engine, Benoit turned to Lila.

"Brent Meyer and his family are not in good standing." She held up a finger. "Let me amend that, Brent and his father are not speaking to each other. The rest of the Meyer family is a bit willy-nilly in their loyalties."

"He failed to mention that."

"It's not something he's proud to admit. There's some bad blood between the Meyer men, but Brent hasn't seen fit to reveal to me what exactly it was that caused the falling out with them."

"Could it have anything to do with the Kauffmanns?"

Benoit shook her head. "It's something more personal than that. Something so deep, it has left a wound on his soul. If he told you about the two families' feud, then you know about his mother's familial history."

"Yes."

The sheriff stared out the windshield.

"This rich, loamy soil brought a whole slew of immigrants to this area. Farmers looking to make a better way of life for themselves. Crops aren't the only things that ripen around here." Benoit looked at Lila once more. "Be careful." And with that ominous warning, she exited the SUV.

Three days into this job. No dipping her toes in the water here. Lila was thrown headfirst into the churning waters.

She followed Benoit to the school front. There was no wait to be buzzed in; the door's electronic locks clicked the moment they approached. Benoit allowed Lila to enter first. Before them was a flight of stairs leading to the second floor. To the left was a wall of reinforced glass, and a heavy metal door. Benoit headed toward the door.

"Principal Ericksen asked that I show you in as soon as you got here, Sheriff," the secretary was saying.

"Expecting me, was he?"

The middle-aged woman gave Benoit a grim smile. "Unfortunately, he was." Her gaze landed on Lila, and she frowned.

"This is my newest deputy. Deputy Dayne is Eckardt County's investigator."

With an acquiescent nod, the secretary led the two behind the counter to a pair of closed doors at the back of the office. The school secretary knocked on one.

"Enter."

"Mr. Ericksen, Sheriff Benoit and her investigator are here." She opened the door wider for them.

Ericksen was a tall man in thick, black-framed spectacles, with graying temples and a houndstooth wool jacket that gave mind to a posh gentleman from Oxford or Cambridge.

He circled his desk, hand outstretched. "Sheriff, thank you for stopping by."

As the two officials shook, Lila scanned the office, cataloging the framed certifications and awards, pictures, and school paraphernalia. Her attention swung back to the principal and she started at the offered hand. Face heating, she gripped the man's hand.

"Deputy Dayne, nice to meet you," he said.

"Hmm."

"Well." Ericksen looked between the two women. "When the news broke last night about the young woman, I knew you'd be paying us a visit." He stepped between them and gestured for them to follow him out of his office through a side door. "After her parents had contacted me earlier, I had all the security tapes and her information pulled and set aside."

He led them down a bright and gleaming hall.

"That was fortuitus thinking there, Mark," Benoit said.

Lila eyed a pair of girls lugging an armful of textbooks, who stared at the passing officers and their principal. One flushed bright red and turned away after meeting Lila's gaze.

"Yes, well, students skipping school is a common occurrence."

The two girls kept glancing back. Between those two, news was going to spread fast that cops were in the building. A hazard of the job when dealing with teens. And if someone knew about Maya Wagner and didn't want to be associated with her activities, all element of surprise would be gone.

Principal Ericksen made a right turn into another room, flicking on the light. Benoit and Lila entered behind him.

"I have the recording over here." Ericksen moved to a filling cabinet.

Lila walked up to the bank of computer screens. Students were moving about in one hall, near the gym, and an area she thought looked like a shop of some kind. Everyone appeared to be acting normal. There weren't cameras in the classrooms.

"Why are the classrooms not covered?" she asked.

The principal turned to her. "The teachers have a setup that allows them to monitor the kids through their computers' camera."

"That doesn't help you out if there's an incident in the room."

"If there were funding for that, we'd take advantage of it. We're lucky to have what we have." He held up a disc case. "The day Maya Wagner was last in attendance."

The sheriff nodded. "I'd like to watch through it here with you. If that works for you?"

"I expected as much." He popped the case and slipped the disc in a player connected to a blank screen.

Lila's gaze shifted back to the monitors. She spotted the two girls they had passed in the hall. The two walked up to door, paused outside it, looked up in the direction of the camera. Running her fingers through her hair, Lila let her hand slide along her head and then cupped the back of her neck, watching the girls as they spoke to each other and then entered the room. A classroom.

"What class hour is this?" she asked Principal Ericksen.

"It's the end of fifth hour. In ten minutes, the first lunch hour rotation starts."

"How many rotations are there?"

"Three twenty-minute cycles to accommodate all the students. We do have an open campus, so some of the students will go into Juniper to grab something fast."

Twenty minutes to drive into town for fast food didn't seem like a productive use of time.

"How many students ditch school during the lunch hour?"

Ericksen's cheek muscles twitched. Touchy subject. "Frankly, more than the state likes. We're considering measures to end this ritual."

Bouncing from one monitor to the next, Lila studied the scenes. Whoever had knowledge on Maya Wagner would use this time to ditch, and they'd be left drifting in the wind.

"Mark, take me to the point where you know Maya was last caught on camera," Benoit said.

Lila dragged her attention away from the real-time footage and joined the sheriff. The principal was forwarding the recording at a fast clip. He stopped at the halfway point and let the disc play.

A bevy of students was streaming through the hallway, some stopping at lockers along the way to switch out books or grab gym bags.

Ericksen pointed at a particular girl in the upper left portion of the screen. "This is Maya."

They watched as she walked toward the camera, stopped next to a locker, opened it, and shoved her bag and books inside, then closed it.

"I'll need to look over her locker," Benoit stated.

"We'll go there next."

Lila squinted at the timestamp. "Which hour is this?"

"Maya was in the second lunch rotation. She'd just left a study hall."

The girl headed straight for a staircase and went down.

"Where does that lead?" Lila asked.

"To the west exit, right out into the parking lot." Ericksen stopped the player and exchanged discs. "This is the recording from the video camera directed at that parking lot." He advanced the disc to the point where Maya left the building.

The teenager skipped down the sidewalk right up to a rusted, white two-door sedan. She bent down to wag her fingers at the driver, then opened the door and slid into the car. The moment she shut the door, the car pulled away. Lucky them, the camera caught the Illinois license plate.

"Has to be her cousin," Lila said.

"We'll run the plates to be sure. But we need to put out a BOLO for the car." Benoit jerked up her hand. "Stop it there."

Principal Ericksen paused the video. "What is it?"

Benoit pointed to a shadow at the edge of the screen, right at the corner of the building. "What is that?"

Lila studied the shape. "Looks like someone standing there."

"You're right." Benoit tapped the screen. "Do you know who that is?"

"It could be any number of students who are coming and going."

Lila picked up on the strain in Ericksen's voice. "But it's not, is it?"

Clearing his throat, he removed his glasses and pinched the bridge of his nose. "No, it's not. It's a former student, if I could call him that."

She turned from the paused scene and walked over to the bank of computers. The bell pealed, releasing the students. She found the monitor manning the west side parking lot and spotted the shadow in the corner of the building. "Your visitor is here today."

Benoit squinted at the monitor. "It appears he's expecting someone. Who is that?"

"Dillon Reed. He loiters there, usually smoking, until his girlfriend comes out. She's in the senior class, and from the moment we realized she was seeing him, her grades have plummeted."

"How old is he?" Lila asked.

"Twenty-one."

"And you say he was a former student?"

"He didn't graduate. Halfway through his senior year, he dropped out. What could we do? He was eighteen, and in the law's eyes he met the age requirement. To be frank, I was relieved. I don't like to see students fail. But there are just some kids that no matter how much you try to reach them, you never get through, because they don't care."

"Reed?" Benoit tapped her holster belt. "His father is Dillon Reed Sr.?"

"Yeah. You remember him?"

"Apple. Tree."

"Exactly," Ericksen said.

"The Reed family has a history," Benoit filled in Lila. "I want to talk to him. He was standing there when Maya left.

He saw who was in that car."

Movement on the screen showed Reed Jr. moving into the camera sight as a twig of a girl dressed in a long, black overcoat exited the school. "On the move. We better hurry."

"I'll have Maya's locker open when you get back," Ericksen said as the two women left.

"Have the discs ready for us to take too," Benoit told him as she strode down the hall.

"Which way to the west parking lot?" Lila asked.

"Faster to go out the front entrance," Benoit said, leading the way.

Bypassing the office, the two pushed through the doors and out onto the sidewalk. Benoit hung a right and jogged up the sidewalk. Ahead of them, Dillon and his girlfriend were strolling away from the school toward a cluster of cars parked along the street.

"Dillon Reed," Benoit called out.

The couple froze and turned. Lila's pulse jumped as panic hit his face. He was going to run.

She'd no sooner thought it and he bolted. His girlfriend let out a yelp when he shoved her.

"Shit," Lila spat and sprinted after the kid.

Benoit peeled off to see to the girl.

"Dillon! Stop!"

Lila's commands seemed to fuel him. He topped the hill and cut across the street, ignoring the cars coming. Lila, yards and closing, threw up her hand to warn the drivers and dodged around the vehicles. Her quarry ran along the street, oblivious to the oncoming traffic. What was this kid worried about that he'd run from cops?

"Dillon! Stop running!"

He continued to pump his arms and legs, his coat waving bye-bye at her.

Sucking air, Lila found her next gear and put on the afterburners. She closed the gap between them. Dillon took a hard left around a corner like a Bears running back avoiding a tackler and clambered onto the sidewalk.

"Damn it." Lila swung wide, avoiding the stop sign, and remained street side. Getting positioned just outside his right shoulder, she drew closer to the curb, ready to hop it.

They were coming up on a large yard dominated by a huge house. Jumping the slight curb, Lila shaved off the last few feet between them and tackled the kid.

Both slammed into the hardened earth, sliding a few feet. Bouncing over the top of the kid's lithe body, Lila came to bumpy halt with her legs draped over Dillon's back. She scrambled around and grabbed his arm before he could get it under his body.

"Stay where you are."

Dillon spewed a litany of colorful words.

"Shut your mouth," she snapped, hooking her hand under his arm. "Get on your knees."

"No."

She leaned down and looked in him in the eye. "Get on your knees, or I'll cuff you."

"What did I do wrong?"

"You ran from the sheriff."

"Nothing illegal about that."

Oh, a genius. "No, there's not. But when you catch sight of a cop and run, you look real suspicious. So, what is it that you're hiding you don't want the sheriff or I to know about?"

"I ain't sayin' nuthin'."

"Well, that's just too bad, Mr. Reed."

Dillon lifted his head, groaned, and let his forehead plop onto the ground.

"Up we go." Lila hauled the kid onto his knees as Sheriff Benoit approached.

Coming down to Dillon's level, Benoit eyed him. For a few agonizing moments no words passed between them.

"What?" he snapped.

"Apple. Tree."

Lila chuckled.

"What is she talking about?" Dillon demanded.

"On his feet, Deputy," the sheriff said and rose.

"Up." Lila helped him onto his feet but kept a hand gripped on his arm.

"Are you arresting me?"

Benoit crossed her arms and regarded the young man. "Should we?"

"Like I told her, I ain't done nuthin' wrong."

"I thought you weren't saying anything more?" Lila interjected.

Dillon blinked, then clapped his mouth shut.

"Mr. Reed, all Deputy Dayne and I wanted was to ask you a question or two about an incident that happened on Monday. Instead of allowing us this opportunity, you ran. As I'm sure Deputy Dayne explained, when someone runs from us, it looks suspicious."

"Questions about what incident on Monday?"

Lila had to resist the urge to roll her eyes.

Sighing, Benoit dropped her arms. "Will you give us the courtesy of staying here and answering our questions without Deputy Dayne restraining you?"

"I guess."

Lila released him and stepped back, but remained within arm's length right behind him.

Benoit inched closer. "Do you pick up your girlfriend every day at lunch?"

Dillon shrugged. "Most the time."

"And drop her off when her time is up?"

He scratched the back of his head. "Sure."

"I'm going to show you a picture, and you tell me if you recognize the young woman in the photo."

No answer. Benoit unzipped her coat, reached inside, and pulled out a crumpled picture. She held it up facing Dillon. He squinted at the image of Maya Wagner in a happier moment of her life on a sunny patch of grass.

"Hey, is that the chick that was found dead yesterday?"

Lila groaned.

Returning the picture to her inside pocket, Benoit gave Dillon a forgiving grimace. "That would be the unfortunate girl. Do you remember seeing her on Monday as she left the school?"

"Yeah, I remember her. She annoyed Frankie."

"Frankie, your girlfriend?" Lila asked.

Dillon scowled at her. "Duh."

"What about her annoyed Frankie?" Benoit asked, catching the man's attention.

"That Maya chick had it in her head that Frankie knew

how to get in contact with some dude who had some friends she wanted to meet up with."

Benoit's confusion mirrored Lila's.

Dillon held up his hand. "Look, this chick was wanting to hook up with some dealer. Said her cousin was coming to town and they were going to want the good stuff."

"The good stuff meaning drugs?" Benoit asked.

"Yes. But Frankie and I aren't into that."

"I'm not here about that, Mr. Reed. Let's stay on topic. On Monday, Maya came out of the school while you were there? Right?"

"I just dropped Frankie off, and needed to catch a friend before I left. The Maya chick came skipping out of the school."

The video had confirmed that part.

"Did you see a rusty white car with Illinois plates waiting for her?" the sheriff pressed.

Another unamused duh expression. This kid would try the patience of Saint Monica.

"Work with me here, Mr. Reed. Did you happen to see the driver?"

"Yeah, I did. It was some dude."

Lila jolted. "A dude?"

"Didn't I just say that?"

Benoit's features pinched. "Yes, you did. You're sure it was a male driver, and not a female?"

"I know what a guy looks like versus a girl."

"Have you seen him before?"

Dillon shook his head. "They must have known each other. She got all giggly and waved at him like a little kid."

Another confirmation of what they'd seen on the video, but that was when they'd assumed it was Regan in the car.

"Was there anyone else in the car?" Lila asked.

"Nope. Just the dude driving and Maya when she got in."

"Did you happen to see which direction they went after leaving?"

"Nope. My friend came out then."

Benoit sighed. "Okay. I think that's what we needed, Mr. Reed."

He huffed. "You know what you did is considered police brutality."

"Actually, it's not, Mr. Reed. You ran when there was no need to. Deputy Dayne asked you to stop, and you ignored her. Therefore, she stopped you. Had you just waited and let us ask our questions, all of this preamble would have been avoided."

He gaped at her, blinking.

"Sheriff, I think we've done enough education for the day." Lila gestured for the sheriff to walk with her. "Go home," she said to the confused Dillon Reed Jr., and the two women left him standing there dumbfounded.

"Are you okay?" Benoit asked. "You didn't reinjure yourself?"

"Fine. His body cushioned me."

A good thing too. Not once had she second-guessed herself the moment Dillon bolted. She was finding her way back. As long as this murder investigation didn't take a sidetrack down memory lane.

CHAPTER TWENTY-THREE

O N INITIAL EXAM, the contents of Maya Wagner's locker appeared that of an ordinary teenage girl. Elizabeth and Lila bagged many of the items, and along with the security footage from the school, they took everything back to the department to sort through. Missing was the one item every teenager in the world owned: her cell phone.

Upon arriving at the bullpen, Georgia waved a pair of pink message slips for Elizabeth. "Call the ME first," she said.

She beckoned for Lila to follow her into the office, where Bentley greeted them, and she closed the door. Taking her chair, Elizabeth called Olivia's office, putting the call on speaker.

"Doc, it's Sheriff Benoit and Deputy Dayne. Have you got any information for me on Mrs. McKinnley?"

"Sorry, Ellie, it took me an hour to convince Jason this was the best idea. He's adamant that he doesn't want his mother cut up like that. I think Amy did more in convincing him than I did."

"But you can, right?"

"Yes. I'll do it here midafternoon. I had something else pull me away." Olivia's sigh brought a weight to Elizabeth's shoulders. "I did a double-check on Regan's and Maya's autopsies. Something was nagging at me that I didn't tell you about yesterday."

Elizabeth met Lila's piercing gaze. "What?"

"Maya was alive longer than Regan."

"Wait. Are you saying she wasn't killed at the same time Regan was?"

"Taking in account air temps, rate of decomposition, and entomology activity, I had to adjust my findings. Ellie, I'm not saying you weren't wrong in your thinking about the first victim. But Maya Wagner was killed shortly before her body was dumped under that tree."

"You're sure?"

"I'm not sure of anything at this point. But the science points to a difference in their times of death."

Elizabeth sighed. "Thanks, Olivia. Let me know when you have Mrs. McKinnley's results ready for me."

"You're not coming in?"

"Other pressing matters."

Elizabeth ended the call. "Maya was alive longer than Regan?"

Lila stared at her, the answer nowhere on her face.

Elizabeth massaged her scalp. "Is every case going to be this complicated?"

Shaking her head, Lila glanced down at the box in her arms. "No. Some of them can be cut and dried, and it makes you glad you do the job you do."

"Well, though she's not here to confirm it, we can rest assured that Neva McKinnley heard what she heard Tuesday night or early Wednesday morning." Elizabeth slapped the top of her desk. "We just need to figure out if Maya was actually in that house and who had her there. And was she killed there?"

"Check with DCI to see if they have the DNA on the blood back. And we need to get toxicology results ASAP."

Elizabeth made a note. "I'll call them."

"Maybe when Meyer and I ride out behind the Barrett place, something will come up."

"We can only hope."

Lila rummaged through the bags of evidence from Maya's locker. "I'll go catalog these and take a peek. I wish we had either one of the girls' cell phones."

"Maya's parents are working on getting her cell phone records and tracking down Regan's mother. But they don't hold out much hope we'll learn anything. In the past the girls used burner phones to keep the Wagners unaware of what they were doing."

"We know more than we did when Regan was found. But the clock is ticking. If my suspicions that Mrs. McKinnley was killed bears out, we might have a panicky killer out there who will stop anyone from pointing fingers at them."

"All the more reason you and Meyer need to get to the Barrett place and scope it out. Process that evidence and head out."

Rapid-fire knocking put a hold to whatever Lila was about to say.

"Yes?"

Georgia poked her head in, then gave Elizabeth a look she reserved for the troublemaker visitors. "Pratt Meyer wants to meet with you. Now." How she controlled her voice in these situations amazed Elizabeth. The visitor was never the wiser to her faces.

"Now?"

Now! Georgia mouthed.

"Deputy Dayne—"

"I got my orders, don't worry. And we'll go update Fitzgerald."

"That would be a good idea. Deputy Fontaine will give you the information on the ATVs."

Cradling the evidence box against her chest, Lila exited the office.

Time for the show. "Come on in, Mr. Meyer."

As Pratt Meyer entered, he made it clear he was watching and analyzing Lila before he rudely closed the door, nearly clipping the deputy with the door handle. "Who is that woman?"

"My newest investigator."

"An investigator? Does the county have the budget to pay for that?"

"She's a law officer with more years of experience than all the other deputies and myself combined." She narrowed her gaze. "I believe that's well within the county budget."

Pratt adjusted his tie. If only he'd tighten it a little more around that chicken neck and cut off his inflated ego. Bentley huffed and he jerked. His gaze dropped to the dog on sentry duty next to her desk.

"I was under the impression that dogs were not allowed in county-owned facilities."

"That would be your impression." Crossing her arms, Elizabeth grasped the threads of her patience. "Mr. Meyer, I believe I made myself clear over the phone this morning that I did not have time for a meeting with you today."

"What I have to discuss with you will not wait. I have put off this conversation long enough."

Oh goodie. This should be scintillating.

Pratt glanced around the office, pausing on Bentley's chair. Her border collie abandoned her post and hopped onto her throne, settling in a curl with her eyes lasered on Pratt. The corners of his mouth twisted, and he sidestepped to the remaining seat in the room, then sat.

Okay, so they were doing this. Elizabeth eased onto her chair, resting her arms on the desktop. "I can give you five minutes, Mr. Meyer, no more than that."

He leaned forward. "It will take as long as needed."

She humored him with a feral smile. "I don't know what type of working relationship you had with Sheehan, but I will not be pandering to your toeing the party line."

White streaks popped at the corners of his eyes and mouth. "Sheriff Benoit, despite whatever you were told or what you heard, there was no such relationship. After the outburst I was subjected to yesterday, I can only imagine the fabrications spun about me and mine."

"You and yours." Elizabeth tilted her head. "Four minutes."

Nostrils flaring, he stiffened. "Very well. Word has reached me that Martha Kauffmann has instigated a witch hunt against me. Laying claim that I was the perpetrator in the death of her son Daniel."

Coughing out a laugh, Elizabeth covered her mouth and cleared her throat. She drew a breath and released it.

Cleansed of her amusement, she resumed her stare down with Pratt. "Forgive me. This farce of a meeting is nothing more than a tattling session."

"Excuse me. There is nothing in this situation that makes it juvenile in any way. That woman has long spread lies and dissension to smear my family name. Claiming I had anything to do with her son's accident is just another ploy on her part to make me look bad in front of the populace."

"Why would that matter to her?"

He slapped the chair arm. "How should I know?"

Elizabeth narrowed her gaze. "What do you expect me to do about it?"

"Stop her. Tell her to cease and desist. Effective immediately."

"No." She pressed her hands flat to the desk. "This Kauffmann-Meyer feud has gone on for a century or more, and, frankly, I don't care to see it played out any longer. You and Ma need to wrap up your differences and end it."

"You fail to see the implications in this."

"I fail to see nothing. What I see are two grown adults acting like children. And what's unbelievable about this is the familial relationship between your wife and Ma that has nothing whatsoever to do with the Kauffmanns and the Meyers." She leaned forward. "Tell me, Pratt, what is this feud about?"

He sat back, interlacing his fingers, regarding Elizabeth. "I understand now."

"Do you? And what is it that you understand?"

An ugly twist of his lips revealed his canines. "Martha has managed to pocket you."

Heat infused Elizabeth's face. She stared at her clenched hands, composing herself before she climbed over the desk and ripped out his throat. How dare he imply her position as bought and paid for.

"For the sake of the dignity of this office, I will ignore your unfounded accusation. I had difficulties understanding why your son hates you." Elizabeth pushed to her feet and peered down at Pratt. "I think I fully comprehend it now. This meeting is over. Show yourself out."

Rising, Pratt straightened his suit jacket, leveling her with what she assumed was his most withering glare. "This is far from over, Sheriff."

"I hold no illusions that it will ever end."

Crisply turning on his heel, he moved to the exit.

"If Ma is right."

He stopped before opening the door and turned back to Elizabeth.

"And you had something to do with Daniel's death, I promise you, I will tear your life apart. And I fear the horror it will bring down on Sophie's head."

"Do not lodge idle threats against me, Sheriff."

She smiled. "Who said they were idle?"

With a sneer, he jerked the door open and marched out, slamming the door in his wake.

Bentley let out a growl, baring her teeth.

"I feel the same way, girl."

CHAPTER TWENTY-FOUR

"**I** HATE THIS," Meyer blurted out as he drove them both to Fitzgerald's home.

Lila glanced over. "You hate what?"

"Going about my duties as if nothing horribly wrong just happened to a resident of this county. We should be looking for her killer."

The man was beating himself up over this. This morning he'd tried to roll Mrs. McKinnley's stiffened body onto her back to administer CPR, but Lila knew it was a lost cause. Meyer nearly howled the second he realized what was wrong.

She reached over and gripped his forearm. "When we have a suspect to tie to her death, we'll track them down and bring them to justice. Right now, we don't have one clue to point fingers in any direction."

"How about the Kauffmann family?"

Frowning, she released her hold. "That's a fairly specific guilty party. Why would they want to kill Neva McKinnley?"

"We're going over to the timber behind the Barrett place to see if the killer left anything behind. People use it all the time for their clandestine activities. It's no secret Ma Kauffmann hasn't had that house torn down because of the shady dealings going on in and around it. And she's had it out for the mayor since he had the county condemn the building. Matters aren't helped when his mother lives nearby and spies on the place."

"Bitter much?"

He flinched, jerking the car across the center line. He guided the unit back to their side of the road. "No."

"Oh, come on. If your fangs could drip poison, they would. You admitted that your father and the Kauffmann family have had it out for each other. Sure you're not invested in that feud?"

"Absolutely not."

"Try again, and with a little more emphasis."

"I'm serious. Whatever feud my father has with other people is not my fight."

"Then let's go ask him."

"No!"

Impressive. Lila could rate that flat-out rejection right up there with the one she'd received each time she'd arrested a juvenile delinquent and told them their parent was about to receive a call from protective services.

"Never mind," he said. "I'm just venting."

Well, the sheriff had warned her to be careful with Brent's family history. "It's fine. What we found this morning would shake any seasoned police officer. Believe me, we'll find whoever killed Mrs. McKinnley and those two girls."

Silence ruled the remainder of the drive, which wasn't far.

Meyer pulled into the tiny drive of a house that looked more like a trailer than a modular home, and then cut the engine. He didn't move to exit the unit, just stared at the back end of a powder-blue, boxy-styled Ford pickup.

That truck looked like it should be sitting in a car museum somewhere and not out exposed to the elements.

"He's going to give you attitude," Meyer said.

"Let 'im."

"Maybe I should talk with him?"

"Will he listen to you?"

Meyer huffed. "Ben only listens to himself."

Lila popped the door. "Time to change that, huh?" Out of the vehicle, she hunched her shoulders against the cold, and without waiting for Meyer, she marched up to what appeared to be the front door.

Banging the side of her fist against the screen door, noting how it bounced under her blows, she gave Fitzgerald two minutes and banged again. Meyer joined her on her third round.

"Fitzgerald, get up!"

"His bedroom might be in the back."

"This thing has thin walls. He can hear me."

Raising her fist for another loud knock, she paused as the bolt clicked. A bleary-eyed Fitzgerald wearing a rumpled T-shirt and shorts peered through the glass partition.

"What the hell?"

"We need to talk." Lila flicked her hand at his door. "Open up."

His sleepy look was exchanged for a perturbed one. He glanced at Meyer, and then jabbed the latch, pushing the screen door out. Lila grabbed the door before Meyer could and gestured for him to enter first.

They stepped into a sparse yet tidy living room. Fitzgerald had all the necessary items a bachelor required. Leather recliner, massive flat screen, and the latest videogame console for all his gaming needs. Unlike his peers, Fitzgerald's mother had done him right by teaching him the value of cleanliness being next to godliness.

He meandered into his combination dining room-kitchen, separated by a dark wood partition wall that doubled as a bookshelf, which carried a varied array of books from Jim Butcher to a biography on John F. Kennedy.

"A fat lot of good it does me to get a full eight in when you come banging on my door." Fitzgerald rattled the metal pot in his state-of-the-art coffeemaker.

"I'll hang later in my shift," Meyer said, shoving his hands in his coat pockets.

"It's the middle of the afternoon. You got enough sleep." Lila inched around Meyer and parked herself in line with the partition. "We've had another death."

Pausing in his coffee prepping, Fitzgerald leaned against his counter. "And that justifies waking me up?"

"It was Neva McKinnley."

This revelation earned her a confused frown.

"Her death looks suspicious. The sheriff is running with the theory it's a murder, but she wants it kept quiet until we have an actual confirmation from the ME."

"This couldn't have waited until I got to the department?"

"No."

He cocked his head, eyeing Lila.

Meyer shifted into the open space next to her. "Ben, stop being an ass."

"Up yours, rich boy."

Meyer twitched, his body posed to make a move. Lila's hand shot out and slammed against his chest. He was a powder keg about to blow. Guiding him behind her, she kept her gaze locked on Fitzgerald.

"Meyer, take a breather outside."

She sensed the deputy's hesitation. Two heartbeats passed and he obeyed her command. Lila eased into the dining area.

"All you women keep mother-henning him and he's never going to grow up."

"Jealous?"

Fitzgerald snorted. "Of him? Never."

"That monkey must weigh a ton."

He blinked, confusion marring his usual sourpuss face.

Lila clicked her tongue and gave him a thumbs-up. "Not a word out of your mouth about Mrs. McKinnley's death." She turned to leave.

"Or what?"

Leaning her head around the edge of the partition, she said, "Or I'll make your life even more miserable than it already is. For some reason, the sheriff sees something in you. I don't. I don't like you, and I don't like how you act. Later."

The house trembled under the force of her closing the door. "Shoot. This thing would blow away in windstorm."

Meyer scowled but followed as she headed back to the squad car. "Why did you make me leave?"

"To save you the embarrassment of having to explain to the sheriff why you lost your cool with a fellow deputy. And why I kicked your butt for doing it."

He snagged her coat sleeve and dragged her around. "I can't make you out."

She scrunched her nose. "What is that supposed to mean?"

"Back at the McKinnley house, before we went inside, you acted like you had no idea what you were doing. Just now, you took charge and did something any seasoned deputy would do. I don't get it."

Sighing, she studied the road and the driveway where the car sat. How did you explain to a rookie the hell she was still trying to navigate through without scaring him off? Oh, right, she didn't.

"Let's go. Deputy Fontaine is supposed to meet us with the ATVs at the Barrett place. It's going to be dark soon, and I'd rather not be out there in the woods in the dark."

"It's not safe back there at night if you don't know where you're going."

"All the more reason to get this show on the road."

AN ECKARDT COUNTY Sheriff's Department Dodge Charger and a dark gray Ford F250 with a long flatbed trailer were parked in the yard. Meyer drove his unit into the overgrown driveway and parked beside Fontaine's Charger. Lila and Meyer exited his vehicle as Fontaine and another man with similar features emerged from behind the decaying house.

"Joel," Meyer called out. "What are you doing here?"

The other man shook Meyer's hand. "Rafe asked me to help out."

Lila met Fontaine's steely gaze. "Did he now? And why would Deputy Fontaine include a civilian in this matter?"

"Because that *civilian* is my brother, the owner of the ATVs we're using, and he knows these woods as well as I do."

Brother? Oh, this must be the ex-husband the sheriff wasn't keen on. Lila gave Joel Fontaine the once-over. Come to think of it, Fontaine didn't like his brother all that much.

"We're losing daylight. If we hope to find anything to tie into these murders, we need to move now," Fontaine said. "Joel and I will take the four-wheelers, covering north and east. Meyer, you and Dayne take the side-by-side and run southwest to west." He held out Motorola radios. "We'll keep in contact this way."

Lila squawked hers. In good working order. "And why are we taking orders from you?"

"Like I said. We know this area best. And the sheriff isn't here to give orders."

"But she didn't give you permission to be out here." Lila poked Fontaine's chest with the Motorola. "Now did she?"

Joel chuckled. "I like this one."

His brother grunted. "It'll go faster with more of us." He turned and strode to the red four-wheeler.

Joel stuck out his hand. "Nice meeting you, Dayne."

She gripped his gloved hand, stunned by the strength pouring from him. That's right. Hadn't Benoit said he was Delta Force? And Lila could see why Elizabeth Benoit had fallen in love. In his youth he must have been a real looker.

With a nod, he mounted the navy-blue mate to Fontaine's ATV. The side-by-side she and Meyer would use was parked to the right of the four-wheelers.

"Do you know how to drive one of these things?" Lila asked the rookie.

His face scrunched. "Excuse me? Are you implying that I, as a *rich kid,* wasn't allowed to slum it with the boys?"

Crap! Dog with her nose in the trash.

Meyer laughed. The knots loosened in Lila's neck.

"My non-approved buddies and I used to race these things. Get in. You'll be fine."

The Fontaine men started their machines as Meyer and Lila climbed inside their designated vehicle. Lila noted with glee the GPS monitor in the cab.

She tapped the power button on the device. The brothers tore out of the yard and sped off to the tree line. Meyer followed on their trail, running alongside the mashed grass of the path that she and Sheriff Benoit had spotted the first time she'd been here. Once the grass met the tree line, the path disappeared under a blanket of pine needles and brown leaves carpeting the forest floor.

"Not that I don't trust you to know where you're going," Lila said as they bumped along, "but I need a better idea of where we are in relation to the house."

"No offense taken." Meyer peeled off the Fontaine brothers' tail and headed west.

Lila watched Joel's backside as he bucked over a slight dip in the pathway. He stayed straight on the path while Rafe went east.

"You get the impression that Deputy Fontaine isn't happy about this arrangement?"

"He probably had to swallow a lot of crow to ask his

brother for these ATVs. And knowing Joel, he probably demanded to come along since he was providing the vehicles."

Meyer slowed the ATV, allowing them to get a better look at the area around them. Lila's gaze bounced from the GPS to the timber floor. Winter's bite had withered a lot of the underbrush that managed to grow despite the thick stand of trees. Meyer had to pick a careful path over downed limbs and rock outcroppings.

"Why would he ask his brother? Aren't there other people that have equipment to borrow?"

"Not everyone can keep their silence like Joel. We'd have a lot of busybodies once word spread. And the last thing we need is Ma Kauffmann to discover we're out here."

"I was under the impression the sheriff asked permission for us to be back here."

"She probably did, but it's safer to have the brothers out here with us in case Ma changes her mind. She won't ever cross those two."

Lila pulled her attention away from their surroundings to look at Meyer. "And why is that?"

Slowing the ATV to a halt, he looked at her. "Family."

"Family has many different meanings to you people."

"Us people?"

She gave Meyer a smile. The kid was growing on her. But she shouldn't consider him a permanent partner. She couldn't afford to get close to anyone.

Swinging her gaze back to the woods, her eye caught a weird break in the scenery. She pointed to their right. "What's that?"

Meyer turned the vehicle in that direction and bumped over the rough terrain to the spot. Lila hopped out before he had it stopped. She knelt beside the tracks.

"I think we found the location where they entered and existed." She followed the tracks as far as she could see. "I'm going to walk them. Follow me, but stay off the tracks."

As she walked, she scanned the ground, hoping that whoever came this way had dropped something. The shadows lengthened. Pausing, she checked her watch.

"Lights?" she asked.

Meyer flipped the headlights and dug into a floor compartment, producing a flashlight. Taking the handheld device, she flicked it on and kept moving.

The Motorola squawked. "Dayne, progress?" Fontaine's voice echoed through the trees.

She grasped the radio and cued it. "I've found some tracks cutting through our area. I'm following them to see where they go."

"How far are you from where we started?"

Meyer held up two fingers.

"Two miles." She squinted at the tree line. "Heading northwest."

"Watch yourself. The area gets rocky, and about another mile or two there is a ravine."

Scowling, she marched forward. "A ravine? Like the one we found Regan in?"

The side-by-side growled after her. She paused and jumped inside as Meyer pulled beside her.

"I think it is," Fontaine said.

"Why did no one tell me this?"

Silence met her inquiry. She pinned Meyer.

"I don't know this place that well," he said.

She cued the radio again. "Rafe."

"I wasn't putting two and two together."

"Damn it." She slapped the dashboard. "Meyer, step on it."

"The tracks?"

"Kick me later, but screw the tracks. Let's go."

CHAPTER TWENTY-FIVE

DEPUTY LUNDQUIST WAS waiting for Elizabeth in the hallway leading to the morgue.

"What do you have for me?" she asked as he fell in step with her.

"The prints that I did find matched with Mrs. McKinnley's. I found dirt clods on the cellar steps. Since she has no exposed dirt on her property, I had the DCI take it, and they're testing it tomorrow."

"Any footprints?"

"No, just the clumps."

They rounded a corner and made a beeline for the swinging doors at the end of the hall.

"Kyle, are her clothes with DCI?"

"Yes. I went over them and took pictures as soon as the body arrived."

"Did you find any anomalies?"

He shook his head. "The doc found bruising on the upper part of her arms."

Elizabeth came to a halt. "Bruising like what?"

"Like she'd been restrained by a strong person."

She closed her eyes and lowered her chin. Neva McKinnley likely had been restrained and probably dragged to the basement door where she was thrown down the steps.

"Murder," she whispered.

The whoosh of rubber suction detaching brought her head up. Olivia came through the doors, removing her blood-splattered yellow gown.

"I'm finished," she said, crumpling the gown into a ball.

"And?"

"I've determined the manner of death as homicide." Olivia gripped Elizabeth's shoulder. "Her neck was broken, but it was the cranial fracture and the brain hemorrhage that killed her."

"Kyle said you found bruising on her arms."

"Yes. They distinctly look like handprints. I'd say male by the size and width."

"A male would be capable of lifting even her small frame and throwing her down the steps."

"But why?" Lundquist asked.

"I think Deputy Dayne might have hit on it earlier. Neva knew too much. She was known to have filed complaints about activity at the Barrett place. And whatever she heard the other night might point fingers at Maya Wagner's killer." Elizabeth pointed at Lundquist. "The blood from the house, has a DNA match come back yet?"

"DCI said it matched Regan."

"Okay, so, Regan was in the house. But she was dead the night Neva heard the sounds. And why throw Regan into the ravine?"

"It's still possible Neva had her nights mixed up," Olivia said.

"Possible, or we still have another victim out there. But it still doesn't explain why Regan and Maya were killed at separate times," Elizabeth added.

"Drugs and sex," Lundquist said.

"Wait, did we ever get a hit on the DNA from the semen?" Elizabeth asked.

"No," Lundquist answered. "Either he's never been arrested or he's not had a full workup due to incompetence."

"Toxicology?"

"Still waiting," Olivia said. "I'm hoping to see something from DCI tomorrow."

Elizabeth drew in a breath and held it two heartbeats before releasing it. "I can't believe we have all this evidence and it amounts up to nothing."

"Any luck with the search on the Barrett property?" Lundquist asked.

"Dayne and Meyer haven't checked in yet." Elizabeth turned to Olivia. "Do you need me for anything more?"

"I'm getting my recordings transcribed. I want to review my report and then I'll send it over. Otherwise, I have nothing more for you."

"Call me if anything new arises." With that, Elizabeth and Lundquist backtracked and headed for the exit. "Kyle, was the meth we found under Maya ever tested?"

"I don't think so."

"I want it tested. We can determine if the batch was fresh and what components are in it."

"Yes, but we don't have anything to compare it against. We don't have any records of drug busts around here. Sheehan never bothered with it."

And why was that, pray tell? "I know. But I have a sneaky feeling it's going to come up. We need to track it.

Contact DCI and get on that." She threw her arm into the door's push bar.

"Where are you going?" Lundquist asked.

"It's time me and the old sheriff have a little tête-à-tête."

LILA HELD HER flashlight aloft and scanned up. "I'll be damned."

Meyer splashed around on the edge of the stream. "Regan was dumped up there. But how do you get up and down from there without climbing gear?"

Swinging her light about, Lila let the beam fall on the tracks they had followed to this point. They disappeared into the streambed. "There has to be an outlet or a trail leading up that we're not aware of."

Her Motorola crackled. "Dayne, report?"

She jerked it free of her duty belt and cued it. "Fontaine, I'm at the base of the ravine where we found Regan. Meyer and I are going to check this area out to see if there's a way to get up and down from the road to here."

"It's getting too dark for that. We'll have to come back in the morning and look. We'll start up top."

She checked her watch. It was nearly five, and the dark was getting stronger. "Fine. Do you have anything?"

A radio squawk made her flinch. "You could say we did."

Her stomach skipped.

"Put these coordinates in your GPS and head this way." Fontaine rattled off numbers that Meyer logged into the ATV's GPS. "Be careful. There are some deep holes and breaks in the ground that the side-by-side will get stuck in."

"Roger that."

She and Meyer loaded up and crawled through the timber at a reasonable pace, avoiding the holes and crevices. After twenty minutes of driving, she spotted the four-wheelers' headlights. Meyer parked the ATV to the left of one four-wheeler and directed the lights on the structure before them.

Exiting the side-by-side, Lila let out a whistle.

Rafe and Joel appeared out the dark, both men armed.

"What is this?" she asked Rafe as approached her.

"Some sort of meth lab." He directed the beam of his flashlight at the top of the building. The beam glanced off the mesh material stretched over it. "They used a camo netting to disguise the whole thing from the sky. A way to keep it undetected even in the winter when the foliage is gone."

Lila blew air through her mouth. "Sheriff is not going to be happy about this."

"But we found the source for our drug problem."

"Do we know who's been using it?"

Joel walked past her with a pair of bolt cutters. "We're about to find out."

"Can we just enter without a warrant or anything?" Meyer asked. "I mean, it just looks like a regular building. Nothing says meth lab."

"Except for the pile of empty propane tanks in the back and the equipment inside," Fontaine said.

"It actually has a window?" Lila asked.

"Not just one but three. They probably figured no one

would find it and they needed some natural light. And, Meyer, if we don't know who uses it, who are we going to serve a warrant to?"

"In the case of a drug situation, I don't think a judge will care," Lila added.

Meyer shrugged. "I'm just saying, we're treading on shaky ground here."

A snap of metal drew the three of them to Joel. Flashlights poised on the sliding doors, Joel dragged the heavy chain out of the loops and yanked one door open. It slid on well-oiled hinges, not making a sound. How convenient for subterfuge.

All four entered cautiously, Lila arming herself as they went. She watched Joel closely, impressed with his quick sweep of the area before walking over to a bank of switches.

"Prepare your eyes," he warned and flipped the switches.

Light flooded the building. Blinking past the sudden change, Lila felt her jaw drop.

"Holy hell," Meyer muttered.

"Someone has deep, deep pockets." Rafe nudged a bank of glass beakers, connected to a sophisticated maze of tubes and burners.

This was no run-of-the-mill, backwoods doublewide meth lab. Above them was a state-of-the-art ventilation system, keeping the fumes from the cooking process away from the chefs. In a corner to their left were four stacks of boxes. Lila inched closer to read the stamped sides. Lighter fluid, pseudoephedrine, iodine crystals, rubbing alcohol, and hydrogen peroxide, all the base components for meth. And boxed, no less. Someone certainly had deep pockets to gain access to boxed ingredients before they hit the stores. "It's like we stepped into an episode of *Breaking Bad*," Meyer said.

"I think this is more sophisticated than that." She walked past a table with an open cardboard box. "We've got Tyvek suits over here. And masks with ventilators."

"Did they happen to label their names in them?" Rafe asked.

She held up one. "Nope."

Joel cleared his throat. "Um, you should come see this."

The other three wandered over to his position in front of a shiny metal door.

"Oh my God," Lila said, her gaze meeting Rafe's. She dug out a glove and donned it. She tugged on the handle; the latch popped and a blast of cold air escaped as she pulled it open.

Among the cold food items, stacks of metal racks, and cases of beverages and pills, the body lay in a fetal position.

"Meyer, it's time to call the sheriff."

CHAPTER TWENTY-SIX

H E WAS RIGHT where she expected him to be. On his throne, surveying his kingdom.

Elizabeth weaved her way through the bodies of The Watering Hole's Friday night crowd. Marnie was nowhere in sight, which meant no detour from Elizabeth's objective. And that objective was sipping his whiskey, watching her advance.

"Well, if it isn't our illustrious sheriff. Sit, have a drink with me." He set the glass tumbler on the table and smiled.

"I'll pass on the drink." She grabbed a chair from an empty table nearby and tossed it backrest-up against the table, then straddled it. "But I'll sit."

A salt and pepper brow lifted. "The news has been interesting the past few days."

"It has at that. And yet, wherever I turn, your name keeps coming up."

He lifted the whiskey bottle and poured a finger in his tumbler. "Does it?" The bottle *thunk*ed down on the table. "Wonder why that is?"

"Yes, I do wonder." Elizabeth adjusted her seat, stacking her arms on the top of the chair. "Daniel Kauffmann."

"What about him?"

"How did he die?"

Sheehan calmly sipped, his cold eyes staying on Elizabeth.

"Maybe the better question should be, why did he die?"

Staring inside the glass, he swirled the liquor. "You know how he died. You have the reports." His gaze flicked up to Elizabeth. "And there is no why. It was a tragic accident."

"Ma firmly believes that it was not an accident."

"She's a mother who can't get past her grief and wants to lay blame at someone's feet instead of facing the facts."

"And what facts are those?"

One corner of Sheehan's mustache lifted. "That she's a terrible mother and her children are nothing more than the trailer trash she brought them up as."

"Harsh."

"Truth." He leaned forward. "You've stepped into a dark world, Sheriff. If it's not your speed . . .?" He swept his hand across the table as he sat back. "Well, you could always relinquish your position."

"Not on your life." Elizabeth straightened. "What would lead her to think Pratt Meyer has anything to do with Daniel's death?"

Silence met her inquiry.

"What is your connection to the Meyer and Kauffmann feud?"

More silence.

"You're just full of answers, aren't you?"

With a smile, Sheehan brought up the tumbler once more.

"Neva McKinnley was killed."

The glass stalled. His smile faded and the flinty look in

his eyes turned dark. "How?"

Vindictive, greedy, arrogant, and a dirty cop all best described Kelley Sheehan, but the crooked man had a soft spot for people like Neva. Elizabeth had spied him assisting some of the long-term residents of Eckardt County by bringing them meals or groceries or even providing a ride to their doctor appointments. Whether it had been for selfish gain or actual kindness, no one but Kelley knew.

"Someone was invited into her home last night, and as payback for her hospitality, threw her down her basement steps. Broken neck and cranial fracture leading to a brain hemorrhage killed her. God only knows how long she lay at the bottom of the steps before succumbing to her injuries."

His tumbler slammed onto the tabletop. "Enough."

Elizabeth blinked at him.

"I won't play your game, Elizabeth." He gathered his bottle and glass and stood. "You wanted this job, and you got it."

"Yes, I got it. As I promised during my campaign, I will expose the corruption left unchecked all those years." She stood, meeting him eye-to-eye. "You will answer for your crimes, Kelley. And I will be the one to make certain of that."

"Sheriff."

Sheehan's eyes flicked to her right, and then he smirked. "Duty calls." He exited his alcove.

Elizabeth turned to Lundquist. "What is it?"

"We have another crime scene."

JOEL ARRIVED AT the edge of the timber on his four-wheeler.

"What are you doing here?" Damn it. First, dealing with Sheehan's nonanswers. And now this. Joel was not supposed to be here.

He idled the engine and rose up on the running board. "Simmer down, Ellie. Rafe asked to use the ATVs."

"And you felt the need to blackmail him by letting you come along."

"Right now, you have a major homicide scene to process. Picking a fight with me is the last thing that needs to happen." He patted the seat behind him. "Get on and let's go. Brent can come back and switch with Kyle."

Lundquist, standing next to the squad car, waved her on. Fitzgerald was supposed to come this way and stand guard. DCI would be here as soon as they could, but it sounded like that wouldn't happen until morning.

Anger spiking through her, she mounted the four-wheeler behind her ex. Joel eased down between her thighs, and kicked the throttle into high, then swung the ATV around and back into the timber. Elizabeth tried to maintain her balance, but the constant rocking and weaving forced her to grab on to Joel's waist.

"You don't have to go so fast," she yelled over the sound of the engine and the whip of the trees as they blew past.

"I'm not going that fast. Besides, you need to get there."

"This is all kinds of not legal for you to be involved with this."

"Consider me an honorary deputy."

She pinched his side.

"Careful, Sweetness. We don't need an accident."

"I don't care if you have more expertise than all of my deputies combined. I can't afford to have a lawyer destroy evidence at the scene if it was compromised by a civilian."

"I won't get in the way."

"I'm holding you to that."

He jumped the four-wheeler over a divot in the earth and rooster-tailed debris from the ground. Adrenaline surged through Elizabeth's veins. Such a macho display. Yet no matter how old she got, she still loved the thrill of action. She was the crazy woman still climbing onto the wildest rollercoaster rides and throwing her hands skyward, screaming for the thrill of it.

Moments later, Joel slowed the ATV and pulled into the square of light spilling from the open bay doors of the Morton shed. He parked the four-wheeler beside its mate and killed the engine. Joel swung his leg over the handlebars and hopped off first, holding out his hand for Elizabeth. Sighing, she took it and allowed him to help her off the four-wheeler.

Leaving him sitting on the ATV, she strode to the open bay doors. Elizabeth came to a hard stop at the edge of the cement flooring.

"Are you freaking kidding me?"

Deputy Dayne turned.

"What the hell is this?"

Covering her mouth, but not before she caught the smile her deputy tried to hide, Dayne cleared her throat. "Umm, well, it's a meth lab."

"I can see that." Elizabeth gestured at the rows of cooking equipment. "This is not your typical meth lab. Those are usually in mobile trailers. Or run-down houses. Abandoned buildings."

"Yeah, typically." Lila hooked her thumbs on her duty belt. "It seems whoever has been cooking the meth here made major, and expensive, upgrades. This is high-grade stuff. Someone has invested a lot of capital behind this."

"Who has that kind of money? No one around here would be able to invest in a facility of this caliber."

"This whole place would beg to differ." Lila jabbed her thumb toward the back of the building. "Sheriff, you need to see this."

She led Elizabeth to the part of the building where Meyer and Rafe were standing guard beside a closed shiny metal door.

Lila gripped Meyer's shoulder. "Head back to the cars and wait for the ME. Make sure we have a way to get the body back there."

The younger deputy nodded and headed off to do Lila's bidding. Elizabeth tamped down the golden bubble expanding in her chest. She'd made the right choice in appointing Lila Dayne.

"Keep that up, and he's going to be working with you a lot."

Pulling on a glove, Lila shrugged. "He's eager to learn."

"He's clicking with you."

Rafe made a disturbed noise in his throat. Elizabeth swung a glare his way.

"You and I are going to have a long discussion about your choices."

"I'm no more happy about having to grovel at Joel's

feet," Rafe remarked. "Besides, I'd rather he be here than someone else. At least we know he can keep his mouth shut."

Leave it to Rafe to hit the nail on the head. She could be angry until the cows came home about Joel being here, but he could be trusted to stay mum about the whole ordeal, and his involvement. He wasn't a secret Delta operative for the fun of it.

Lila popped the handle on the door and swung it open. Cold air hit Elizabeth full in the face.

"Could this have been where Regan's body was held?"

"It's a possibility." Lila pointed inside the walk-in cooler.

Elizabeth entered the cooler and pulled up short when she spotted the body. "Who is he?"

"We don't know," Rafe said.

Rubbing her forehead, Elizabeth studied the young man curled in the fetal position. "He's going to be fun to get out of here and into the ME's van."

"Dr. Remington-Thorpe might have a good idea on how to accomplish that," Lila said.

"Do you think he's been dead as long as Regan?"

"Maybe longer. Maybe shorter. It's going to be hard to tell."

Groaning, Elizabeth about-faced and exited the cooler. "Both of you get on finding out who he is." An idea hit Elizabeth. "Deputy Dayne, get a photo of his face and track down Dillon Reed. See if this was the man he saw in the car with Maya."

"Worth a shot. We might want to check with the Wagners too."

"I'll do that," Elizabeth said. "They were supposed to

meet with me in the morning." She grimaced. "Crap, what time is it?"

Rafe checked his watch. "Seven thirty."

"Well, county council is going to be mad I didn't show up."

"Let 'em," Lila said, taking her glove off. "We have more pressing matters."

"Knock, knock."

Rolling her eyes, Elizabeth stalked out to the middle of the building. "Joel, you're not supposed to be anywhere near this building."

"I get that, Ellie, but you have a visitor."

No one was with Joel. Elizabeth scowled. "Where are they?"

He beckoned her outside. Stalking out of the building, she followed him to the darkened edges of the timber. He held up a pair of binoculars with night vision.

"Look a bit to the north."

She did, scanning the horizon until her sights caught what he pointed out. A figure lingered near an indescribable shape. A vehicle of some sort. Elizabeth tried to focus the binoculars to get a clearer image, but it didn't work.

"I can't make out who and what is there." She lowered the binos and held them out to Joel. "Get it to look better."

"That's as good as it gets."

"What is it?" Lila asked.

"Someone is out there watching us, but I can't make out who it is."

"Then we go get him," Rafe said.

"It's too far away. By the time you'd get there they'll be

long gone." Joel lifted the binos. "They can see us, and they know we see them. Whoever it is picked a good spot to stay unnoticeable."

"It's probably someone involved with running this meth operation." Elizabeth turned back to the Morton building. "And they're going to alert the big man in charge. They'll pack up shop and move somewhere else."

"They might already have another lab squirreled away somewhere else in the county or in the next," Joel pointed out. "You do remember how much of the land is made up of timber and state parks."

"I'm well aware of what's in my county, Joel. Deputies Dayne and Fontaine, when Lundquist gets back here, bag and tag everything we can. Once Olivia takes over the body, we can begin the process of identifying him." She faced her ex. "Are they still there?"

"Looks like they're leaving." He lowered the binos. "You need to contact Iowa's drug task force for this."

She sighed. "In the morning." She wagged her hands at her deputies. "We've got a long night ahead of us. Let's get going."

CHAPTER TWENTY-SEVEN

Day 4: Saturday

L ILA AND THE other deputies were running on fumes by the time DCI arrived. After a drawn-out argument with her ex-husband, who left only when she pleaded with him to go take care of Bentley, the sheriff had sent everyone off on their respective errands.

Lila and Meyer made a beeline for the nearest gas station to fill up the car and grab their own refueling needs. Once they had that accomplished, Lila set him on the path to find Dillon Reed. They were grungy, dead tired, and both badly needed a shower, but duty trumped personal hygiene.

"I know where we can find him on a Saturday morning," Meyer said as he pointed the car toward Juniper.

"In a bed somewhere sleeping off whatever fun he had the night before?" Lila bit into her hot egg and bacon on an English muffin.

"He wishes." Meyer tore into his breakfast sandwich.

Washing down her food with a gulp of milk, Lila swiped a napkin across her mouth. "You going to tell me? Or do I have to guess?"

He smiled. "Maybe I'll just take you there and you can wait."

"Meanie."

"I aim to please."

While he drove to town, they finished their meal, followed up with a less-than-stellar cup of gas station sludge. Meyer passed the just-waking retail district of downtown Juniper, waving at a few store owners who had flipped their signs to open, hung a hard right past the courthouse, and headed straight for the north side of town.

Lila double-checked her battery level on her phone. It would make it a while longer before going critical.

Meyer directed the car through a rougher neighborhood. The majority of the buildings were from before the turn of the twentieth century. Some of them looked ready to cave in, while others showed signs that the citizens were trying to make a go of keeping them up and running. Most of the area homes and business were darkened, the owners not ready to rise and shine, sleeping off their preferred form of poison.

Outside of town limits, Meyer slowed the car and turned onto a gravel road. He drove a mile before turning onto a gravel lane. The lane led them to a set of barns and a large fenced-in pen. A handful of horses milled about in the enclosure, steam rising from their backs in the cold morning air. The animals lifted their heads and watched as the squad car approached.

Meyer parked next to a barn with an open door and cut the engine. He nodded at the building. "He'll be in there mucking stalls."

Lila glanced at the barn and then back to Meyer. "He works as a stable hand?"

"He doesn't have a choice unless he wants to get a whipping he'd like to forget. His father owns the property and people board their horses here. But his father is rarely around."

"What does the father do?"

"A little of this, a little of that. Mostly he drives semis. On the road all the time. Dillon Sr. isn't trifled with. He might act like a slacker, but he expects more out of his kid."

Lila grunted. "Not how the sheriff and the principal made it sound yesterday."

"The Reeds are a take 'em as you see 'em."

"I'll say." She grabbed the handle. "Be ready to grab him if he makes a run for it. He tried to outrun me yesterday."

"I doubt he does it again today, now that he knows who you are."

"Right," she said as she exited the car.

The horses tracked her progress across the barnyard. When she stepped into the open doorway, they continued on with whatever it was horses did.

Lila was greeted by the pungent odor of manure, urine, and the sweet scent of dried grass. She listened for signs of Dillon. It came with the scrape of metal against wood followed by the sight of debris flying out of a stall and into a wheelbarrow sitting in the middle of the aisle. She wandered to the stall and jumped back as poop and soiled wood shavings sailed in front her.

Peeking around the edge of the stall wall, she found Dillon with his back to her, earbuds in, and shovel in hand. Staying back out of the way in case he flung a pile at her, Lila waited for him to turn. Dillon lifted the laden scoop, turned, and looked up as he went to toss his new load. He saw her and yelled. The shovelful fell short of its target, flopping on the stall floor and on the aisle.

Yanking out his earbuds, he glared at her. "What the hell? What are you doing here?"

Baring her canines, Lila inched forward and leaned against the stall wall, blocking any escape attempt. "Thought I'd check in on you after our little escapade yesterday."

"I hurt all over. Thank you for that, by the way. My old man sees all those bruises, he's gonna think I got into a fight."

"You only have yourself to blame." She cocked her head. "Is he going to be mad if you were in a fight?"

"I'm a grown man. I don't have to answer any of your questions. You saw me, so leave." He went to put the earbud back in.

"Hold on there, Dillon. I also came because I need you to look at a picture."

His gaze narrowed. "A picture of what?"

"A guy. We want to know if this was the man you saw in the car with Maya Wagner."

Sighing, Dillon draped the earbud over his shoulder and leaned the shovel against the wall. "Fine." He scratched the side of his nose, leaving a brown streak.

Lila pulled out her phone and unlocked it. "You like horses?"

"Yeah. Used to ride a lot."

She glanced at him. "Why'd you stop?"

His face flushed and he looked away. Lila felt certain she wasn't going to get an answer out of him. With his head lowered, he scuffed the toe of his boot into the exposed dirt floor. "My mom got real sick, and there wasn't any time anymore."

What she gathered was that he lost the joy of it after his mom died—the hurt little boy expression said it all—and riding horses was something Mom used to love to do.

Lila opened the up-close photo of the mystery man in the meth lab walk-in cooler. "A word of advice."

His features scrunched.

"Start riding again. It's what she would have wanted."

He blinked at her, then shrugged. "You gonna show it to me?"

Turning the phone, she held it up. "Look familiar?"

His eyes widened. "Yeah. That's the guy I saw."

Well, that ruled out their John Doe being dead before Regan. This had been someone Maya Wagner knew well enough to get in the car with and leave the school. Maybe the sheriff would have better luck getting an ID on him from the Wagners.

"Thanks, Dillon. I'll let you get back to work."

When she stepped out into the cold morning, she glanced back and spotted Dillon watching her. She saluted him and left.

In the car, she shivered. "Brrr."

"What did he say?"

"It's the guy he saw in the car with Maya. Let's hope the sheriff has some luck with the Wagners." She adjusted the vent. "Start this baby up. I'm cold."

Meyer backed out of the spot and drove down the lane. "I forgot to ask. Did you and Lundquist find any tracks from our mystery watcher?"

"Nothing to distinguish who it was and what they were

driving. The path they chose was on purpose; it wouldn't leave any trace behind."

"Wish I knew who it could have been."

"You and everyone out there last night." Lila lifted her cup of sludge and grimaced. "Is there any place we can get better coffee? And use a restroom?"

"Close by?"

She gave Meyer a sidelong look. "Yes, close by."

He grinned. "I'll see what's open on this side of town. There won't be any good coffee."

"I can wait for that."

Meyer located a more respectable convenience store with a restroom inside.

She leaned down. "If they have good coffee, you want some?"

"I doubt it, but you can try."

After dumping their trash in a bin, she hurried inside. A quick scan of the store and she found the restroom. Giving the cashier a wave, she bolted for the women's. Business done, hands scrubbed up, she peeked at her reflection and winced. She looked like she'd taken a fast pitch to the face from a Cubs pitcher. Splashing some water against her cheeks, she dried her face and left the restroom.

She browsed the cooler section—they carried two flavors of frappuccino. Did Meyer like cold coffee? She peered around the shelves in the middle of the floor and saw the coffee counter.

Hot would warm them up.

Lila abandoned the frappuccinos. But was she willing to chance the quality of a real coffee?

A crack rent the air.

Lila's hand dropped to her sidearm as she spun to the door, sliding her weapon from the holster.

"Oh my God!" the cashier screeched, ducking down.

Running to the door, she slammed through and burst into the lot. Her head on a swivel, she caught sight of the backend of a small white pickup and bolted out to the street to see if she could read the license. If the damn thing had one.

"Meyer?" she called out, still squinting at the vanishing truck.

No answer. She turned and stiffened.

Meyer's window was down, and he was flung back against the backrest, mouth gaping like a fish out of water.

"Meyer!"

She holstered her sidearm as she ran to the car and ripped the door open. A to-go coffee cup fell out and hit the pavement, the lid popping off and spewing coffee all over Lila's pant legs. Blood dribbled from his mouth.

Lila grasped his face. "Meyer! Look at me."

Color leached from his features, and his eyes rolled. "Help," he groaned and then coughed, blood sprayed from his mouth, hitting Lila in the face.

"Shit!" She fisted his coat and dragged him out of the car, grabbing his shoulder radio as she lowered him to the pavement. "Officer down!" she screamed. "Officer down! We are at a gas station on the north side of Juniper. Send medical!"

Letting the handset fall, she ripped his coat open, pausing as her fingers met liquid warmth. The lower half of his uniform top was soaked in blood. "Oh-God, oh-God!"

He'd been gut shot. The shooter had managed to avoid his Kevlar. Lila reared back, pressing her hands to her mouth. What did she do? If she didn't do something, Brent was going to die.

Lila scrambled onto her feet and toppled inside the car, looking for anything to help stem the flow of blood. Where the hell was the first aid kit?

"Lila! What gas station?" Georgia's voice penetrated her brain.

Falling out of the car, Lila grabbed up the radio. "I don't know what street. We're at . . ." She stared at the sign above her. "Casey's?"

"Hang on. I know where that is."

The radio slipped from her hands and cracked against the red-speckled pavement. Brent's head rolled her way, and he pawed for her hand.

"It . . . hurts," he slurred.

Squeezing her eyes shut cut off the wet heat building. Lila grasped his and squeezed. "I know." God, she knew how bad it hurt. The fire ripping through her flesh. The hot gush of blood. God, the agony. Black ringing her vision. A voice echoing through her mind. She couldn't remember everything, but she knew it had been Cecil, begging her to hold on. Not die.

Meyer coughed more blood. His body convulsed.

"Brent, help is coming." She dragged his torso into her lap and clung to him. "Just don't die."

CHAPTER TWENTY-EIGHT

ELIZABETH AND RAFE ensured the meth lab was locked down after DCI finished and left, then set up cameras to hopefully catch someone coming back here. But Elizabeth doubted anyone would return if their mysterious visitor had passed the word along that the lab was compromised.

"Now what?" Rafe asked as they walked back to their vehicles.

"Have you made any progress on looking into Ma?"

"Little. Neva's death, getting Joel to agree to let us use the ATVs, and last night have eaten up my time."

"Get on that. Today." Elizabeth rubbed her eyes. "I'm going to check on Bentley and make sure Joel hasn't decided to play house."

"Then what?"

"Pay a visit to the Wagners." She turned. "Rafe, I'm calmed down now, but you bringing Joel into this would have been a nice heads-up."

He grunted. "You were married to the man for how long? He was never going to stay out of it."

"One day Joel's going to learn he can't be lord over all." She grasped the SUV's handle. "If I can, I'm going to catch a nap in my office after I talk to the Wagners."

Rafe's hand covered hers and stopped her from opening

the door. "I don't think you should drive."

She faced him. "I can't leave my vehicle here."

"You're in no shape to drive. Let me call Fitzgerald and Lundquist down here to pick it up."

"Rafe, stop coddling me. It's not going to look good to the voters if you have to bail me out. Like I can't stand on my own two feet."

"Ellie, no one will fault you if you're exhausted, which you are. It's been a trying week."

She scowled. "This is crap Joel would pull on me. I'm not a weak woman in need of rescuing when things get rough."

"No, but you are human. A human who is sleep deprived, and it will get you killed."

She slapped the side of her fist against his chest. "Stop it. Now."

As she went to repeat her beating, he grabbed her wrist and ceased her movements. "Stubbornness got nobody anywhere but hurt."

"Speak for yourself," she snapped.

The proximity to his body, his musky scent, and her weakened will was playing hell on her mind. What was it Marnie had told her yesterday? *Time to screw Rafe.*

What the hell.

Rolling up on the balls of her feet, Elizabeth smashed her lips into his. There was the barest hint of stiffening from him, more of shock than hesitation, and then Rafe returned the kiss with a ferocity Elizabeth craved. He backed her against the SUV and devoured her mouth.

From inside the cab her radio screeched. Elizabeth ignored it. By God, she was finally kissing Rafe and nothing was stopping her now.

Rafe's radio squawked, and the voice penetrated their heavy panting.

"Officer down!"

Pushing Rafe off her body, Elizabeth ripped his radio from his shoulder. "Georgia?"

"It's Brent, Ellie. Brent's been hurt."

Her legs wobbled, and she started to slide. Rafe's strong hands caught her and stabilized her.

"Not Brent," she whispered.

He took the radio. "Georgia, where?"

"An ambulance is on scene. Deputy Dayne is with him. I sent Lundquist to help her." Georgia's voice cracked. "Just go to the hospital."

Rafe grabbed Elizabeth's hand and dragged her to his Charger. "It'll be all right." He opened the door and ushered her inside. "He'll make it," he said before closing the door.

Elizabeth stared ahead, her brain playing over every moment she'd had with Brent.

He couldn't die.

THE CHARGER CAME to a squealing halt outside the hospital entrance. Elizabeth bailed from the car. Rafe left the car parked where it was, lights flashing, and followed her inside.

She'd made it halfway down the hall.

"Ellie!" Olivia rushed from a side hall toward Elizabeth.

"Olivia, what happened?"

Olivia latched on to Elizabeth's arm and escorted her down the hall. "He was shot. I don't know any more than that. I've got Lila in a room. She's in shock."

Elizabeth looked over her shoulder. Rafe was following. Assured he was near, she let Olivia lead her.

"Has anyone told Sophie?"

"Georgia is calling her. No doubt she will be here quickly."

But would Pratt come as well? His not coming would be better for all involved.

Olivia took Elizabeth to the walk-in clinic and straight to a closed door. Pushing it open, she stepped in. "Lila, the sheriff is here."

Lila lifted her head. Sucking air at the sight before her, Elizabeth hesitated. Dried blood war-painted her deputy's face, stained her hands and clothing. Her eyes revealed the shattered woman inside.

"Is she hurt?" Elizabeth asked Olivia.

The doctor shook her head.

Elizabeth gestured for Rafe to remain outside. He nodded and took sentry. Sighing, she moved over to the exam table and sat next to Lila. She laid her hand over Lila's shaking one, and stayed that way until the shaking stopped.

From her post by the sink, Olivia waited.

"Is he going to live?" Lila's voice, small and raspy, was like shards of glass to Elizabeth.

She met Olivia's troubled gaze. The doctor shrugged. When she wasn't the one in the operating room, how would she know the outcome? Even in the best of circumstances, it was hard to know.

Elizabeth squeezed Lila's hand. "Brent is a fighter. Dominic is the best surgeon we have."

Slipping her hand free, Lila tucked it under her arm.

"Lila, what happened?"

Staring at the wall, the deputy remained locked up. Rafe's warnings trickled through Elizabeth's mind. Had Lila met her breaking point and this was the outcome? A shell of a police officer?

"I was in the gas station. I had to use the restroom. I was looking for coffee for us, and then I heard the shot." She faltered but kept her gaze zeroed on the wall. "I ran outside."

Lila squeezed her eyes shut and bowed her head. She sat that way, taking deep breaths. Elizabeth feared she'd go light-headed and pass out. As she reached for Lila, the deputy's head came up and her eyes flared open.

"It was a white Chevy pickup. It had a huge dent in the tailgate and looked like it should have been in the junkyard. There were two people in the cab. No license plate. Bald tires. Bits of a bumper sticker, red, blue, green. The bumper hung off the backend, like it was ready to drop off."

Elizabeth gaped at the details rolling from Lila. Suddenly the woman's head snapped in her direction. The shattered look that had met her entering the room was gone.

"We need a BOLO on that vehicle."

"I'll get it out as soon as I walk out of here. What else can you recall?"

Lila went on, everything spilling out in crisp, clinical detail. She spoke as if she were writing her report, detaching from the moment. Elizabeth sensed under Lila's words, she was trying not to rehash the fear her own attack had left on her soul. Between this incident and her actions at Neva McKinnley's house, Lila was trying to piece her life and her career back together.

It had been a good decision to add her to the department force.

Elizabeth gripped Lila's shoulder. "You did good, Deputy Dayne."

She shook her head. "I shouldn't have left him alone in the car."

"We can't fight the call of nature. By what you're describing, I don't think the shooter would have stopped at Brent. Did he say who did it?"

Lila shook her head. "I was too worried about saving him to even ask." She lifted her hands as if to rub her face, but halted, staring at the dried blood on them. "Why shoot him in the gut?" she whispered.

A knock on the door kept Elizabeth from answering.

Rafe poked his head in. "Lundquist is here."

"Good. Rafe, we need a BOLO on a white Chevy pickup with a big dent in the tailgate, no plates, two armed suspects."

"On it," he said and disappeared.

Lundquist stepped into the doorway and entered when Elizabeth beckoned him forward. He too had streaks of blood on his uniform. "Sheriff, I've got the area around the shooting taped off and the car is on a wrecker headed for the department. DCI and the PD investigator are on the scene. I left Fitzgerald to stand watch."

"Did you get a coffee cup that came out of the car?" Lila asked, her voice firm.

"I did, left it with the DCI team. I'm doubtful there will be any prints aside from Meyer's, but we might get lucky."

Lila stood suddenly. "I want to go over that car."

"Whoa." Elizabeth came up. "Deputy, you've had a shock. You need to take some time."

"No. Don't make me sit this one out. I owe that much to Brent."

"I know that, and I respect it. But I really must insist."

"Sheriff, if I don't get back out there, that gives Brent's shooter more of a chance to disappear. I'm done running."

Her statement had more meaning than the other two would ever realize.

A smart sheriff would bench her deputy. Would tell her to rest and look at this with fresh eyes. But Elizabeth's intuition warned if she did that, she'd have a rogue deputy on her hands, and that was not good.

"At least go home, clean up, and put on a fresh uniform. Lundquist will take you there and then to the department."

"Thank you, Ellie," Lila whispered.

"Go."

The two left.

Olivia shook her head. "I hope you don't come to regret that."

"I have a lot of regrets in my life, but listening to my gut has never steered me wrong."

CHAPTER TWENTY-NINE

THERE WAS BLOOD on the driver's side, but not as much as Lila expected. Blood droplets from Brent's cough dotted the interior, but most of that had hit her in the face.

She swept her flashlight over the cab, scanning the passenger side. Looking for what? She didn't have a clue. The surgeon had been given word that the bullet had not exited Brent's body. Once they had the piece of shrapnel, they'd have a better idea of what type of gun was used.

Lila eased out of the squad car and straightened. She'd heard that shot. It was a crack. Loud enough to break the sound barrier. Small gun. Small caliber? A pistol.

"What?"

Lundquist's question jolted her. She drew in a breath and shrugged. Backing from the open door, she closed it.

"Did you remember something?" he asked.

"Not really. Mulling over what I know." She angled her body and lifted her gun arm. "I don't think the shooter was inside the cab of the truck when they pulled the trigger."

"Outside? Standing next to Brent?"

"Why else would he have the window down? And he had a cup of coffee. I dumped all the trash from our quick breakfast when I went into the gas station."

Lundquist moved out of her way as she sidestepped closer to the car. "What you're suggesting is that it was someone he knew. Someone he wouldn't suspect of malice."

"And that's pretty much everyone in this town. The entire county." Lila thrust her shoulders back as she realized she might be in the right position for the shot. "Shooter stood here." She stood with her frontside facing the car, her shooting arm just above the side mirror, acting like she was walking away. "The shooter knew how to avoid his vest."

"Why not in the head?" Lundquist stood next to her. "If you wanted to kill him"—he placed his finger right against her temple—"it would be easy to do it here."

Lila narrowed her eyes. "I don't think they wanted to kill him outright." She pulled Lundquist's hand down. "Or they didn't have the stomach for it."

"If it was someone Meyer knew, he was probably friendly with them. But it doesn't answer the question of why target him? Do you think it has anything to do with what's been going on?"

She turned on her heel and paced away from the car. Brent Meyer had a family legacy and a father who despised him. Could his father have been the shooter? Lila shook her head. If Pratt Meyer had it out for his son, he wouldn't have waited this long. No, this was something different. What was it Meyer had said yesterday in a fit of anger? That they should look real hard at Ma Kauffmann.

"Lundquist, what do you know about the Kauffmann and Meyer feud?"

"Are you thinking a Kauffmann did this? That's far reaching, Dayne. That feud has never resorted to violence. Not once in all their history."

"Who says it hasn't come to that point?"

"What would harming Meyer bring them? He and his father are estranged—there would be no gain. And I can't see Ma ever putting out that order. She might be a hard woman, but she'd never purposely kill someone."

"People change, Lundquist. They grow meaner and harder. She might have been pushed to the brink and decided this was how it had to go."

He shook his head. "Not likely. It's just not possible. Her dead husband, maybe, but that man wasn't working with a full load. Ma's the brains in that family."

"How did he die?"

"The story goes, he tried to play hardball with some punks that had moved into the area from Chicago. They didn't like his attitude and shot him." Lundquist scowled. "Speaking of which, I don't think Sheehan investigated that too hard. I read up on that in the papers, since it happened before my time in the department. Sheehan claimed the punks had skipped town and he had no details to go any further. Henry Kauffmann's death is technically still an open case."

"Is there an actual case file in the department?"

"We can find out."

As they headed back to the courthouse, Fontaine's Charger pulled into the parking lot. The deputy himself stepped out, alone.

"Where's the sheriff?" Lundquist asked.

"Meeting with DCI and PD at the gas station. What are you two doing?"

"Looking at some old case files," Lundquist said. "Hey,

do you remember when Henry Kauffmann died?"

"Yes? What does that have to do with Brent's shooting?" Fontaine asked.

"Probably more than we think," Lila said. "Inside, Fontaine, you can help us. After all, you're family."

"Only on Ma's side."

"All the better."

THEY FOUND ONE box with evidence on the Henry Kauffmann death, and together the three of them dug up a few more case files with connections to the Kauffmann family, per the sheriff's wishes, according to Fontaine. Lila hit on a juicy file with a connection to a Meyer family member, which she added to their growing pile.

"I can't believe Sheehan left this here for us to find," she said.

Fontaine dropped a folder into a full box. "When Elizabeth won the election, she didn't give him a chance to clear out."

"He was so mad. He was screaming at anyone who'd listen, which wasn't many. She even barred those deputies who were most loyal to him. They couldn't even touch his stuff," Lundquist added.

"Unfortunately, he kept anything that could have incriminated him out of the department. And files were scarce." Fontaine shoved the box back on the shelf from where it came. "Most of this stuff happened before his time. But those previous sheriffs were as bad as Sheehan."

And what did that say for the county as a whole if the people kept voting in corrupt sheriffs? Yet they had voted for Elizabeth Benoit. Perhaps the tide was swinging toward better?

"Let's take these upstairs and see what we have," Lila said, stacking her two boxes.

They carried their findings up to the department floor and under Georgia's watchful eye spread out the cases between their three desks.

"Any news from the hospital?" Lila asked.

Georgia shook her head. The old adage, no news was good news, fit perfectly here. But was it? The unknown was hell on the nerves. Lila slid a file onto a stack. She knew all too well that feeling.

How many times had the doctors hovered over her, refusing to divulge what they knew for fear of causing panic? She hated it then, and if the lack of news on Meyer continued, she would hate it again.

"Should we be leaving Fitzgerald out there to man everything alone?" Lundquist asked.

"He's not," Georgia said. "The sheriff asked for assistance from the state troopers."

Lila let a pile of folders slap onto her desktop. She tipped the empty box onto the floor and made room for more files.

"How do you want to do this?" Lundquist asked her. "What should we be looking for specifically?"

"Anything that ties Ma, her husband, or her family to criminal activity. If a Kauffmann name appears in any way, write it down. Is that what the sheriff was wanting, Fontaine?"

"For the most part."

"Let's get to work."

As they combed through the reports, Georgia kept them fueled. At one point, she joined Lila reading through a file, abandoning her forty minutes later to answer the phone.

"I'll let them know." Georgia set the handset on the receiver.

News. Had to be about Meyer. Lila's hands dampened.

"Brent's out of surgery." Georgia sank into her chair. "He's alive but critical. They have him in the ICU."

"Any more details?" Lila asked. She forcibly pried her fingers out of a fist.

"The sheriff said she'd relay that when she got here." Georgia massaged her forehead. "In all my years of dispatching, this has never happened."

Lila turned from the woman. How she wished that had been true for her. She could still hear his voice in her ear as he drove the blade into her body. *Hush, my darling.* Spreading her fingers wide over her abdomen, Lila gritted her teeth. He had taken much from her—her sanity would not be one more.

Her gaze flicked toward her fellow deputies, and she locked eyes with Lundquist. He glanced down, his forehead wrinkled. Aware of what she was doing, she jerked her hand from her body, and angled her back to him. Picking up another report, she flipped the file open, trying hard to ignore the sensation of his eyes drilling holes into her back.

Lila had a nearly empty page of notes after another half hour of work. Even the file she'd pulled on the Meyer family member was nothing more than a property dispute with another farmer whose cattle were breaking through the fence and destroying crops. Frustrated, she tossed the file into a box.

"Are you having any luck?" she asked her male counterparts.

Fontaine shook his head. Lundquist looked up from a report he was reading and paused. The whoosh of the outside door opening echoed down the hall, followed by the squeak of rubber on polished cement.

They all looked to the doorway as the sheriff entered.

"What is going on?" she demanded.

"We're doing what you asked," Fontaine said, slapping a file down on his desk. "And it's getting us nowhere."

"Not exactly," Lundquist piped up.

Benoit frowned. "Doing what I asked?"

Lila ignored her boss. "What do you have?"

Lundquist held up the open report in his hands. "I don't know if it's strong enough, but it's on Henry's death."

Abandoning her post, Lila joined him. She skimmed the report over his shoulder, until he pointed to the part he thought worth mentioning.

"Pratt Meyer was questioned about Henry's death?" Lila's head snapped up. "Why would he be questioned if gang members were the supposed killers?"

"Let me see that."

Lundquist handed over the report to Benoit. The sheriff read through, her features tightening.

"Because Ma threw Pratt under the bus." Benoit slapped the file shut. "She was deflecting the investigation away from her and her family. And Sheehan went along with it."

"What is her beef with Pratt Meyer?" Lila asked.

"There seem to be numerous reasons, but none make sense except to her." Benoit handed back the file. "I have something for you." She dug into her coat pocket and withdrew a plastic baggie she held out to Lila. Inside was a mushroomed bullet. "The bullet tore through his bowels. There was a lot of blood loss, but Dr. Thorpe did what he could for now without putting any more stress on Brent."

Lila took the baggie and stared at the stunted piece of lead. This small, almost insignificant thing had ripped through a man's body and left him hanging on for his life by a thread.

"If I had to hazard a guess, that looks like the remains of a twenty-two," Lundquist said.

Crumpling the baggie in her hand, Lila let it fall to her side. "Up close. They wanted to kill him."

"I want this bastard," Benoit said in a low voice.

Not as bad as Lila did.

"Sheriff," Georgia broke in, "the Wagners are here."

Benoit blinked. "I'll take them into my office."

"I want to be there," Lila said.

Benoit frowned. "Are you sure?"

"Yes."

CHAPTER THIRTY

"MR. AND MRS. Wagner, thank you for coming in. I'm sorry I had to ask this of you. Meeting at your home would have been more comfortable." Elizabeth closed her office door, gesturing at the two chairs. Lila had grabbed the extra from the bullpen.

As the couple sat, offering the typical platitudes of quite all right, and no trouble, Elizabeth took a position sitting on the corner of her desk. Lila had gingerly eased her body onto Bentley's chair.

"We have Maya's phone records from the last three months." Peter Wagner held out the half-inch thick stack. "And I was able to gain access to her app history. She had some we'd forbidden her to have, and we have no idea how she managed to get them on her phone and past all the firewalls we installed."

Elizabeth took the papers. "Today's teenagers are re-sourceful. They know how to do things we only dream of being able to do. Some of those apps can delete the history and we would have to get a warrant to even get access to that information. And if the company complied, it would be months before we got all that information." Months Eliza-beth wasn't about to risk in solving Maya's and Regan's deaths. She skimmed through the top sheet. Call and text history. "Did you see anything in here that indicated contact with Regan?"

"There's a few odd names and IDs that might be her, but we aren't certain." Mary fiddled with her hair. "I haven't connected with my sister. She could be on one of her binges and there's no finding her until she's ready and willing. Then there's the chance she doesn't care."

"As Regan's next of kin, we can release her to you."

"I'm afraid that might be the only option we have."

Elizabeth read through the next page. A new ID popped near the bottom of the page. Flipping to the third, she saw that it continued, and the contact with it grew in frequency. "Do you know if this Bandino45 was in contact with her before you moved from Illinois?"

Peter shook his head. "It's hard to say. Like we mentioned, the girls used to get prepaid phones and made all their contact that way."

"How did you keep her from doing that again?" Lila asked.

"Wasn't much we could do if she did get one," Peter said. "I haven't found one in her room if she did have one."

"Maya could have kept it with her, and her killer took it. The phone you said she did have is still missing," Elizabeth said.

"Is there any way you can track it by the GPS?" Mary asked.

"The techs with DCI are working on that," Lila said. She stood and joined Elizabeth next to her desk. "Best we can do is learn her movements before the phone was disabled."

"There has to be something you can tell from that." The

tone in Peter's voice was bordering on pleading.

How Elizabeth wished she could tell the couple more, but there just wasn't much to go on.

"Once the techs are done, we will," Lila assured them.

Obviously, her investigator knew or suspected something Elizabeth didn't.

"Mr. and Mrs. Wagner, may I show you a picture?" Lila asked, pulling out her cell phone.

The couple blinked at each other. Elizabeth listed a bit to the right. What was her deputy up to?

"I guess," Peter said.

Lila opened the image, angling her phone just enough for Elizabeth to see the photo of the mystery man from the cooler. Enlarging the image, Lila turned the phone to the couple.

"Do recognize this man?"

Peter took her phone and stared at the picture. "Yes." His gaze flicked up to the women. "This is Regan's boyfriend." He looked to his wife.

"I think his name was Robbie or Bobby. Something like that." Mary took the phone from her husband. "He's dead too, isn't he?"

"Unfortunately, he is." Lila took her phone back and closed out the photo gallery. "We learned from school security footage that he picked up Maya on the day she went missing. An eyewitness places him inside the car with Maya."

Peter cast a look at his wife. "It makes sense he's here. He followed Regan wherever she went. She had this weird pull on him."

Elizabeth crossed her arms and leaned back. Betting

woman that she was, she bet when the DNA came back on Robbie or Bobby it would match the sample from Regan's swab. They just needed to learn how he died and his real identity.

A knock on her door put everyone on pause.

"Yes?" Elizabeth called out.

Georgia poked her head in. "There's a call from the hospital on line one. You need to take this, Sheriff."

"If you'd follow me," Lila said and led the Wagners out of the office.

Once the door was closed, Elizabeth circled her desk and picked up the line. "Sheriff Benoit."

"Sheriff, this Israel. We need you to come down to the hospital."

"Has something happened with Brent?"

"Not yet. But there's a problem with the family."

"I understand. I'm on my way. Thank you, Israel."

"Just hurry."

She hung up and exited the office. "Georgia, I'm going back to the hospital." Her gaze swung to the remaining deputies. "Keep doing what you were doing."

"Ellie, what's wrong?" Rafe asked.

"Nothing to worry about." She headed for the hall. "Georgia, call Joel and have him give you an update on Bentley."

"Sheriff, do you need me to come?" Lila asked as she met her in the hall entrance.

"No. I've got it. You keep tracking down who would have a reason to shoot Brent. And why someone would want to kill three young people who had no connections to this community and a beloved teacher."

Lila saluted her.

Elizabeth hurried out of the building and to her SUV. Israel's meaning was loud and clear. Sophie Meyer may have very well reached her limit with her husband's animosity.

ISRAEL POINTED HER in the right direction, but the act was unnecessary as the raised voices echoing down the hall were indication enough for Elizabeth. Two security personnel barricading the hall parted when they spotted her coming, allowing her to pass. Their movements caught the attention of a nurse and Dr. Thorpe, who waved her forward.

"For the last time, Sophie, I won't allow it."

Elizabeth stepped into the doorway and grimaced.

"You gave up your right to make demands over our son the day you decided he was no longer a Meyer."

Wearing a long jean skirt and a white blouse under a tooled leather coat, Martha Kauffmann stood in front of the waiting room windows, watching the couple bicker.

Elizabeth sighed. Not the family drama she expected.

"Pratt. Sophie."

Her bark brought a halt to the verbal lashings. A corner lifted on Ma's mouth, her eyes sparking.

"Dr. Thorpe, are you allowing visitors?"

"For a short time."

"Please take Mr. Meyer to see his son."

Stunned, Pratt gaped at her. Angling her body, she gestured for him to follow the doctor. As he passed, he gave her a stilted nod. Once the two men and the nurse left, Elizabeth dismissed the security guards.

She crossed her arms and sized up the situation. "Ladies, would you mind explaining what this is all about?"

Sophie looked to Ma, then turned her back on Elizabeth. The mouthpiece of the pair stepped forward.

"It appears to be a simple thing, Ellie. Brent is family, and Sophie asked me to come. Since her daughters are out of state and Pratt—well, Pratt being Pratt, it only seemed fitting."

"Your relation to Sophie is more distant than, say, her relation to Rafe and Joel." Elizabeth stared into the woman's back. "Why not ask them to come?"

"The boys are otherwise occupied. I was available."

"Sophie, I'm asking you the questions, not her."

The distraught blonde faced Elizabeth but remained closemouthed. For all the spit and vinegar she spewed at her husband, she was reverting back to her submissive ways now?

Ma sighed. "She's been through the wringer, and Brent ain't out of the woods yet. Let her be."

How . . . Christian of her. This, coming from a woman who had been nothing but a flagrant thorn in the side of Pratt Meyer for years. Far as Elizabeth knew, not once had she ever lent a giving hand to the Meyers. And the same for them, even after Henry's and Daniel's deaths.

"You, above all people, know the distress your being here puts on Pratt." Elizabeth stepped toward the Kauffmann matriarch. "And you relished the chance to poke that beast."

"I relish nothing. In times of tragedy, I take the high road. Family is family, no matter the distance or the estrangement. When I lost my Daniel, Sophie was there for me."

Now that revelation Elizabeth found suspect. Why would Sophie support Ma when the older woman had it out for her husband every chance she got? And was Sophie aware that Ma was still throwing around accusations against Pratt for Daniel's death?

This whole thing made no sense.

Unless there was an ulterior motive on Ma's part. Elizabeth didn't put it past the woman. Inching closer to Ma, she lifted a finger to the other woman's face. "I don't know what game you're playing, but I'll see that it ends."

Ma glared at the appendage, and her features tightened. "Fine words coming from you."

From the corner of her eye, Elizabeth caught movement. She looked over her shoulder. Hovering in the doorway, features strained, Stephen glanced from his mother to Elizabeth.

"Mama?"

"It's all right, baby. The sheriff was just asking me a few questions," the old crow croaked.

Elizabeth backed from Ma. Stephen's taut expression melted into a lopsided smile.

His gaze tracked to Elizabeth and settled there. "Mama, we need to depart," he said, his tone more cultured than that of his family.

Speaking of which. "Where is Karl?"

Ma passed Elizabeth to join her son. "He's working. Like a good boy."

Karl, a good boy? Only in the eye of the beholder.

"Sophie, dear, Stephen has a meetin' he needs to be at. I'll be back quick as a flash if you need me."

"Thank you, Martha."

With parting smirk, Ma left. Stephen right behind her.

Elizabeth's taut muscles slackened, and she nearly collapsed. Was this what Joel referred to as situational awareness fatigue? An adrenaline crash of sorts after a tense confrontation. She didn't like it.

Her refereeing skills no longer needed, it was time to move on. "Sophie, I will speak with Pratt. Please avoid any more clashes with him." She quit the waiting room.

Her forced march slowed the farther she got from the waiting room. The last twenty-four plus hours had been hellish, and the next twenty-four did not look any better. She needed sleep, she needed peace, and she wanted everyone to stop finding ways to drive her batshit crazy.

Rounding the corner, Elizabeth reached the bank of elevators and caught one going up—alone. Tucked in a corner, she sagged into the juncture and wedged her head inside the V, closing her eyes for the brief ride. Knotted muscles in her shoulders tightened. Prickles raced up her neck, into the back of her head. A jolt of energy would be much appreciated.

"Fifth floor."

Disembarking, Elizabeth followed the signs directing her to ICU. A nurse in dark blue scrubs spoke to Dominic. The doctor turned and lifted his chin to Elizabeth.

"Thank you for that," he said in a lowered voice when she joined him.

"I still don't get why she was even here, and what Sophie

was thinking asking her to be here." She peeked past his shoulder. "Is Pratt still with him?"

"Yes. I gave him a few extra moments." Dominic massaged the back of his neck. "Brent's blood pressure isn't stabilizing. If my measures don't work, I'll have to take him back into surgery."

The exhaustion took on a deeper level. She wanted to sink to the floor and not get up.

"Honest opinion, Dominic." Elizabeth leveled her best pleading eyes on him. "Will Brent ever return to law enforcement?"

"Honest opinion? First, I want to make sure he doesn't die." Right there was the reason Dominic Thorpe, even in all his arrogance, was the best.

"Can I see him?"

"For a few minutes. Brent is still out of it, so he won't talk." He turned and started walking down the hall. "Did he say anything to Deputy Dayne about who shot him?"

"No. She didn't even think to ask."

Elizabeth followed Dominic to the lone room with beeping and whooshing machines. She lingered outside the sliding glass door, glimpsing the IV in the hand of her young deputy when the doctor parted the curtains. A moment passed before Pratt and Dominic exited the room.

Coming to a halt at her side, Pratt stayed facing the wall behind her. "Elizabeth."

"Pratt." She kept her gaze glued to the slit in the curtains revealing a sliver of the young deputy's body connected to all those machines.

"The deputy who was with him."

"Deputy Dayne."

"Thank her for doing what she could to save him." He closed his sheeny eyes. "Please."

Gripping Pratt's shoulder, she squeezed. "I will. She and Brent were getting along well together."

They stood that way for a few clicks of the second hand. Pratt straightened his shoulders, and Elizabeth's hand slipped away.

"Do you have any regrets?" he asked a moment later.

"More than I care to express."

"How do you cope with them?"

She sighed. "I let them go." Shoring up her walls, she took a step into the ICU room. "Pratt." She looked back, meeting the man's troubled gaze. "I will find who did this. And they will pay for their sins."

A mere twitch of his head was all the acknowledgment she got before he walked away. Elizabeth didn't bother to watch him leave. Instead, she stepped into the sterilized atmosphere.

"Hey there, Brent. It's Ellie."

CHAPTER THIRTY-ONE

S HE WAS GOING cross-eyed from all this reading and thinking.

Closing her eyes and lowering her head, Lila rubbed her forehead. She couldn't recall the last half hour's worth of reading.

A clack on her desktop. Lundquist swung a chair around, slid up flush to her desk, and straddled it. A cream-colored cup sat between them.

"What's that?"

"Chai tea." Lundquist scooted the cup closer to her. "My sister says it's better for you than coffee."

The Viking had a sister. Was she as imposing and nosy as her brother?

Lila took the hot beverage and sipped. Hallelujah! The sister knew how to make a proper cup of chai. Lila's last good one came from a little hole-in-the-wall café in a part of Chicago only the foolishly brave ventured. Two weeks before the attack, she'd been there running down a lead on a turf dispute that had killed a ten-year-old girl. If incidents like that had been the only type of homicides she'd had to deal with, she wouldn't have come onto her attacker's radar.

"You still with me?" Lundquist's inquiry dragged her back to the present.

Setting the cup down, she shuffled through her notes. "I never left."

"Looked like you were off somewhere."

Head cocked to the side, she crisscrossed her arms over her mess. "Is there a reason why you're bothering me?"

"I got results on the DNA."

"That quick?"

"I asked a favor to get it fast-tracked. Having some comparable evidence helped move it along." He reached over to his desk and snatched a sheet of paper dangling on the edge, then held it out to her. "Our freezer guy matches the semen sample from Regan."

"Which makes sense if he was her boyfriend." Lila took the page and studied it.

"As a bonus, his prints were in the system."

Her eyes widened. "He had a record?"

"Meet Robert 'Bobby' Pelham. A notorious Narcos wannabe. It seems he wanted to get into the big-time drug dealing game, but mostly ripped off small-time dealers."

"You called the Romeoville and Oak Park police departments?"

"Part of my job description. Mr. Pelham decided to take on the wrong gang and ended up on the bad side of an undercover operation that landed him in jail. He did his time and when he got out, he met Regan."

"In the middle of this comes Maya, who thought her cousin hung the moon. And all three formed a group of drug buddies."

Drugs. It always came back to the drugs. The girls using, the meth lab in the middle of nowhere, the sheriff's determination to end the drug and criminal problem in the county. Drugs. What was it Cecil had always drilled into her?

Follow the most obvious angle.

In this case, it was the drugs. The girls had a history of using heroin or cocaine. Meth wasn't their preferred drug, but it wasn't out of the question for them to change it up. Try something new. More exciting than the same-ole, same-ole.

"What was Pelham's drug of choice?"

Lundquist sorted through some notes and pulled out the page he wanted. "He was a bit of an all-arounder but preferred cocaine."

"What were the dealers pedaling when he tried to steal their wares?"

"Coke and crystal meth."

There was the connection. Yet, Maya showed no signs of using either one of those—she was a heroin user. And they still didn't have the toxicology reports back on either one of the girls. Lila had to connect these threads.

"Maya's parents wanted to separate her from Regan." Lila tapped a steady rhythm on her files. "Regan was dating a known criminal with aspirations of being a kingpin. What am I not seeing here?"

"Money?" Lundquist provided.

Lila ceased her drumbeat. "With Pelham's record, their little group decided they wanted more than to just get high." She slapped the top of her notepad. "That's it!"

Her outburst startled Fontaine, Georgia, and Fitzgerald, who had come in an hour ago.

Lundquist scowled. "What's it?"

"Our little trio wanted to be a merry band of thieves. That's why Maya was asking around the school for information on who was selling in the area." She stood up. "Think about it. Why would Regan and Bobby come over here when they could have their choice of any place in the Chicagoland area?"

"Because all of you Illinoisans think we Iowans are backwoods hicks," Fitzgerald said.

"There's that, I guess," Lila conceded. "No, it's exactly what they would have thought. Easy targets. They'd think if there was any operation worth taking over it would be in some small town with a tiny police presence. Few gangs—"

"Try no gangs," Fontaine corrected.

"Okay, no gangs but crooked cops. Or at least there used to be."

"But if that Morton building we found last night is any indication, we've got more than just a simple, small-time operation going on around here," Lundquist said.

"And somehow Bobby, Regan, or Maya found out about it. Here was their pot of gold."

"We don't even know who was running that lab."

Lila stepped out from behind her desk and marched over to the huge corkboard Fontaine had been tacking on pictures and information throughout the morning. An old-time version of the present day dry-erase evidence board.

"We all agree that building had someone with deep financial pockets funding that operation. Who around here has that kind of money? Or, better yet, who didn't before but is now suddenly flush with cash?"

The three men blinked at each other. Lila glanced to

Georgia, sitting back in her chair, arms crossed, watching the four deputies, amused.

"Who, Georgia?" Lila threw at her.

"Pratt Meyer is the only one in this entire county who has that kind of money."

"But?"

"But he's too far above soiling himself with the likes of drug manufacturing."

Lila smiled. "Ma Kauffmann then."

Fontaine barked. Lila looked at the man.

"You're smoking weed if you think Ma has any kind of capital. That family barely has two pennies to squeeze between all three of them."

"So you think." Lila leveled him with a point-blank stare. "The ones who are sophisticated and smart don't flaunt their fortunes. They kept it all lowkey and out of the public eye."

He scowled. "Pratt Meyer is more likely to be the man behind that operation than Ma ever will be."

"I find that insinuation suspect."

They all turned as Bentley tore into the office with a bark, her owner hot on her trail.

"On what basis, Sheriff?" Fontaine snapped.

"The basis of seeing that man in utter shellshock after witnessing his son hooked up to a bank of machines keeping him alive." Sheriff Benoit joined Lila in front of the cork-board. "And finding out that Ma has somehow ingratiated herself with Sophie Meyer."

"Come again?" Fontaine sounded incredulous at this bit of news.

"Yeah, had me confused too." Benoit looked at Lila.

"You're onto something. What is it?"

"She thinks our three victims were trying to rob or take over that meth operation," Fitzgerald said.

Benoit's gaze didn't waver from Lila. "And?"

"And . . . I'm not off base with this."

Shifting to put her back to the board, Benoit gestured for Lila to take the floor. "Prove it."

Public speaking had not been her forte. Lila glanced at the people in the room, heat consuming her body.

"We are all colleagues here."

Lila frowned at the sheriff. How did that woman—? Never mind. Drawing her shoulders back, she took command, laying out her thoughts. As she reached her conclusion, there was an expression of pride on Benoit's face.

"Neva McKinnley? How do you place her in all of this?" Benoit asked.

"Her autopsy showed she'd been restrained, and her death was caused by a fall down the steps, which we can conclude she was most likely pushed."

"Well, though she's not here to confirm it, we can rest assured that Neva McKinnley heard what she heard Tuesday night or early Wednesday morning." Benoit tapped the side of her thigh. "We just need to figure out if Maya was actually in that house and who had her there. And was she killed there?"

Lila turned to the board. "The house is in the general vicinity of that meth lab. I think she ran from the lab when Regan and Bobby were killed." She looked at Benoit. "She was hiding from their killers in that place, but they found her."

"Seems logical to me," the sheriff said.

"But why leave Maya's body in that open field?" Fitzgerald asked.

"She was a message," Benoit supplied.

"To who?" Fontaine asked.

Lila's gaze traveled to the notations on Meyer's shooting. She turned to the sheriff. "You say Martha Kauffmann and Sophie Meyer are suddenly buddy-buddy."

"Ma claims family support."

"But why would Ma want to have anything to do with a Meyer? Even if Sophie is her distant cousin?" Lundquist asked. "It makes no sense."

"Brent knew his shooter." Lila's gaze strayed back to the board. "Neva McKinnley knew her killer." She tapped her chin, squinting at the pictures and reports hanging there, conjuring them together to give her the answer. "She's keeping tabs on Brent's situation."

"Why?" Benoit asked.

"Because she knows who shot him. If Brent talks . . ."

The sheriff's features paled. "Deputy Dayne, are you certain?"

"Her husband dies under suspicious circumstances. Her son is killed in an accident she claims is more than it seems. Both men were connected to drugs in some way. That's an awful lot of coincidences piling up with her name on them."

"I still say you're barking up the wrong tree," Fontaine interjected. "There's no way Ma has any kind of financial means to create a meth lab like that."

"She would if she went into a partnership with someone."

"We find that partner," Sheriff Benoit said, "we find our shooter. And we find our killer." She turned to Georgia. "Call the police chief. I need to talk with him."

She gripped Lila's arm and escorted her into her office. Once through the door, Benoit kicked it shut and freed Lila to circle behind her desk.

"Give me your honest assessment. Who do you think is Ma's partner?"

"It can't be Pratt Meyer—they hate each other. And she keeps lobbing complaints against him."

"Maybe it's someone from outside the community?"

"That could be possible, but my gut says it's local. How does one get to Ma?"

Benoit faced her windows that looked out on the courthouse lawn and the backside of the veterans' memorial. Pensive lines marred the sheriff's features. "Ma is crafty, a regular old pit viper. You don't come at her." She pressed her knuckles to her lips.

"If I'm right about her, then maybe she isn't wrong about how her son died."

Benoit lowered her hand. "But who would have wanted to see Daniel dead? Surely not her partner in all of this?"

"Do you see Pratt Meyer doing it?"

"What would he have to gain by killing off Daniel?" Benoit rotated. "Do you think Pratt is in the drug business?" She frowned and shook her head. "I just can't see him lowering himself to that level. Fraud, now that I can see him doing."

"Sheriff, what caused the rift between Pratt and Brent?"

Sighing, Benoit pulled out her chair and sank into the

large leather beast. "Anything I tell you is speculation on my part. Brent has never revealed to anyone what drove him and his father apart."

Grabbing a chair, Lila slid it closer to the desk and sat on the edge. "Would his wife know? Would she be willing to say?"

A knock on the door preceded Georgia's entry. "Police chief on line one."

Benoit grabbed up the phone and punched the blinking button. "Ed, I need a favor. Would you be able to spare an officer or two to stand guard outside my deputy's hospital room?"

Lila leaned closer.

"I think whoever shot him might make a go of it again. And I think it's someone trying to get close enough to the family to have that access . . . I appreciate it greatly, Ed. I'll owe you one . . . Okay, make it two." She hung up the phone. "Brent will be protected for now. I'll call the hospital and give Dr. Thorpe strict instructions to allow only specific people into Brent's room."

"Sheriff." Lila stood, and Benoit paused in picking up the receiver. "I'm going back to the Barrett place and the meth lab. Something about that whole area . . ." She sighed. "It's the key."

Benoit nodded. "I agree. Go with Lundquist. Both of you stick together, and watch your sixes."

"Yes, ma'am." Lila quit the room, allowing the sheriff to make her call. "Lundquist, with me."

He scowled. "What for?"

"Sheriff's orders. I'm running on a hunch here."

CHAPTER THIRTY-TWO

ELIZABETH VACATED HER office moments after Dayne and Lundquist. She found Fitzgerald and Fontaine loitering.

"Ben, I need you to do some snooping."

His face fell. "Why?"

"Think you can pull off an undercover job for us?"

Fitzgerald sat on the edge of his desk and crossed his arms. "Who would I be snooping on? And why?"

"Sheehan. He thinks you're still batting for his team, which makes this a prime opportunity. That man knows something about what's been going on. He won't talk to me, or any of us for that matter, but he might let it slide in front of you."

"You're dreaming," Fitzgerald said. "I told you, he never trusted me. So, why would he talk with me?"

Elizabeth glanced at Rafe, drew in a fortifying breath, and let it out. "Do you trust me, Ben?"

As he stared at her, narrow-eyed and sullen, Elizabeth practically willed him to answer yes.

"Say I do go along with this, what do I get out of it?"

Rafe rolled his eyes and groaned.

Elizabeth just smiled. "Why, my undying gratitude, Deputy Fitzgerald."

Bentley pressed against her leg and huffed.

"That's it?"

"Be lucky she isn't sacking you," Rafe snapped.

"I wouldn't do that even if he refused." Elizabeth stroked Bentley's muzzle. "Marnie assures me Kelley will be in his usual spot in two hours. Plenty of time for you to run home, change out of your uniform, and come up with a legit reason for me to have kicked you to the curb." She held up a finger. "That, Ben, is your ticket to getting an audience with him. He wants dirt, so give him dirt."

Rafe chuckled. "Right up your alley."

"You're so certain he'll fall for it. The man is as twisted as barbed wire and just as sharp. He'll figure out what I'm doing."

"Play him. You don't trust him any more than he trusts you. If you act like you're not willing to divulge, then he'll press the matter. He's the shark and you're the fisherman; fight him too long on the line, and he'll get away, but if you wage a steady battle of tug-of-war, he'll eventually tire and you can reel him in."

Fitzgerald wrinkled his nose. "Where do you come up with these metaphors?"

She shrugged. "They come to me."

"She's not wrong in that," Rafe said. "You know the game, Ben. Sheehan is arrogant enough to believe you're nothing more than a pawn for him."

"Exactly. Feed him whatever line of bull, truth or not, that will hook him. He's ripe for gossip to use against me. Use that to your advantage."

"If you two think this is so easy, then why aren't you doing it? Or better yet, send Dayne in there. She's fresh meat. He'll be all over that."

"I need Deputy Dayne doing what she was brought into this department to do: investigate."

Fitzgerald looked down at the floor, tapping his thumb against his bicep. Rafe settled back in his chair and cradled his head in his intertwined hands. The silence broken only by the tick of the wall clock and Bentley's tail swishing over the wood flooring.

"Fine, whatever. But I ain't guaranteeing success." Fitzgerald stood. "You better have a backup plan."

"I always do."

Once he exited the building, Rafe rotated his chair.

"Now what?" he asked.

"Now, you and I are going to the hospital."

How she managed to convince Rafe to let her drive was a wonder. Elizabeth relished the momentary victory. However, it seemed Rafe had an agenda, and their privacy left her trapped and on the spot.

"Ellie, we need to discuss what happened this morning."

She flexed her grip on the steering wheel. "You'll have to be more specific. A lot has happened this morning."

"No runaround. I'm not in the mood. We crossed a lot of professional, ethical, and personal lines by kissing."

"I admit it was wrong professionally and ethically, but there were no personal lines."

"You're my brother's wife."

"*Ex*-wife."

"When it suits you. Damn it, you two were going at it like teenagers a few nights ago."

"I was drunk."

"Not an excuse." Rafe sighed. "If you truly didn't love Joel anymore, you wouldn't have let him seduce you."

"What's between me and Joel is complicated."

His attention snapped in her direction. "I don't eat off another man's dinner plate."

"No, you just covet what he eats."

Face flushed, Rafe ripped his gaze from her.

"I'm tired of the same song and dance with you, Rafe. We've been tiptoeing around this attraction far too long, and it's about damn time we did something about it."

"Not at the cost of your position. All it takes is for your detractors to catch you in one heated moment and you'll be voted out. Sheehan is wanting an excuse to get you ousted—fooling around with me will be just the scandal he'd love to get word about." His shoulders sagged as he shook his head. "Having an affair with your ex-husband won't tarnish you in the eyes of your voters like an affair with a deputy."

Elizabeth let his statement hang between them as she drove into the hospital parking lot. Once she parked the SUV, she killed the engine and sat there.

"I know," she said softly. "But it doesn't make it any easier for me."

His gaze dropped to her hand, still clenched around the steering wheel. Elizabeth wanted him to take hold of her hand, but, clearly, his desire to keep it professional was winning out.

"We'll find a way," he said. Drawing in a breath, he looked outside the SUV. "Why are we here?"

"I want to talk with Pratt and Sophie, without Ma around."

"And I'm here to deter Ma."

"In a way, yes. I'm done with Ma sticking her nose where it doesn't belong and stirring up trouble. But first, I want your honest opinion on something. What's Stephen really like?"

Rafe scowled. "What do you mean?"

"What I mean . . ." Elizabeth grimaced. "I don't know what I mean. Is he really not like his family?"

Rafe shrugged. "I guess. He's never been in trouble with the law like Karl or Daniel. Ma treats him like a prince. And intelligence wise, he runs circles around all of them. Stephen is Ma's ticket for a better life."

"No way she'd ever allow anyone to screw that up?"

"You could say that."

His answers didn't ease the niggling in her brain. There was more to what was going on with Ma. Maybe Lila's suspicions about the Kauffmanns were leading somewhere.

And maybe Pratt Meyer could shed a little more light on that suspicion.

THERE WERE NO raised, angry voices leading her into a family showdown this time. The soft, sterile quiet hospital setting was all that greeted Elizabeth and Rafe as they strode down the hall.

Olivia spotted them, and joined them at the elevators. "I hope you didn't come for the autopsy. The victim hasn't thawed enough for me to start."

"We're not, but have you at least done the X-rays?"

"Yes, and given him a full external exam. I'm afraid his death is similar to Regan's and Maya's, but I can't pinpoint exactly what caused it. I won't know more until I can cut into him."

The elevator doors whooshed open. Rafe stepped on.

Elizabeth turned to Olivia. "Did the Meyers move to the ICU waiting room?"

"Yes, they are there."

"Ma?"

"I don't think she's been back."

Rafe's hand shot out to stop the doors from closing.

Elizabeth cocked her head to the side. "Interesting."

"Ellie, let's go," Rafe said as the alarm rattled.

She stepped on the elevator. Up they went.

"If Ma isn't here, then I'm here for what reason?" Rafe asked.

"To keep an eye out. Maybe take Sophie for a stroll and see if she'll reveal anything to you."

"I highly doubt that."

"Won't hurt to try."

"Fifth floor."

She found Sophie alone in the ICU's private waiting area designated for Brent's room. Maybe cornering Sophie would get her answers.

"Change in plans." Leaving Rafe outside to derail Pratt's reentry, Elizabeth entered the waiting room.

Sophie sat on a comfortable-looking sofa, staring out the window. Dressed to the nines in a midnight-blue blouse and khaki slacks with her hair swept up in a French twist, Sophie looked better suited for a school board meeting than a hospital waiting room. How had she survived the transition from working professional to a stay-at-home mother of three and housewife to an extremely successful businessman?

"Sophie?"

Her red-rimmed eyes landed on Elizabeth. Frowning, she stood, smoothing nonexistent wrinkles from her clothing. "Sheriff. What are you doing back here?" Panic splashed across her features. "Has something happened to Brent?"

"No." Elizabeth held up a hand as she would to a panicked horse. "Far as I know, he's in the same condition he was when I left."

Sophie sank down onto the sofa once more. "Oh, thank God."

"Is Pratt still here?"

She flapped her hand. "He needed some air or something." Remaining in her stiff posture, she angled her body to stare out the window once more.

Elizabeth ignored the blatant dismissal, hiked her duty belt higher on her hips, and took the armchair positioned to face Sophie. "I know this isn't the best time, but I need to ask some questions."

"Sheriff"—she tilted her head to look at Elizabeth—"must you?"

"If it's not me, then it'll be one of my deputies."

"I rather think that's unfair."

"And siccing Ma on me wasn't?"

"Martha does what Martha wants. I was . . . in a fog. My son is fighting for his life because of the job he chose."

"I was under the impression you were okay with Brent becoming a police officer."

Silence met her inquiry.

"We've come to . . . believe that whoever shot Brent may keep tabs on his progress in order to ensure he doesn't survive."

Horror masked Sophie's features. "What?"

"Brent knows the shooter. I don't think he was meant to survive, because he could finger the person who did this."

"Why?"

"I don't know." Elizabeth calmed her jiggling leg. "I'm afraid that his being shot might have connections to the homicides we're investigating." She swallowed hard. "It might even have some connection to the long-standing tensions between Pratt and Ma."

"Ridiculous. That is utterly ridiculous." Sophie slapped her hands into her lap. "You've completely lost your mind, Elizabeth."

Biting her tongue was for the best. "Maybe I am way off base here. But can you explain any other way?"

"How does my son being a cop and having to deal with the hairy unwashed on a daily basis work for you?" Sophie leaned forward. "It's because of you that he's even doing this. Brent was going to be a lawyer or a state representative, a senator. That was how he was going to make a difference. But instead, he was swindled into believing the way to help was by being a cop. Now look at him."

Sophie had moved to a different stage of her grief: blaming.

Movement by the doorway caught Elizabeth's eye. Rafe had moved his sentry duty to better see both women.

Not daring to touch the other woman, Elizabeth cleared her throat. "I know it seems unfair, but we need to look forward. It's the best way to protect Brent and you and Pratt."

Eyes wide, Sophie paled. "Are you insinuating that his shooter might come after me and Pratt?"

"I'm not insinuating anything, I'm flat-out warning you. The police chief has allowed me use of two of his officers to post as guards outside of Brent's room. I will not allow anyone except those of my choosing in his room. However, I can't offer that same protection outside of the hospital. You and Pratt need to be on alert and protect yourselves."

"This is absurd."

"This is reality, Sophie. And I would strongly suggest you stay away from Ma and the rest of the Kauffmanns until we either clear them of any wrongdoing or the shooter is caught."

"She was right. Pratt has turned you against her."

Elizabeth narrowed her eyes. What lies had Ma spun to snag her cousin? It didn't help matters while Brent was suffering.

The sharp rap of knuckles jolted Sophie. Rafe beckoned Elizabeth.

"Yes, leave," Sophie hissed.

"Heed my warning, Sophie."

As Elizabeth exited the waiting room, Rafe pointed down the hall. Pratt was returning. She met up with him before he stepped into the room.

"Sheriff? I just came from my son's ICU room, and there is a police officer there who will not allow me to enter."

"I've asked for this. Pratt, we believe Brent's life is still under threat. I will clear with the officer and Dr. Thorpe who are allowed to enter."

"You're serious? Who would dare attempt such a thing in the hospital?"

"A determined killer."

His face blanched.

"Pratt, I also recommended to Sophie that the both of you be on alert for a threat to either of you."

His features hardened. "I told her the same. Martha Kauffmann is not to be trusted."

How she wanted to agree with the man. But he was still under suspicion, and the last thing Elizabeth wanted to do was give him an opportunity to avert attention from himself and place it solely on Ma.

"Be diligent." And with that parting advice, Elizabeth walked away.

Once they were on the elevator heading down, Rafe asked, "What did you learn from that?"

"That someone is pulling strings. And I refuse to dance to their tune."

CHAPTER THIRTY-THREE

L ILA STOOD BEFORE the rickety house, staring up at the caving roof.

"What do you hope to find here?"

"Answers." She marched past Lundquist and up the back steps.

"It's not safe to be in there," he called after her.

"Well aware of that," she shot back.

Picking her way around the damage done by the fallen porcelain tub, she entered the kitchen. Behind her, Lundquist muttered expletives as he followed.

"The sheriff will have my head if you get hurt again."

"She won't if you're hurt too."

"You're a sadist, aren't you?"

She smiled at his deadpan. Inching into the dining area, she studied the room, its rubble, and the adjoining rooms. Lundquist stood in line with her but a few feet apart.

"It would help me to know what you're looking for exactly."

"If I'm right about Maya trying to hide out here, maybe she hid her phone or phones. Possibly Regan's or Bobby's. Anything of theirs that would be overlooked."

He frowned, looking about. "Better hope it wasn't under the bathtub."

Lila sighed. "I am." She headed for the living room/parlor.

"Lila."

Stiffening, she turned casually. "What?" Well, that was weak.

"Be careful."

The obvious concern in his tone unsettled her. One minute he acted like she was a thorn, the next she was a liability to the department, and then he'd flip it all on its head and suddenly he was worried for her welfare. She put her back to him. Deputy Kyle Lundquist was a riddle Lila did not want to unravel.

"You too. My little body can't lift your Viking butt to safety."

There was a strangled sound from him that made her grin. Good. He did have a sense of humor.

"Why don't you check over the kitchen, lightweight?"

"If we strike out everywhere else, we'll go there. The kitchen is too obvious of a hiding place. The killer or killers would look there first."

"You are talking about a teenager with an underdeveloped brain in a panic."

"True." Lila lifted the edge of the ripped up carpet. "But I'd like to give Maya the benefit of the doubt and say she was being logical." She dropped the carpet, stirring a cloud of dust.

"Not that it would matter to you, but I wouldn't create a dust bowl. There's a lot of nasties in the dirt in here that can cause lung problems."

Lila saluted. "Aye, aye, Captain."

His face soured, and he stared at her.

"What?"

Face relaxing, he shook his head. "Nothing." He lifted an edge of the broken table.

Shrugging off his odd reaction, she went to work, taking his warning in advisement and not disturbing the dirt and dust too much. Together, they cleared the first floor with no success. At the bottom of the steps, Lila looked up.

"I don't know if we should chance it." Lundquist squinted at the upper level.

"You want to run the risk of missing crucial evidence being left up there because you're worried the floor will collapse?"

"Yes. As you so eloquently put it, my Viking butt is too heavy for that questionably stable floor."

"Just because a porcelain tub caved in the floor of a bathroom, where I'm sure there had been water damage to weaken the integrity of the wood, doesn't mean the rest of the upstairs is compromised."

Lundquist gestured for her to climb the steps. "Be my guest. I think I'll stick to the first floor."

"All right." Lila looked down at her duty belt. "Better still." Nimble fingers went to work removing her belt. "Hold this. A little less weight."

He took her belt. "Be quick about it."

She mounted the first step. "Not how an investigator does their job. Fast work is sloppy work." Which steps were the ones she had to avoid or risk falling through?

"You know what I mean."

Lila peered at him over the stair railing. "Do I?"

His features hardened. Guess that answered her question. Setting aside the oddity that was Kyle Lundquist, Lila crept up the stairs, locating the weak steps as she went.

"I'll look over the stairwell," Lundquist said when she reached the top.

"You do that."

Start from the big hole that was the bathroom and work her way back to the stairs? Or begin from where she stood?

A creak at the end of the hall made her shiver.

End of hall back to the stairs it was.

As she passed the smear on the wall, she hesitated and looked at it closely. If memory served her right, the condition of Regan's body didn't determine if her bloodied injuries were caused peri- or postmortem. Lila studied the sweep and angle of the smear. Turning her back to the hole, she swiped her hand through the air in the same direction of the stain.

Before it plunged into the hole, she thought the tub had blood in it, but it was pockmarked by rust, making it difficult to determine one way or the other.

"Lundquist?"

"Did you find something?"

"Not yet. Hey, think about the condition Regan's body was in when she was discovered."

After a few seconds of silence. "Okay?"

"Do you think it's possible she'd been beaten? Tortured?"

Lila looked down the hall, picturing the bathroom once more whole. The image that came to her turned her body cold.

"Are you thinking, whether she was alive or not, the killer brought Regan here to torment Maya before they killed her too?"

Bile burned the back of Lila's throat.

"My God," Lundquist groaned. "Who the hell does something like that?"

"Someone bent on protecting their identity."

Lila turned to the bedroom behind her, the room where the possum carcass stank up the place. She entered the room, gagging on the sickly sweet stench. Last time, she'd only glanced at the room, repulsed by the corpse. Finding a sturdy, rusted curtain rod, she used it to leverage the body up and flipped it over.

"Maya, you clever girl. Found them!"

Digging out gloves and a baggie, she picked up the two cell phones, gagging through it, and dumped them in the bag. She hoped the body fluids hadn't ruined the SIM cards and computer components. A tiny part of her felt sorry for the tech who was going to have to deal with the juiced over devices.

She double-timed her way out of the room and down the hall. She waved the bag at a relieved Lundquist as she picked her way down the steps.

Lundquist handed over her duty belt and took the bagged cell phones. "Let's get out of here."

"I can't believe my hunch proved right," Lila said as she stepped out into the fresh winter air.

"You're just lucky you didn't fall through the floor again."

Rounding the corner of the house, they pulled up short

at the shotgun pointed at them. Lila clutched the nylon straps, itching to grab her gun. How could she have let her guard down?

"Don't even think of doing it. Give me the phones."

CHAPTER THIRTY-FOUR

E LIZABETH CAME TO a screeching halt. "What are you doing here?"

Fitzgerald, wearing his civvies, was camped out at his desk. "I waited for Sheehan for an hour and he never showed. Marnie told me it'd look suspicious if I continued to sit there all afternoon not drinking and sitting in his spot."

"What if he's there now?"

"Marnie promised she'd call me if he showed up," he bit back.

"Why does she know what you're doing?"

Fitzgerald blanched.

For the love of all that was holy. "You told her?"

"No," he snapped. "She figured out what I was doing. She wanted me to tell you that this idea is crap and it never would have worked."

"Damn it." Elizabeth looked at Rafe. "On today of all days, he pulls a disappearing act."

"He only has so many places to go. That we know of." Rafe settled into his desk chair.

"We just can't have Ben show up at his home pretending to be defecting."

"If he's not at The Watering Hole, he's probably at the Elks or the country club," Georgia supplied.

Elizabeth made a face. "The Elks and the country club allowed him membership?"

"If he pays his dues, they have to. Doesn't hurt when your cronies run the place."

Growling, Elizabeth stalked to her office. "I'm getting exactly nowhere today but further in the hole." She slapped a hand on the doorframe. "Have Dayne and Lundquist called in?"

Georgia shook her head.

Curling her hand into a fist, Elizabeth pressed her knuckles into the wood frame. A good scream would feel great right about now. Every muscle strained, pulling on her bones until she felt like they'd snap. But no. She must be in control. She was the sheriff. To show even an ounce female response to stress would set back any progress she'd made as an authoritative figure.

Bentley curled herself around Elizabeth's legs, gazing up lovingly at her. Stroking her companion's head, she let the motions soothe her frazzled brain.

"Ellie, all is not lost," Rafe said. "We know more about what happened to our victims than we did two days ago."

"But we don't know why Brent was shot or who shot him."

The phone rang, making her jerk. Georgia answered.

"We're all tired," Rafe continued. "Rest and give Dayne and Lundquist a little more time."

"I can go to the hospital and keep an eye on Meyer," Fitzgerald offered.

"Wait to see if Marnie calls you. If nothing happens in the next hour, we reassess. I'm hoping Olivia is able to get to the Pelham autopsy before the day is out."

"Ellie," Georgia said. "It's Joel."

Scowling, Elizabeth stepped over Bentley and stalked to her desk. She grabbed the receiver and punched the blinking line. "What?"

"Ellie . . . your . . . house. I'm shot."

Her exhausted brain took a moment to unravel what he said, then her legs gave out and she landed hard on the chair. "What?"

Rafe and Ben appeared in her doorway, probably summoned forward by Georgia.

"Elizabeth, I'm . . . shot . . . " The line went silent.

Elizabeth's body went slack, the receiver slipping free and cracking against the edge of her desk. A strangled sound ripped from her lips.

Rafe was at her side. "Ellie?"

"Joel's dying."

He rocked back on his heels, his body slamming into her desk. "No. Where is he?"

"My house." Elizabeth didn't recognize her voice.

Fitzgerald swore and ran out of the office. "Georgia, send an EMS unit to the sheriff's place. I'm on my way."

Rafe took hold of Elizabeth's face. "Look at me."

She met his gaze.

"We have to go to him. Now." He straightened, grasped her hand, and helped her to her feet. "Bentley, stay."

Numb, feeling like she was floating, Elizabeth let Rafe lead her out of the building.

"This isn't happening," she uttered.

But it was. Decades of living in a constant state of readiness as an army wife, prepared for that inevitable call, she thought she knew how she'd react. But she was divorced. This was not her life.

Rafe bundled her inside his car. She was losing it again. Letting him take charge.

Damn it all! She was the sheriff.

He slammed the driver's side door and held up a finger as she turned and opened her mouth. "No arguing. Buckle up. We're leaving."

ELIZABETH BAILED FROM the Charger before Rafe had even put the car in park. The ambulance was rolling to a stop on the street as she ran up the drive. She mounted the porch steps two at a time.

As she grabbed the screen door, Fitzgerald appeared and caught her before she could enter the house. "Sheriff, no." He wheeled her backward.

She slammed her fists against his chest. "Let go of me."

Grimacing under her blows, he held fast, wrangling her out of the way as Rafe and the paramedics raced into the house.

"No!" she screamed, sagging into Fitzgerald's arms.

"Sheriff, listen to me." He hauled her up, but she gave up caring. "Listen, Joel is still alive. Let the medics do their job."

"I need to see him."

"Not a good idea. Stay out here."

How was it possible to hurt Joel? Who in this town was

capable of hurting him? Joel was an expert solider. He was trained in the art of war. He wasn't easily waylaid.

"Marnie, take her," Fitzgerald said over her head.

In the transfer from his hold to her sister's, Elizabeth's body gave out and she crumpled to the porch, dragging her sister down with her. Marnie cradled Elizabeth, allowing her to watch the door.

"Did you hear it?"

"No. I heard only the sirens." Marnie stroked her head. "He'll survive. He's too damn stubborn to die."

Clattering wheels stopped both women. A medic backed the gurney through the screen door. Elizabeth scrambled out of Marnie's arms and bolted to her feet as the men wheeled her ex out of the house. Crimson bandages covered his chest, blood streaked his bare abdomen. Following next to the gurney, Rafe squeezed an oxygen bag. Elizabeth took two wobbling steps to follow but was blocked when Marnie stood.

Over her sister's shoulder, Elizabeth watched the medics load Joel into the ambulance, then Rafe scrambling back as the doors were closed. The slap of the doors slammed home the reality of this for her. A man who had suffered nothing more serious than bruises and a few broken fingers was fighting for his life. Joel had lived through war only to be cut down on his home turf by someone breaking into her home.

Rafe's face was a mask of agony and fury. Whoever did this would regret their decision to take down a Fontaine brother. Swiping a bloodied hand against his pant leg, Rafe turned and ran to his Charger. He roared out after the ambulance, leaving her behind.

Elizabeth felt something rip inside of her.

"Sheriff."

A .22 dangled by the trigger guard on a pen Fitzgerald held out. Blood smeared the slide and handle. Joel's blood.

"He was holding it when I came in."

"He tried to stop them." Marnie gripped Elizabeth's shoulder. "I bet that's how he got shot."

"Call Lundquist. Get him back at the office. I want that thing dusted for prints." Elizabeth snapped her spine straight. "I want my house processed top to bottom. They're not getting away this time."

As Fitzgerald put through the call to his fellow deputy, Elizabeth staggered into her house. The puddle of blood beside the partition was the lone thing to prove a crime had been committed.

"Sheriff, he's not answering," Fitzgerald said.

"Keep trying."

"I'm sorry, but I can't."

She wheeled around. "Try harder!"

"His phone goes straight to voice mail. It's been turned off."

"Call Lila."

"I did. The same thing happens."

"What the hell!?"

The screen door screeched open, and Elizabeth's blood pressure rocketed. He would *dare* show his pompous, corrupt face in her presence. Her hand slapped to her sidearm. Shoot him now. Shoot him and be done with this whole affair. For Bre. For all the other people he had hurt or swindled. Their cry for justice deserved it.

"Get out of my home."

Looking about in his typical nonchalant way, Sheehan ignored her.

Elizabeth drew her weapon and stalked past Fitzgerald, right up to Sheehan, aiming the gun in his face. "Get! Out!"

He swiped her gun to the side and stepped into her personal space, preventing her from rising her hands. "Careful, Sheriff. The last thing you need on your watch is a police shooting."

"In this instance I'm not the sheriff or a law enforcement officer. I'm a woman defending her home."

His gaze narrowed. "No. In every situation you are the sheriff." He backed away from her. "He's reacting. You learned too much, and now he's cleaning up. Your deputies are in trouble."

"He who?"

A wicked grin gave his bearded face a macabre look. "Holster your weapon, Sheriff."

Sliding her sidearm home, she crossed her arms. "He who?"

"What I tell you gives me immunity from anything you learn about any perceived involvement I might have."

"Perceived or not, I'm coming for you, Kelley."

"Immunity or I walk."

Elizabeth glanced at Fitzgerald, who shook his head. Marnie shrugged. Her gaze returned to Sheehan, who was tapping a finger against his watch face.

God forgive her for this.

CHAPTER THIRTY-FIVE

L ILA SQUARED OFF with the shotgun-wielding woman. "Dangerous game you're playing here."

One leather-clad shoulder lifted. "I've been courting danger the whole of my life, missy." She jerked her chin at the open doorway behind Lila. "Join your boyfriend."

The chill from the walk-in cooler buffeted Lila's back. There was no way in hell she was going to be frozen to death.

"Move." The shotgun came up. "Or I let my boy have his way with you, and we let lover boy watch. And once he's finished, he throws your used body in there."

"He's not my boyfriend or my lover."

"Lila," Lundquist growled.

"You're a real piece of shit work. What kind of woman threatens sexual violence against another woman?"

Martha Kauffmann's features turned ugly. "I don't have to threaten it." She raised the shotgun to eye level. "But I'm not against just shooting you and letting you suffer a horrible death."

"And how is freezing to death any better?"

"You have some real sass in you, girl."

"Must be my Chicago upbringing."

Lundquist grasped her arm and tugged her back as Karl advanced. Dragging her inside the cooler, Lundquist stepped in front of Lila. Karl smirked as he stood in the doorway.

"This isn't going to end like you think it will," Lundquist said. "Sheriff Benoit knows where we are."

"She'll be too busy to worry about you two." Karl's swing was blinding and landed hard in Lundquist's gut. With a laugh, he stepped back as Lundquist fell to the floor.

Lila glared at the brute as he sneered at her.

"I'm all up for a good hump."

"Pay a visit to Rosy Palms and her five sisters. They're always willing."

Spitting a cruel word, he slammed the cooler door.

Lila's body wobbled. If it had come down to it, she would have fought, risking a gut full of buckshot before she let Karl touch her. She slid to her knees next to Lundquist.

He heaved and moaned.

"Breathe through it."

"I'm tryin'," he gasped.

Settling her hand on his shoulder, she eased him through the pain. He rolled onto his back and stared up at her.

"Now what?" he asked, his breath a cloud.

She looked around at the steel racks and the packages of food DCI had left in the cooler. No windows. The door was most likely locked. And she'd watched Ma turn the temp down on the thermostat. How long did they have before hypothermia kicked in and weakened them to the point of death?

Ma and Karl had stripped them of their coats, belts, boots, vests, and any device that could be used to free them or alert anyone to their predicament. Left in socks, pants, and their undershirts, the cold would do its damage long before anyone would figure out where they were.

"Why didn't she just shoot us?"

"It's a control thing for her." Lundquist groaned as he sat up. "I don't think Ma is really keen on watching people die."

"She just has others, her son in particular, do it for her." Lila noticed the dark blue ink peeking from under his shirtsleeve. She gently lifted the sleeve, revealing the anchor tattoo. "I thought so."

He grasped her hand and pulled it down. "We need to figure out how to get out of here."

"Would it have bothered you if Karl had raped me in front of you?"

"Yes." He scowled. "Why would you think it wouldn't?"

She shrugged and backed away. "Isn't there another son?"

"Stephen."

"Where is he?"

"Good question."

But it was Karl's taunt before he punched Kyle that she couldn't shake. "What do you think he meant by the sheriff being too busy to worry about us?"

Lundquist winced. "Ma did something to divert attention."

"Maybe that's why Brent was shot. To throw us off her trail."

"What if they shot Ellie? She'd be the only one to remember we're out here."

"Didn't she and Fontaine set up cameras out here?"

"Ma probably disabled them."

Clambering to her feet, Lila moved to the wall. "This is

an exterior wall, right?"

He studied the cooler. "I think so. What are you thinking?"

Lila shivered. Grunting, she shook it off. Grasping the steel racks, she jerked, but they didn't budge.

"Even if you got them loose, we wouldn't be able to make a dent in the wall."

She squatted and examined the base. The rack's braces were screwed into the cement. She grabbed the leg with both hands and wiggled harder.

Lundquist joined her, squatting down. "Lila, it's not going to move."

"Defeatist. Use those Viking muscles and help me. Best-case scenario we keep our bodies warmed up to stave off the hypothermia."

Shrugging, he wrapped his hands on the bar above hers, and together they worked the metal leg back and forth until there was movement in one of the screws.

"Keep going," she hissed.

A clatter at the door jolted them to a stop. Standing, they turned as the door suddenly opened. Ma barged in, shoved a shocked Lundquist aside, and grabbed Lila by the hair, dragging her out.

Lila cried out, slapping at the woman's hands as she tried not to trip with her body bent over at an awkward angle. She glimpsed Lundquist trying to make a break for the door as Ma pulled Lila through it, but a weapon was rammed into Lundquist's face and the door slammed shut.

"Shut up!" Ma barked, and then flung Lila forward, releasing her hair.

Unable to stop her momentum, Lila landed on the meth lab floor and slid across the smooth surface. Shockwaves reverberated through her, piercing her scars. Curling into a ball, she swallowed the cries.

"I'll shoot her."

Peeling open an eyelid, Lila found the shotgun barrel pointed at her head, Ma towering over her.

"Martha, that's not why I'm here, and you know it."

Bile pooled in Lila's throat. That snake oil salesman voice. She tilted her head back and sighted the man ten feet away.

Sheehan.

"I warned you, Kelley. You had your chance. It's too late."

"And you think threatening to kill that outsider in front of me makes a bit of difference?"

"I can make it look like you did it."

Sheehan shook his head and chuckled. "You really have lost your grip." His eyes narrowed. "They warned me to keep an eye on you. Told me you were going senile in your old age."

"Lies. Malicious lies to turn us against each other."

Sheehan looked at someone off to Ma's left. "Tell me, Martha, have you ever worked it out how and why Daniel really died?"

The shotgun lifted from Lila's head. "Say another word and I'll fill you so full of lead, you'll look like ground meat."

"You don't have the stomach," Sheehan taunted.

A creak echoed through the building, and a door slapped shut.

"What is he doing here?"

"Stephen, perfect timing, baby."

Lila scooted a little bit by little bit away from Ma so as to not draw attention to herself. The young man who emerged from the back of the meth lab brought Lila's progress to a halt. He moved with a swagger that didn't match his stick-thin frame. His reptilian eyes darted about the area, falling on Lila.

He paused. "Who is she?"

Ma's head snapped to Lila. "She's the sheriff's new investigator."

"Investigator," he repeated, his voice dropping into a frosty tone.

"Stephen, are you bleeding?" Ma asked.

Lila swallowed, her arms shaking. Stephen's clothing was covered in blood.

He lifted his jacket away from the speckled mess that was his shirt. A cruel smile tilted one corner of his mouth. "Naw. Mama, this isn't my blood."

"What did you do?" Ma's voice rasped.

Karl's laughter bounced off the walls. "Like you don't know."

"Shut up, you damn fool," Ma screeched.

Karl kept laughing until she walked over and slapped his face.

Sheehan clucked his tongue and shook his head. "Stephen is the one who shot Joel Fontaine. Oh my, Martha, you just set off a fuse."

"You idiot! If Rafe figures it out, he's going to be all over us like a hound of hell."

Lila jolted at the violent crack of Stephen's fist smashing into his mother's jaw. She scrambled back as Martha careened around and hit the floor, the shotgun clattering out of her reach.

"Wrong choice of words, *Mama*." Stephen stepped over his mother's trembling body and picked up the shotgun. "Now"—he swung the barrel in Sheehan's direction—"what were you going to tell my mother about my dearly departed brother's death?"

Sheehan slowly lifted his hands. "Nothing she hasn't already figured out on her own."

"And what is it exactly that you've figured out, Mama?"

Martha scrabbled away from her son. "Nothing," she croaked.

Sniffing, Stephen jabbed the shotgun into Sheehan's stomach. "Poor Daniel. Got too smart for his own good."

"Always knew to keep an eye on you," Sheehan sneered.

Keeping an eye on the shotgun-wielding teen, Lila crawled over to Martha's side and touched the woman's bruised cheek. The Kauffmann matriarch peered up at the brush of Lila's fingertips. Abstract fear filled the woman's eyes, setting Lila back on her knees.

"I have never liked you, Kelley." Stephen moved toward Lila. "Your agreement with Mama ends today." Like his mother, Stephen reached out and snagged Lila's hair and wrenched her to her feet.

Biting her tongue to quell the cries of pain, she stumbled over Martha's prone body. Claws bared, she scratched the back of his hand. He gave her a violent jerk, her neck muscles tearing as her face lifted to meet his.

"The older girl tried to fight back, fancied herself some kind of martial artist. Her neck snapped like a twig."

His taunt broke through the thin wall of fear she'd let build. This was the type of person she had trained herself to fight back against. His kind had been the one to attack when her guard was down, ripped her career out from under her, and left her to die.

Psychos like Stephen Kauffmann would never harm her again.

She stared into his cold, lifeless eyes, and it all clicked into place. He had killed his brother—why, only he knew—killed the trio of thieves, threw Neva McKinnley down her basement steps, and shot Brent.

"It's been you all along."

"It appears the sheriff was wise in choosing you as her investigator. Her wisdom will be your undoing."

Lila's mind raced with how to free herself and disarm him before he could shoot her or break her neck. The only logical one demanded she go straight for his throat.

"Stephen, baby, this isn't you," Ma pleaded.

His derisive laugh reverberated through Lila's head. So reminiscent of her attacker's it made her want to vomit. How could two different people be so alike?

"Oh, I've always been this way. You were too stupid and blind to see it. But that was what made it all together perfect." Stephen waved the barrel of the shotgun. "Get up and join your partner, *Mama.*"

Out of the corner of her eye, Lila watched Martha gingerly rise from the floor and shuffle over next to Sheehan. Gone was the sadistic woman who threatened to have her son rape another woman. Cowed and bruised by one of her own, Martha Kauffmann looked every bit her age and more.

"By now the sheriff has pieced it all together," Sheehan broke in. "If I were you, Stephen, I'd be hightailing it out of here. She's going to be coming with a full force behind her."

"Karl," Stephen barked. "Get the other prisoner."

"Karl. Stay where you are."

Lila smiled at that voice of an angel. She glimpsed Sheriff Benoit behind Stephen, her weapon leveled on his torso.

"Release my deputy, Stephen."

"You brought them here," Stephen spit at Sheehan.

He remained silent, only lifting his hands higher in surrender.

"Put the shotgun down and release my deputy," Benoit ordered.

Stephen jerked Lila closer, jamming the barrel into her stomach.

"Give me a reason to put you down." Fontaine's deep growl came from somewhere behind Lila.

"This will not end how you think it should, Sheriff." Stephen rotated, dragging Lila around. "You are tangling with forces that will see you torn to pieces and scattered to the far corners of this county."

"I assure you, son, I'm fully aware of that, and I don't plan on allowing them, or you, any part of me and my own."

Lila felt the vibrations in Stephen's body. He was making a decision, and it wasn't a good one. Her time to act was now, and it was going to hurt like a mother. With his focus on the sheriff, Lila twisted away, the hunks of her hair wrapped in his fingers ripping free.

Spinning on the balls of her feet, she brought her left fist around and punched him hard in the kidney. The pain would be instantaneous, creating a paralyzing effect on his body. His mouth gaping, his legs buckled; he was going down. Before Lila could react, Sheehan shot forward, grabbing the shotgun from Stephen's slackening hand and tugging away the gun. Stephen hit the floor on his knees, gasping and moaning.

Sheehan leveled the shotgun on Ma. "I wouldn't if I were you." He gave Lila a nod to proceed.

Lila stepped behind Stephen's quaking form and bent down near his ear. "Hey, tough guy, Regan might have fancied herself a martial artist, but I'm actually trained to kick your ass." She held out her hand. "Cuffs."

The warm steel clanked in her hand. As she brought Stephen's arm around, he collapsed face forward. Lila cuffed him and left him writhing on the floor.

Assured that all were covered, Lila ran for the cooler. As she passed Karl, he reached back and grabbed her arm. He was swinging her around, most likely to use as a hostage, but Lila was having none of it.

Using the energy of him trying to right his body and drag her in front of him, she kicked her leg out and swept his braced leg out from under him. Like all great trees, he went down hard, dragging her with him. Aiming her elbow, she rammed it into his breastbone as she landed on him. His head cracked against the cement, and his grip loosened. Lila rolled off him and stood.

"Keep this trash away from me," she said to Fitzgerald and stalked over to the cooler.

Jerking the door open, she let it fly back. Lundquist, shivering, sat on the floor by the door. She held out her hand to him. With a shaking hand, he took hers, and she helped him out of the cooler.

"Took you long enough," he stuttered.

"Tell them." She nodded at their fellow deputies and the sheriff.

"We're here now," Sheriff Benoit said. "Let's wrap this mess up."

CHAPTER THIRTY-SIX

ELIZABETH LEFT DR. Thorpe and made her way to the fifth floor.

Joel would live. He had come to right after arriving at the hospital and managed to explain what had happened. He'd surprised Stephen, who had been waiting to ambush Elizabeth. Joel, not knowing what Stephen was capable of, grappled with the young man for the gun. Despite Joel's training, somehow Stephen managed to turn the gun on Joel and shot him. The bullet went through the upper part of his chest, the angle of the gun sending it through his clavicle, shattering it, and the piece of lead had just enough energy to exit out of his neck. It had clipped an artery, but Joel was able to slow the loss of blood before passing out right when Fitzgerald arrived at the house.

With the Kauffmanns in custody, Elizabeth was moving onto her next problem. While she'd been escorting Martha to the jail, Martha let it slip what had happened to Deputy Meyer. The matriarch was so shaken by her son's betrayal and the events leading up to her arrest, she was more than willing to throw any and all under the bus.

The ICU lights were dimmed for the evening hours. Brent's condition had improved to the point Dr. Thorpe felt he didn't need to operate again, but the young deputy wasn't out of the woods yet. She bypassed the empty rooms and came a stop in the open doorway of the Meyers.

Pratt was absorbed with his tablet, glancing at the wall-mounted TV and the talking head droning on about the stock market. Sophie was perched on the sofa, sitting in the exact position she had been in when Elizabeth left her earlier.

Rapping her knuckles against the door startled the couple. Pratt remained seated, setting his tablet aside, but Sophie jumped to her feet.

"Sheriff," Pratt said casually. "Has there been a change since we last spoke?"

"Yes, there has." She stepped into the room, mindful of the grime and blood that still spotted her uniform. "We have taken several people into custody. A confession from one has revealed Brent's shooter."

Sophie crossed her arms, gripping her elbows. "Who was it?"

"It was Stephen Kauffmann."

"What?"

Pratt bolted upright. "I knew it was one of those bastards."

"Pratt, sit down," Elizabeth snapped.

Shocked, he obeyed. Elizabeth kept her attention zeroed on Sophie.

"Stephen and Karl are also under arrest for multiple homicides, including the death of Neva McKinnley."

"Why would they kill Mrs. McKinnley?" Pratt asked.

"Because she had become too aware of their activities. It seems that along with murder, the Kauffmanns were into the illegal manufacturing and sale of methamphetamine. They had quite the sophisticated meth lab out behind the old Barrett place."

"My word," Sophie breathed.

"Yes, it was shocking, because word from the Iowa DEA estimates the cost of that whole lab close to half a million dollars in equipment, the structure, ingredients to make the meth, and distribution. They believe the lab as a whole was generating over a million in revenue."

"Here in Eckardt County?" Pratt asked incredulously.

"That's what DEA tells me."

"But why are you telling us this?" Pratt asked. "What does that have to do with Stephen shooting Brent?"

Sophie's eyes narrowed, but she remained solid, her gaze locked with Elizabeth's.

"My informant stated Martha and her partner had a falling out because of an attempted robbery on the facility and the not so subtle threat left on a piece of the partner's property."

"Elizabeth? What are you implying?" Pratt insisted, coming to his feet, and moving to stand near Sophie.

"Do you want me to tell him? Or would you rather divulge that pearl of wisdom?"

Pratt's attention swung to his wife. "Sophie, what is she insinuating?"

"You are speculating. Conjuring up rumors and myth."

"No, actually, I have evidence and a signed confession."

"From a woman who will say anything to keep her sentence light."

Pratt stepped back from his wife. "My God, Sophie, what is going on?"

"The signed confession isn't from Martha." Elizabeth rolled her neck, lifting her head higher. "I had to make a deal with the devil to get what I needed."

"Speak to my lawyer, Sheriff. This discussion is over."

"That's your right. But you still have to come to jail."

Pratt sank into his vacated chair, gaping at his wife. "What have you done?"

Sophie looked at her husband, contempt rolling off of her in waves. "I did what you never had the balls to do. Instead, you let some petty feud keep you from what was rightly ours." She smiled. "And to think, all this time, your son thought you were the criminal in the family."

"But . . . why?"

"Because, Pratt, she was never satisfied with being a trophy wife. She was about to start proceedings to divorce you."

Elizabeth hooked her hands on her duty belt.

Pratt shook his head. "I don't understand."

Sophie's huff carried a tone of scoffing.

"I'll admit, in my naiveté about this job, I didn't see it myself." Elizabeth inched closer to Sophie. "Neither did your son. I truly applaud your skills, Sophie—it takes a true genius to hide behind the façade of a domestic goddess to pull off a criminal enterprise the likes this county has never seen before. And all because you were tired of your husband controlling every aspect of your life and your finances. Genius."

"You have no idea who you're dealing with, Sheriff."

"Everyone keeps telling me that. Why don't you enlighten me?"

"I'd rather rot in jail."

Elizabeth turned at the scuff of boots against the polished floor. Lila entered the room, cuffs clenched in her fist.

"Sophie Meyer, you are under arrest . . ."

CHAPTER THIRTY-SEVEN

L ILA LOITERED OUTSIDE the hospital room, cracking her knuckles and shifting back and forth on her feet. She lifted her fist, then dropped it back at her side.

"Just knock," the Viking grumbled.

She glanced at him. "I hate hospitals."

"Imagine how he feels. He's the one stuck in the bed."

"I know exactly how he feels," she muttered.

Lundquist frowned. And with that, Lila knocked and entered the room before she was given permission.

Brent rolled his head her direction. "Hey, Dayne," he croaked.

She smiled. "Hey. Sheriff said you were asking about me."

"Yeah." He tried to push himself upright.

Lila rushed to the bed. "I wouldn't recommend that." She located the button to raise the bed and propped him up at a comfortable angle. "If you strain your abdomen, you'll rip the sutures."

"Apparently, she speaks from experience," Lundquist said from his position by the door.

Brent peered around her. "Kyle."

The Viking gave a curt wave.

"I do speak from experience. Just take it easy and listen

to the doctor." Lila found a safe spot and sat on the edge of his bed. "What did you want to see me about?"

Brent took her hand, he stared at it. "Ellie told me what happened with the Kauffmanns. And about my father and my mother."

"Kinda messed up."

"That's putting it mildly." He cleared his throat, and lifted his gaze, and curled his fingers in hers. "She also told me why you're actually here."

Lila turned cold. "She did?"

"As motivation, for me."

She looked back at Lundquist, who had inched out of his spot in front of the door. He still had yet to learn the truth, and Lila wasn't sure if she was ready for him to know.

"Lila."

Her attention returned to Brent.

"I want to return to the department. Dr. Thorpe isn't sure I'll be able to work as a cop again. Ellie says you were able to do it." He stared at her like he was willing her to give him the answer he wanted. "Will you help me get back?"

Drawing in a breath, she bit her lip. She had suffered greatly at the hands of her attacker. She'd lost her ability to have children and her kidney was damaged, but the worse was the mental scars. She didn't know if she was capable of helping another person do what she had done. Her motives went deeper than just getting back on the job.

"Please, Lila," he whispered.

She laid her free hand over their joined ones. "Let's see how you heal first before we jump into working on getting you back. Okay?"

Brent blinked at her for a moment, then he nodded. He

relaxed into his pillows, fatigue dragging on his young face.

"We'll let you sleep. Believe me, it'll help you heal faster."

He made a soft sound in his throat, his eyes drifting shut. Lila placed his hand across his chest, and reclined his bed.

Lundquist held the door open as she exited. Together they walked through the hospital and to their patrol car. Settled in the driver's seat, Lundquist hesitated before starting the engine.

"Lila?" He looked at her. "Are you ever going to tell me the truth?"

She rolled up onto her hip and leaned across the divide, putting her face next to his. "I'm damaged goods."

His gaze flicked down to her mouth, and then back to her eyes. "What are you insinuating?"

She pressed a light kiss to his lips. "Nothing." She settled back into her seat. "Let's go before the sheriff puts out a BOLO on us."

Lundquist gave her a grin full of promise as he turned over the engine. "I doubt that. She's too busy with her ex."

ELIZABETH CLOSED THE door to the spare bedroom where her ex lay in a healing sleep. Dominic had released Joel to her care since his injuries were not as life-threatening as Brent's had been. And Joel was well-versed in the art of recovery.

She returned to the main living area of her home, stopping in the spot where Joel had bled on her floor. The puddle had been removed by a special team of cleaners days ago. But it would never be erased from her memory.

Bentley jumped to her feet at the heavy bootfalls on the porch. Elizabeth commanded the dog to stay. She opened the door with her sidearm pressed against the doorframe, in sight. Her visitor gave a wicked grin.

"Ahh, she is learning."

"What are you doing here, Kelley?"

He held up his hands as a sign of peace. "I just wanted to check on Joel."

"He's sleeping. There, you checked, now leave."

"Such animosity. Will you ever find it in your heart to let bygones be bygones?"

"With you? Never. We have a temporary truce. Once the Kauffmanns and Sophie become a problem of the state's, that truce will end. I know you're hiding more than your connection with that whole ordeal, and I will see you in jail."

His grin widened. "I look forward to the game, Sheriff."

"I'm sure you do."

With an acquiescent nod, Sheehan turned on his heel and exited her property. Certain he was truly gone, Elizabeth closed the door and set her firearm on the table next to the door.

"Who was that?"

She turned. "You are supposed to stay in bed."

Joel tilted up one corner of his mouth. "When have I ever listened to an order given from you?"

"Those are your doctor's orders."

"Them either?"

Stalking across the floor, Elizabeth invaded her ex's personal space. "For once in your life, don't be such a stubborn cuss."

He hooked his good arm around her waist and tugged her flush to his body. "Ellie, for once in your life, stop trying to control everything and everyone around you. Relax."

"I kissed Rafe."

"Really? About time."

She frowned. "He was upset about it, and you act like it was long overdue."

"Well, it was." Joel pressed his forehead to hers. "Do you love him?"

"I don't know."

"Because you still have a piece of your heart in my hand."

"Joel, I can't go back to what we used to be. I'm not that same person."

"Watching you for the past week, I know that now." He brushed his thumb against her cheek. "Rafe was always the right one for you."

"That is ironic coming from his jealous brother."

"As soon as I'm able, I'm going back to the base. This wound won't stop me from being an instructor. It just seals my retirement from active-duty status."

"Maybe you need to seriously consider full retirement."

Joel kissed her forehead. "That's never going to happen. Just like you'll never give up being a good sheriff. Remember that, Ellie."

If you enjoyed *The Killer in Me*, please leave a review at your favorite online retailer!

Join Tule Publishing's newsletter for more great reads and weekly deals!

ACKNOWLEDGMENTS

I started this project on a few pages and a whim in the midst of a jump back into the life of a college student, while working a full-time job, and, well, a worldwide pandemic. What a crazy time to deal with all of that and write a crime novel. Somehow I did it, and now you hold in your hands the fruits of my efforts.

Many talents aide an author in creating and writing a book. Especially one such as this. First and foremost, thanks go to my sidekicks and first line of defense readers, Rachel and Jennifer. If it wasn't for them, I'd probably still be wandering aimlessly around in a fog. When writing a crime fiction book with cops, you better have a good one on hand. I got it in my old high school mate with a long career as a police officer, Ed, who brought his wonderful wife, Amanda, on the reading journey—and to drive him to get the read-throughs done. Thanks a mil, you two. Huge thanks to David, whose daughter is the wonderful girl I dedicated this book to. He was more than willing to help me figure out how to really jack up someone without killing them, and his long years as a military medic and critical care EMS are invaluable.

Getting a book from rough draft to finished product also takes a crew, and the Tule crew is top-notch. Shout it from the rooftops for one of the best editors in the biz, Julie knows me well enough to get inside my head and pull out what I was missing—or doubting myself on. Tons of thanks to Jane, Meghan, Nikki, Cyndi and all the rest at Tule, as they have made it a truly wonderful place to be an author. Keep up the great work, y'all.

I have some kooky and wonderful kids, leave it to my own spawn to keep me in my place. My boys more than pulled their own weight in keeping us going with cleaning and cooking. And my girl's penchant for showing cattle got us out of the house, even with a pandemic going on. When they're all moved out and on their own, I don't know what I'll do with myself. And to the man who decided I was weird enough for his own brand of weirdness, I love you, and yes, I'm not letting any other author get ahead of me in this business.

Finally, thanks to you reader. Without you, we authors would be lost. Thank you.

If you enjoyed *The Killer in Me*,
you'll love the next book in the…

BENOIT AND DAYNE MYSTERY SERIES

Book 1: *The Killer in Me*

Book 2: *Hush, My Darling*
Coming January 2022!

mation can be obtained
esting.com
USA
6240821
0005B/126

9 781954 894211

ABOUT THE AUTHOR

Winter Austin perpetually answers the question: "were you born in the winter?" with a flat "nope," but believe her, there is a story behind her name.

A lifelong Mid-West gal with strong ties to the agriculture world, Winter grew up listening to the captivating stories told by relatives around a table or a campfire. As a published author, she learned her glass half-empty personality makes for a perfect suspense/thriller writer. Taking her ability to verbally spin a vivid and detailed story, Winter translated that into writing deadly romantic suspense, mysteries, and thrillers.

When she's not slaving away at the computer, you can find Winter supporting her daughter in cattle shows, seeing her three sons off into the wide-wide world, loving on her fur babies, prodding her teacher husband, and nagging at her flock of hens to stay in the coop or the dogs will get them.

She is the author of multiple novels.

Thank you for readir

THE KILLER IN ME

If you enjoyed this book, you can fir great authors at TulePublishing.com online retailer

TULE
PUBLISHING

CPSIA info
at www.ICG
Printed in th
LVHW11117
695998LV(

If you enjoyed *The Killer in Me,*
you'll love the next book in the…

BENOIT AND DAYNE MYSTERY SERIES

Book 1: *The Killer in Me*

Book 2: *Hush, My Darling*
Coming January 2022!

ABOUT THE AUTHOR

Winter Austin perpetually answers the question: "were you born in the winter?" with a flat "nope," but believe her, there is a story behind her name.

A lifelong Mid-West gal with strong ties to the agriculture world, Winter grew up listening to the captivating stories told by relatives around a table or a campfire. As a published author, she learned her glass half-empty personality makes for a perfect suspense/thriller writer. Taking her ability to verbally spin a vivid and detailed story, Winter translated that into writing deadly romantic suspense, mysteries, and thrillers.

When she's not slaving away at the computer, you can find Winter supporting her daughter in cattle shows, seeing her three sons off into the wide-wide world, loving on her fur babies, prodding her teacher husband, and nagging at her flock of hens to stay in the coop or the dogs will get them.

She is the author of multiple novels.

Thank you for reading

THE KILLER IN ME

If you enjoyed this book, you can find more from all our great authors at TulePublishing.com, or from your favorite online retailer.

TULE
PUBLISHING

9 781954 894211